Bright Dawn

As the silent, shaking explosion reached into her depths, she clung to him, tears wetting her cheeks. "Jess . . . Jess," she whispered. "I thought I'd never again feel . . . oh . . . Jess!" She thought he was calling her sweetheart but couldn't be sure because that joy lasted forever, then, slowly was gone.

She realized what he'd done instantly. She pushed him away and he let her. She sat up, furious. She hated him worse than before. He'd actually raped her. Well, in the beginning it was rape, which was just as bad.

She accused him of rape, nonetheless.

"Rape!" she croaked, trying to hide her breasts and thighs.

He was breathing hard. He shook his head.

"No rape, lady. I had your full cooperation, after a certain point."

All at once she wanted to cry. Him and his conceit! But she had a right to revenge. She'd show him what a second course was . . .

Books by
Francesca Greer

Bright Dawn
First Fire
The Second Sunrise

Published by
WARNER BOOKS

Bright Dawn

Francesca Greer

WARNER BOOKS

A Warner Communications Company

WARNER BOOKS EDITION

Copyright © 1983 by Frankie-Lee Janas
All rights reserved.

Cover art by Max Ginsburg

Warner Books, Inc.,
666 Fifth Avenue,
New York, N.Y. 10103

 A Warner Communications Company

Printed in the United States of America

First Printing: March, 1983

10 9 8 7 6 5 4 3 2 1

For my husband, Gene Janas

I

Texas

Chapter One

RAE-ELLEN had never been so stunned and outraged. She ran headlong out of Pa Travis's big living room, out of the sprawling redwood-and-stone ranchhouse, Baby Vic bouncing and yelling on her hip.

Across the graveled driveway she ran, past the gleaming cars parked there, to the hitching post where she'd left Platinum.

She untied the saddle filly, popped the year-old baby onto the horse and mounted behind him, in one swift, fluid motion. She urged the filly into an instant trot, bracing Baby Vic, who had stopped yelling because he loved to ride, against herself.

She was so furious that she didn't notice the great live oaks and the moss draping them, or enjoy the dusty look that August gave them. She didn't see the vast spread of the Star-Bar as she rode. She kept to the shoulder when she reached the highway, busy with cars, a slender, twenty-two-year-old girl with auburn-streaked hair which bounced angrily on her shoulders and almost all the way down her back.

Pa Travis had been delighted when she rode up with the baby an hour ago on Platinum, his gift to her. He had tossed his laughing grandson in the air and caught him with great, sure hands, and they had been a happy sight, the great, homely man and the sturdy, laughing, homely child. He had played with Vic until the baby pulled free and began to crawl along the polished floor, stopping to examine the fringe on the fine, big rug. Then he went into housekeeper Rosita's arms and she bore him away, chattering in Spanish.

Pa Travis grinned at Rae-Ellen, then sobered. "I've got a word to say," he told her, "if you'll listen."

"You're due a word, after giving me Platinum!" she said, smiling. "Talk away, father-in-law!"

"I'll speak my mind, you know that."

"Go ahead, shoot!"

Against the rugged background of the room Vic Travis was Texas incarnate. He was six-feet-one, had tawny, grizzled hair and eyes like those of his dead son, brown and beautiful, while his face was strong and homely.

She was aware of how she looked, that long, auburn-streaked hair and her eyes so vividly blue. She was tall, her figure slim and firm, not out of shape from giving birth. Her features were chiseled, her eyebrows arched, her lips too red. Always, she rubbed face powder on them to tone down the color.

Bewildered, she watched Pa Travis's expression harden. "You've been a widow for a year," he said. "Your boy is being raised by a bunch of women. And that won't do, not for my grandson."

"What are you getting at?"

"It's time you gave Vic a pa, that's what," he said.

"He had a pa! He had the best!"

"He sure-hell did! He had Burr Travis—he had my son! But Burr's dead now, and it's up to you to get Vic a pa as good."

For an instant, she flared with silent rage. Her one interest, outside thoroughbred horse breeding was her son. And here Pa was, ordering her to marry and get a father for him!

"Don't burn them blue eyes at me, girl! You get that boy a proper pa! Send them chums of yours home where they belong before they turn him into a sissy!"

"They're not doing that!"

"Don't tell me! I've got eyes! And I won't by-cracky stand for it! But pick your man with care! Any man'd be glad to get you—just make sure you take the right one!"

"And if I don't marry? What can you do?"

Rae-Ellen's jaw dropped as her father-in-law looked at her coldly and said, "You'll rob Vic of his birthright. Unless he's man-raised, he'll not get an acre of my land or one of my oil wells, or—"

"I've got the Double T. I've got a start on my horse breeding. That's all he needs!"

"You ain't got it yet! I offered it for a wedding present, sure, but the papers ain't final—won't be

13

until after you get Vic a pa! Otherwise, you won't *have* a horse farm!"

Rae-Ellen glared. "Ha! Blackmail!"

"In a way, reckon so. And you won't get land from your own daddy, in North Carolina. We've talked by phone and agreed on what I told you."

"You've got Keith Belisle in mind!" she cried. "Because he's the foreman Burr hired for us, because Burr thought Keith hung the moon—works like a demon! Or else it's Grant Miller, 'cause you admire what he's done with the Leaning K!"

"Six months!" Pa Travis bellowed. "Six months is time aplenty!"

"Never!"

"There used to be a Texas law said if a grandparent can do more for a kid than his parents, he gets custody. I'll use that law—if it don't exist, I'll get it back on the books!"

He had the power to do it, Rae-Ellen thought. And if she did consent to marry, he'd want to approve the man, if not choose him. She was in such a turmoil that she couldn't think.

"Six months!" Pa Travis repeated.

She fled, snatching Baby Vic from Rosita, drawn by their shouts. She made for the door.

"Where you going?" roared Pa.

"To ride the filly you gave me!"

"Where to?"

"I'm going to see Drew!" she snapped. "He's getting a new bronc, and I'll hear about it and catch up on rodeo plans!"

Though she was on the move, he took two great strides and caught her by the shoulder. Jolted to a standstill, she stood, raging, unwilling to jerk away from him, to give him that satisfaction.

"Why don't you go to the hotel at Travis Forks?" he asked. "The manager I hired you is there. He was Burr's sidekick. He'll give your horse-breeding a real boost. You can at least see him, let him know he's to use your dogtrot rooms!"

"I run to no man!" she cried.

Yet here she was, riding like the wind to Drew Knight, to whom she was strongly attracted, because of whom she'd refused sex with two Dallas men. She was heading for the K-Bell, Drew's sheep ranch.

Rage at Pa Travis seethed again. He had no right to order her to marry. He did, according to his thinking, have the right to hire a manager for the Double T because he was furnishing both the land and the money. Yet she resented it. She wrenched her mind off him, urged Platinum on.

The breeze that the galloping filly raised lifted her hair back from her face, and she felt it flying like a shimmering copper scarf. She gave her head an angry toss.

Her misfortune, she knew, was to feel that love was the important thing in marriage. And Pa Travis had bellowed "Six months!" He didn't consider love, and it was his own son he wanted to replace!

Without love—and the wild love she and Burr had known proved this—life would be flat and unbearable. No amount of land, such as Pa Travis owned in Texas, or the many acres of tobacco land her own father owned in North Carolina, no number of oil wells with the name Travis on them, or the uncounted conglomerates, could take the place of love.

She was willing, even eager, to give up such riches, to marry the poorest man alive, if he could measure up to Burr. She had to love and be loved; without that she would know only unhappiness, and never be able to give Baby Vic the sort of home he needed.

And the only man she could possibly want—*did* want, might as well admit it—was Drew Knight. Drew—fine, wonderful Drew of whom it was no use to mention a word to Pa Travis. For Pa was cattle and Drew was sheep and Pa hated sheep. He'd never let his grandson be reared by a sheepman, though he liked Drew personally and was on friendly terms with him.

Six months to decide a lifetime—she couldn't do it.

She slowed Platinum to an easy lope, not wanting to overheat her. Baby Vic squealed and wanted to go faster, but she pointed to a rabbit hopping along in a pasture, and he stared at that as long as he could see it, then forgot about speed.

She thought about Drew as she rode toward his ranch. Not only did he run the biggest sheep ranch anywhere around, but he was important in other matters. He had served one term as state senator in Austin, declining to run for a second term, though he would have been a shoo-in. He said he preferred the ranch to the senate chamber. Now men came from all over the state to get his advice on matters, and followed the advice and were successful. He was widely respected and admired, was, actually, presidential material.

16

He was also head of the local rodeo performances, which were his hobby, and many of which were staged at the K-Bell. He didn't ride in the rodeos himself often, but when he did, won prize money, which he gave to charity.

Drew was perfect, Rae-Ellen thought, not for the first time. Since Burr would one day have a successor in her life, Drew was the only one who could match him. And he wouldn't be easy to win, because he was the most sought-after bachelor in two counties. The woman who got him would be lucky indeed.

Yet Pa Travis would never accept him.

No matter that Drew was a six-foot, russet-haired, true Texan: he had the sheep and a few wild broncs. Further, if he were to marry Rae-Ellen, he'd never let Baby Vic be a cattleman, him loving sheep so much, and Pa Travis knew it.

But for Drew, she might have had sex with one of those men from Dallas. They had been very attractive. Why *have* I held out for Drew? she wondered.

Suddenly she felt almost impatient with him. Because he hadn't tried to get romantic. And she'd let him be just friendly because she was...maybe...frigid now.

Yet, if this were true, would she tremble at the very sight of him, would her heart twist, then begin a wild racing? Would her legs go to rubber? Would she lie awake at night, seeing him in her mind? Would she wonder what it would be like if she were in bed with him, if he were making love to her? Would she toss all night, longing for love? And for whom did she toss? Not Burr. It couldn't be Burr. He was dead, and she had grieved for him, but now she was ready to get on with life. So *was* it only Drew for whom she longed in the long, restless nights? And if not him, then who?

Maybe she'd been wrong to turn down the Dallas men. Now she regretted them, even as she yearned for Drew. Suppose trying out various lovers was the thing to do? She had lost the chance to find out which man of the three might have brought her alive.

Let Pa Travis stew. Let him deprive her and Baby Vic of the Double T. There was room aplenty at the K-Bell, and she was positive that Drew, being so fair-minded, would let her breed thoroughbreds—if she won him. And Baby Vic, when he was grown, could take his choice—be a sheepman or a horse breeder or both. Look at the way Drew managed both sheep and rodeos. And Pa Travis, for that matter; he handled cattle and oil wells and conglomerates with ease.

She decided Pa could see Baby Vic all he pleased if she married Drew. She'd never keep Burr's son from knowing his grandfather and the Star-Bar. And Rosita. As for the old man, he'd never be able to resist seeing the boy. He might be too stiff-necked to make him his heir, but Baby Vic would have his heart.

Now she was riding between fenced sheep pastures filled with grazing sheep. She watched them crossly. If only Drew hadn't inherited a sheep ranch, then fallen in love with it! Even if she could make him fall in love with her, she'd never be able to talk him into cattle.

And she wouldn't want to, not really. He was a

man of conviction, and sheep were his life. She'd not want him easily swayed.

Once, when they were discussing the next rodeo at the K-Bell, Pa Travis's name had come up and Drew had said a couple of things about him. With utter respect—Drew would be respectful to the sorriest saddle-bum—but what he meant was clear. He understood that Pa Travis expected her to marry cattle. And now she had that belief to overcome along with everything else.

Susie Drummon, her chum, too. She had her to overcome. Susie was always in the way. She'd been in love with Drew for months and was now staying indefinitely with Rae-Ellen, and always managed to show up when Drew was around, no matter where they were. The only thing that cheered Rae-Ellen about this was the fact that Susie had a guilty secret and could never actually marry Drew because of it.

As for Drew, he treated Susie fondly. But as a friend, only. Rae-Ellen had never seen him give her an intimate look or touch her unnecessarily. And he was as fondly kind to her as he was to Susie.

She turned into the driveway of the K-Bell. It was lined with big live oaks, as were nearly all the ranch driveways, and she slowed Platinum to a walk. Baby Vic bounced, squealed crossly, wanting to go faster.

She dropped a kiss on his hair. "Patience," she murmured. "You'll soon be the center of attention."

Chapter Two

THE house was of fieldstone and sprawled as much as
did Pa Travis's house. It was big—perfect for a man
and wife and a large family of children. The inside
was perfect, too. Rae-Ellen had been there many
times, loved the bare, polished floors, the braided
rugs, the heavy pine furniture with nubby coverings.

She knew for a fact that there were eight bedrooms, because she'd couted them. All sizable, too,
with air and sunlight—enough for each of seven
children to have his own room. Baby Vic, hopefully,
would be the one to get first choice.

Platinum clattered up to the hitching post, and
Rae-Ellen suddenly realized that her hair was a mess
from blowing in the wind. She slid to the ground,
swiping it back, keeping a hand on Baby Vic.

Inwardly she was boiling. Just when she wanted to look her best, impress Drew favorably, she had to be sweating and have her hair tangled!

"I'll take the boy," said a deep, quiet voice, and big hands lifted Baby Vic down and held him.

Rae-Ellen kept smoothing her hair.

"You look fine, lovely as ever!" laughed that deep voice. "Pay some attention to me!"

She glanced up. "Drew! I look—"

"You've been riding. And so has this fellow."

Baby Vic was patting Drew's face, grinning and drooling from the tooth he was cutting.

Drew's eyes, russet as his curly hair, were on her. His lips were smiling.

No wonder Susie was overboard for him! No wonder all the girls in the county— But she was with him now. And today, even with Baby Vic here, she meant to do something about it.

"Where's Susie?" he asked. "You're usually together."

That was certainly a fact. Rae-Ellen never got to be alone with him. Either Susie was along or some other girl who was chasing him would appear before Rae-Ellen could get in one private word.

"I took Vic to Pa Travis for breakfast," she said, "then decided to stop by here on my way home." She smiled, keeping her eyes on his meaningfully, but he missed the point.

"Have a big breakfast?"

She laughed. "You know Rosita. I think she'd spank me if I didn't simply stuff!"

"I'm just about to have fresh doughnuts and coffee," he said. "Vinnie made some and insisted. Here she comes now!"

When Vinnie, wife of a sheepherder and in her thirties, caught sight of Rae-Ellen and Baby Vic, she began to run. When she reached them, she was out of breath, her plain face wearing a smile.

"Can I hold Vic?" she asked Rae-Ellen. "You know me, without a chick or child!"

Baby Vic stopped patting Drew's face—Rae-Ellen almost winced to see that end—and flung himself at Vinnie. She hugged him and bounced him and he laughed and wanted more.

"Rae-Ellen's going to have coffee and doughnuts, too," Drew said. "Why don't you keep Vic at your place until we've finished?"

Vinnie glanced at Rae-Ellen for permission, and she gave it with a nod and a smile. "I may stay a while," she warned.

"Then I'll give the little darling a doughnut and play games! Shep came in for doughnuts—I'll send him up with yours and the coffee, since I've got this angel!"

She scurried away, and Drew turned to the house, Rae-Ellen with him. "Think you can hold doughnuts after that breakfast?" he asked.

She would have eaten doughnuts with him if she burst. She'd eat them if it made her fat overnight. Or, if he didn't like her plump, she'd diet and exercise and shed pounds and inches. Whatever Drew Knight wanted of her, he was to have.

"I love Vinnie's cooking!" she declared. "I can hold at least three doughnuts, and two cups of coffee!"

"Just a healthy, growing girl!" he chuckled, and offered his arm.

She tucked her hand into it, then had to put the

other hand on top to keep both hands from shaking. This was the first time she'd ever really touched him except for when they had danced—and she found it exciting and unnerving.

He was six feet tall, six inches taller than herself. His height was perfect. She looked up at him fully, and he looked back, smiling, his strong, chiseled features tanned almost to the russet of his hair. His inner strength came through steadily.

Everything about him was strong—his deep voice, his Texan build, which was broad-shouldered and slim-hipped, all of him in top condition from working and riding and doing the strenuous ranch work he did, including shearing and dipping the sheep.

He was a man born for ranching, for life, for love. Her breath stopped as she walked with him across the gallery, down the broad hallway and into the room he used for library and ranch office.

He sat her down on the sofa. "Leave that hair alone," he said. "I like it when the wind's been at it. You get lovelier every day, you and Susie."

"You're just saying that!" she laughed, the pleasure of his words spoiled by the mention of Susie.

"No, I'm not!" he insisted, sitting at the other end of the sofa. "I've watched the two of you getting lovelier until..." He smiled and spread his hands. "Take it easy on the men, both of you! Or you'll have every man in the county out of his mind. And, worse yet, have to make up your minds which one you'll marry, knowing full well that you'll leave a string of broken hearts!"

Footsteps sounded and Shep, Vinnie's husband, came in with a big tray of fragrant doughnuts and a pot of coffee. He was a dark-haired, broad-chested man—one of the best with the sheep.

"Howdy, Rae-Ellen," he said. "That's a fine boy you got. Vinnie says he's cuttin' a tooth."

"Thank you, Shep," Rae-Ellen said, glad all over again that in this free and easy Texas first names were used by one and all. "He's going to be cutting more soon, I think."

Shep grinned. "Well, I'll be back at my fences," he said. "Found a few weak places," he told Drew. "I'm going to make the rounds before I quit, see to every inch of fence. Don't want our sheep gettin' onto the cattle spread either side."

"Thanks, Shep," Drew said. "Had your doughnuts?"

"Stood at the stove and got mine as Vinnie brought 'em out of the grease. Almost too hot to eat, but I can't never wait for her doughnuts." He grinned, and added, "She told me, Rae-Ellen, that she wants to learn you to make 'em. They're Drew's favorite, too. We both say he needs a wife to do for him in this big house, if you don't mind I speak out."

Drew chuckled.

Rae-Ellen's body went hot. Shep saw this and grinned. "My Vinnie, she says you got to get a wife, Drew, to make doughnuts and learn from her how to cook the things you like."

"Vinnie tired of the job?" Drew teased.

"Hell, no!" Shep shuffled his feet. "She's like all women, a matchmaker. Can't stand to see a good man run around loose. In this case, though, I more or less agree with her."

Drew waved him away, laughing. And Shep departed, laughing too. Rae-Ellen ached to cry, "Listen

25

to them, Drew! I'm the one! I can cook the food, bear the babies, breed the horses!"

Drew, still chuckling, met Rae-Ellen's eyes. She felt she was cooling down and maybe not blushing so hotly. While he'd been talking to Shep, she'd probably been fiery!

"Are you still as much in love with Platinum as you were when you got her?" he asked.

"Very much in love," she murmured, looking right at him, knowing it to be truth, hoping he'd get the import and respond. But his face was placid. If he'd got her meaning, he didn't show it. She felt that quiet strength. How could she *not* be in love with him? How could Susie help being in love with him? And all the other girls?

"Want to pour the coffee?" Drew asked.

She poured, his cup first, put the amount of cream in she'd noticed on other occasions that he liked, fixed hers the same way. No sugar. He put warm doughnuts on plates and set them on the coffee table.

They took the first bites in appreciative silence, then they began to talk rodeo.

"Some people say there won't be many rodeoers at this next one at your place," Rae-Ellen remarked. "That most of them will make for the big one they're going to hold in Fort Worth."

"The Fort Worth date is later than ours," Drew said comfortably. "And I've been able to get donations from over the county. We'll have riders. We've got the bait."

"Besides that," Rae-Ellen put in, happy to be discussing a subject Drew was so interested in, "from what I hear there are almost enough riders from the ranches around Travis Forks itself to have a rodeo."

Drew laughed. "Just about. And there are always the loners, the drifters, who go from one small rodeo to another to pick up a few bucks. It's in their blood, you see, rodeoing. There's something about it that draws them. It isn't only the money. In fact, I believe money plays the smallest part with most of them."

"But there *are* rodeoers who go into it for the money?"

"Oh, sure. Just as with anything else. But even they have a love for it or they wouldn't go for it. It's too dangerous."

"Is that why you don't compete much? The danger?"

He grinned and shook his head. "I used to ride, do the whole bit. Won a good part of the money. Gradually, I became more interested in putting on a rodeo than in riding in one. That's why I don't compete often now—I'm too busy with the other end of it."

"And the next rodeo is to be here at the K-Bell?"

"Next of any size, yes. The county rodeo will come next, then the one in Fort Worth."

"And now you're getting ready for yours," she said softly.

He nodded. "We're getting the pens in shape. The boys are practicing."

As he talked rodeo, his face was alert and happy. She kept him on the subject until every doughnut and every drop of coffee was gone.

He looked excited as he explained about the fine, wild saddle-bronc he'd bought, which would be delivered in time for his rodeo. He said this animal would be the star there, and hoped a star rider would draw him to ride.

With him in this wonderful mood, Rae-Ellen carefully pushed her coffee cup away. She was going to do it, she really was. This was the 1980s. Women had been emancipated for a long time. She had no need, none whatsoever, to sit back and wait for Drew to speak. She could come right out with what was on her mind, no matter how frightened she was, how uncertain.

"Drew," she said, forcing her voice to be steady, "there's a . . . wondering I have about you."

He met her look, frowned, puzzled. "What is it?" he asked gently.

"You're thirty-two years old, right?"

"Yes, that's true."

"You have so much—the K-Bell, thousands of sheep, millions of dollars . . . "

"A bit over one million, Rae-Ellen. Not all in cash."

She shrugged. "Money! You're head man of the rodeo, and you have every girl in the county—and her mother—chasing you. You have everything but a wife. Why haven't you married yet?"

Her heart pounded. She'd got the big question out in the open. Now he had to answer it, one way or another.

She put a ringless hand on his wrist, and he almost absentmindedly covered it with his hand. "I don't know how to answer," he said. "I haven't given the matter a lot of thought, actually."

"Why not? You're a bachelor . . . you're a man.

28

Surely you feel the need for a woman!" She gasped at her own temerity, then tried to breathe normally.

"It's not that there hasn't been a woman, now and then," he said. "I'm a normal man, with strong instincts. It's just that I've never got down to considering marriage seriously."

"Why not? Why shouldn't you marry?"

"No reason, none at all. A good marriage is a fine thing in a man's life."

"So . . . ?"

"It calls for the right woman, don't you see? I've looked around some, and only two girls have come up to what I need in a wife."

Her hand tightened on his. "Who are they?" she whispered, voice trembling.

"You yourself, Rae-Ellen, honey. And your best friend, Susie Drummond. So. Tell me, if you can, how to choose between you."

"That's easy! The one you love!"

"Ah, but for a long time I couldn't decide which one that was. It started when you married Burr and put yourself out of reach, and Susie was always in the picture. For a while, I considered courting Susie, since you were taken; then I decided to wait and make certain she was the one."

"But now I'm free, Drew! How do you feel now?"

"Truthfully, I've continued to feel pretty much the same, except . . . Well, the attraction I feel toward you both has come into it. With you and Susie inseparable, even living together, you're almost like sisters. And it's hard to choose between sisters, lest you hurt one of them. When you—well, know—they both favor you."

Rae-Ellen gnawed the inside of her lip. So. He had noticed that she was strongly attracted to him. What was she to do? She could never tell him Susie's guilty secret; that would be competing unfairly. It might even turn him against her.

She cuddled to him so that he had to put his arm around her. She'd wanted to do this for weeks, and it felt as wonderful as she had dreamed it would.

She held her face to him, lips quivering. Half-shyly, she moved them so they touched his, and hesitantly he let their lips rest together. His were warm and throbbing, and they moved gently, but she kissed him back with slow, loving firmness, and clung. Even when he tensed to put her away, she held on to him with arms and lips and closed her eyes and feasted on his reluctant but lingering kiss.

Her knees were shaking, but she kept that kiss. Heat sank into her loins and she longed for all of him. She could feel the wild shaking of her heart; and she knew that he could feel it, too.

He set her, slowly, away from him.

"I shouldn't have let that happen, honey," he said. "My apologies."

"No apology! Another kiss!"

He put out his hand, held her away. "You can't go around kissing men like that," he said. "Surely you must have some idea of what it does to them. Kiss the wrong man, and you'll be in trouble."

"I want to be in trouble!" she cried. "With you!"

He looked at her keenly. "I thought you were just being provocative," he said, "but now—"

"I know what I'm doing, Drew, believe me! I'm

making a play for you! Please, take me now, in this house! Find out for sure what wife you want!"

She moved toward him again, but he held her away. "You don't mean it, you can't!" he said earnestly. "Please, Rae-Ellen— Let's drop the fooling around and be friends, as always!"

"I'm not fooling around! I want to go to bed with you, to show you how I feel, give you a chance to see how you really feel!

"I'm in love with you, Drew Knight," she wailed, "and I want to be your wife, mother of your children! I want you for Vic's pa! He likes you, and you like him! If you don't feel marrying-love after this first time, why I'll wait, because it'll come, it's bound to!"

"Rae-Ellen . . . honey . . . honey, no."

"I'll make a bargain!"

"It isn't a thing to bargain about."

"I'll be your mistress until you realize I'm the one you want! Six months! Give me six months, and I *know* you'll want me!"

"No . . . still no . . . and no. I'd never take such advantage of you. I'd never hurt you like that. It's impossible and, no matter what you're feeling just now, you know it. Please . . . be my own Rae-Ellen!"

"I *am* being your Rae-Ellen! Finally! I noticed you even when . . . Burr . . . and since then it's grown—until now, this moment, it's the biggest thing in my life!"

"I can't do it to you, honey."

"It's Pa Travis, isn't it? His talk has got to you! You know he'd fight our marriage because you're a sheepman! You know he wouldn't consider you a suitable father for Baby Vic—that's the thing that holds you back, isn't it?"

"What the hell are you talking about?"

"Pa Travis wants me to marry within six months— so's Baby Vic'll have a pa! He wants my son to be raised to be cattle-crazy and take over the Star-Bar when he's grown! But that needn't stop you from marrying me! Pa is so crazy about the baby he's bound to relent!"

He pulled her to her feet, held her by the arms. Their eyes met, clung, hers imploring, his curiously sad. "I'm going to tell you what I should have a while ago," he said. "And then everything that's happened between us this morning's got to be forgotten."

"Impossible! You do love me! Your kiss—"

"Honey, of course I love you."

"Then—" She tried to get into his arms again, but he held her away.

"I love you as a dear, dear friend, honey. A darling friend. It's Susie I love the marrying way, has been for months, though I didn't fully realize it until just now, with you. Even when Susie had that crush on Keith Belisle, I half loved her. I've been waiting for her to get over it, I think, before making a move. Today's opened my eyes. I'll not risk hurting other girls as I'm hurting you."

"You really mean it!" she breathed.

"Don't look so stricken, honey. I'm sorry, but I do mean it. I'm going to start seeing Susie if she'll let me. And as soon as I win her love, if I can win it, I mean to marry her."

Rae-Ellen's heart stopped, then thundered. No matter what he said, he wasn't married yet. She'd never give up.

"Had you already chosen between us?" she whispered.

32

"Not for sure—until I kissed you. And—forgive me—I felt like I was betraying Susie."

"It can't be!" she breathed. "Not after what Susie—"

She broke off. She couldn't tell Susie's secret, not even when she wanted Drew so desperately for herself. Yet she ached to uncover the whole, shameful truth. It wasn't right to stand mute and let Drew be hoodwinked.

"What is it, Rae-Ellen?" he asked keenly.

"Susie will have to tell you herself."

He half smiled. "Nothing Susie tells me can be very bad."

Rae-Ellen fled from the room, ran to Vinnie's cottage, and got Baby Vic. She mounted Platinum and went streaking down the driveway.

Chapter Three

GALLOPING down the road, headed for home, Rae-Ellen cried. She let the tears stream down her face, sobbed, hiccuped, blew her nose.

She was stunned by the turndown Drew had given her, stunned and torn. She'd never dreamed any man could make her feel so hurt.

She wiped her cheeks with her bandana, dropped a kiss on Baby Vic's wondering, upturned face, settled him so he faced ahead again.

As she rode, her determination rose, grew. She'd never give up, she wouldn't let Pa Travis boss her. And even if Susie did want Drew, she herself would work all the harder to get him.

She raced Platinum along in a near-gallop. Trees, pastures, streams, a ranchhouse or two, passed in a blur. One thing she decided as she rode: she definitely was going to have sex with some man, learn new arts to use on Drew, entice him into marriage. And she'd also beat Pa Travis at his own game. She'd have both husband and love; Pa could keep his millions.

She walked Platinum up the oak-shaded drive, studied her ranchhouse and loved it more than ever. It was one-storied, built of stone with green wooden shutters. The main body of the house held living quarters and bedrooms; connecting it to three rooms at the far end was a long gallery, called a dogtrot, furnished with two green benches. This section she and Burr had planned for guests. Now Pa Travis—damn him!—had told the manager he'd hired that he was to occupy those quarters. They were handy to the stable and outbuildings spaced attractively beyond the house, the pastures wide and lush behind them.

She dismounted and, holding Baby Vic on her hip, tied Platinum to the rail. Skinny young Johnny Malloy, the stableboy Burr had hired, came running up.

"You going to ride some more?" he asked.

"Yes. After I've tended the baby. I'm going in to Travis Forks."

"Then I'll cool Platinum down," Johnny said, untying the horse.

Leah Crouch, the housekeeper, opened the door for her. Baby Vic squealed and threw himself at Leah, and she caught him, laughing.

"Bet he wants a cookie," she said. "I got some fresh-baked. He smells them."

Rae-Ellen smelled them, too; the house was filled with the delicious odor. The housekeeper was in her mid-fifties, a spinster, weighed a hundred and fifty pounds, and had prematurely white hair, all of which she took pride in. She owned a small farm but rented it out, preferring to work at the Double T, where something was always going on. And where there was a baby to cuddle.

Not that Baby Vic, named for Pa Travis, submitted to cuddling. He was too much like Burr, like Pa Travis, for that. He was a sturdy, bossy baby, giving his smiles where he chose, and he always smiled for Leah because of the cookies.

When he had his cookie in his hand, Rae-Ellen took him again and went into the nursery. She had no more than put him on the bath-table to change him than Dots danced into the room.

"Hi!" Dots sang out. "Thought you'd never get back! Susie went horseback riding, and I've been alone with Leah and her cookies!"

Dots Romano was a rancher's daughter, barely twenty, five feet three inches tall, weighed just about a hundred, had ebon hair with blue lights, ebon eyes and the sexiest build in the state of Texas.

"Not a man has called!" she wailed. "I might's well be home with Moth' and Dad! Reason I talked them into lettin' me stay with you after Burr, it was so's I could be with you all I want and date as I please, and now look!"

Rae-Ellen laughed. She couldn't help it. Dots was so openly man-crazy. And so open about the number of dates she went to bed with.

"You'll not have long to wait," she assured Dots. Expertly she changed Vic while he smeared cookie over his face. "Tom or Bill or George . . ."

"You're just makin' up names, now! It's Wilson I

37

want today. He's the best-lookin' man I ever saw, even if he does live across the county line. I'm going to try him out a lot of times, see if I get tired of him. If I don't, then I'll marry him. Which is what you should do."

"Marry Wilson?" teased Rae-Ellen.

"Oh, you goose! You know what I mean! You should try out men, get a husband that way. Here, give me the baby. What you going to do now?"

"Ride in to the Forks," Rae-Ellen said grimly. "To see a man."

"Make time with him, gal, make time!"

Rae-Ellen blurted out what Pa Travis had said to her earlier. She said nothing about Drew and what had happened with him.

"That bossy old man!" Dots cried. "Worse than my folks! Oh, they want me to get married, but they're afraid I'll get into trouble first. That Pa Travis thinks he's boss of the world!"

"He is—of his world," Rae-Ellen murmured. "But not of me or my son."

"Good for you! You'll be back from the Forks in time to go meet your sister at the airport?"

"Loads of time," Rae-Ellen replied. A lousy day so far, but at least Adah would be here soon.

She washed her face, dusted on a bit of powder, brushed her hair. To keep it from flying again, she made a ponytail and tied it with a narrow black velvet ribbon.

"You goin' to see a new man dressed like that?" Dots gasped. "Jeans and shirt and ponytail?"

"Sure. I'm going to ride."

"Why don't you drive, wear a dress, a pretty one?"

"Jeans and shirt are good enough for this man," Rae-Ellen said. "He's of Pa's picking. I wouldn't turn my hand over to make a good impression on him."

"Still," Dots said, "you never can tell."

Rae-Ellen grinned, winked, said, "You'll get a call soon, see if you don't!" and went running from the room and outside.

Johnny had a different filly saddled and waiting. "Platinum was pretty wet," he explained. "Needs cooling down. So I saddled up Silver Gay—you always like to ride her."

Rae-Ellen nodded, ran her hand over the lovely silver withers of the filly. Every horse and mare and filly and colt at the Double T was a beautiful silver color; she was going to breed only silver horses, ever.

Being fresh, Silver Gay galloped the three miles to town. Rae-Ellen fumed as she rode; she didn't want to call on the manager Pa had hired, was doing so on sheer impulse. She had every intention of letting the fellow see who was the real employer.

She reined up sharply at the hitching post provided for riders at the Travis Forks Hotel, and Silver Gay whinnied and reared. Instantly Rae-Ellen soothed, stroking and patting.

"There, there, lovely Gay, I'm sorry!" she murmured. "I let my temper...You're a good girl, a beautiful girl!"

She dismounted, tied the rein, stood with her arms around the filly's neck, her cheek against the smooth, damp coat, murmuring and singsonging. Silver Gay quieted and nibbled at Rae-Ellen's hair, and all was well between them again.

She went into the bare little lobby of the hotel,

bootheels clicking on the board floor. The desk clerk, gray-haired and thin, greeted her in a friendly manner.

"Jess Tower, Mr. Simmons," she said. "That's who I'm here to see."

"He ain't in," the clerk replied. "I seen him leave a spell back. Likely went to eat. You might try the diner."

Well, she wasn't going to chase the man all over Travis Forks! "I'll wait," she said. "In his room, if I may. We have business to discuss."

She got the key and tramped up the stairway to the second floor.

The room was empty. There was a bed, a bed table, lamp, a dresser and a straight chair. She sat on the bed to wait. The spread was smooth and smelled of sunlight.

She wished she could just tell him to repack his brushes and go back to where he came from. But she didn't quite dare. Pa Travis, like it or not, still held the reins. She had things to accomplish before she could be in charge.

After forever, she heard a footstep, the door swung open and a man came in—six feet one or six feet two, she couldn't tell which—a powerful man, almost frighteningly so.

In his late twenties, he was the handsomest man she'd ever seen, but he reminded her of Burr, who had been homely, and this infuriated her. He had sun-streaked, wavy, brown hair, generous, chiseled features and blue, keen, sunny eyes.

Instantly and instinctively, she knew him for what he was—and hated him for it. Tall, disgustingly handsome, blatantly virile, the kind of man who

40

assumed that he could have—and then discard—any woman he wanted; who drifted through the world, doing what he pleased and then moving on. He might have some claim to the background for the job Pa Travis had been soft enough to give him, but he was, face it, basically a bum—the only term for him—sliding through life on his good looks and his arrogance. And this was what Pa had foisted on her!

Neither spoke.

For Jess Tower, it was hate at first sight. This one was plainly a hellcat. Look at the way she held her head, as if she owned the world. He knew who she was by instinct. Travis had said she was a wild one, on the phone.

"She needs a strong hand," Travis had said. "But she made Burr a perfect wife, even sweet."

Sure, Jess thought now, looking at her angry mouth. She was pregnant then, placid as a mare about to foal. Now she's herself again, mean as a cat. The only good things about her were her shape and that brown, red-tinged hair.

She glared back into his glare.

He attacked: "I saw you rein up that filly!" he accused. "You hurt her mouth!"

"Who asked you to spy on me—Pa Travis?"

"It didn't require spying. I was going into the diner and glanced over this way. You can't get out of it. I saw it happen!"

Pa Travis had said the new manager was all business, but he hadn't said he was so unbearably handsome. Or that he'd have the nerve to jump all over his employer about something that was none of his business.

41

"The way I rein up is none of your affair!" she cried. "Since you were spying anyway, why didn't you wait long enough to see me love and pat my filly and tell her it was an accident and I was sorry? I've got sense enough not to mistreat fine-bred stock—or any stock!"

"So the filly accepted your apology. But don't let it happen again."

"She's my filly, and I'll do with her as I please! If you want to think I'm Simon Legree, go right ahead! For your information, I don't mistreat my horses, but I'm not about to let you order me around!"

"That's for me to decide," he retorted. "I'll order you when you need it. For the good of the stable."

"Who do you think you are?" she demanded.

"Jess Tower. Hired by Vic Travis to run your horse farm and see to the welfare of the horses. And it isn't to be tolerated that a featherheaded female—even if she owns the filly—can rein up like you did today! I suppose you examined her mouth to see if it was cut?"

"I didn't cut it! And never will! I've been around horses all my life!"

"Poor horses!"

He glared at the high-handed beauty perched on his hotel bed—a headstrong girl who had wonderful hair. Except on her it wasn't so wonderful. She was so high-tempered she spoiled her own hair, her own beauty. Plus those blue eyes, way too blue, like electricity, and just as dangerous. She'd stop at nothing to get her own way. Well, she needn't try it on him. He was a match for her.

He recalled the phone conversation he'd had with

Travis when they set up this deal. "You want me to run the horse farm for your daughter-in-law, sir?" Jess had asked.

"For six months. She has a good foreman. With you at the head for a while, everything should go smoothly."

"I think you should know, sir, that I won't take orders from a woman. Not even from your daughter-in-law."

"You won't have to. You'll manage the place, oversee breeding, management of the horses, such like. You're accountable only to me."

Now, seeing this female's stubborn chin, he knew she probably would try to make him follow her orders. She wasn't at all like Susie Drummond, who had ridden in yesterday to meet him. Susie was warm and friendly and reasonable, and he'd felt drawn to her.

"Maybe I should tell you," he said, "that when your father-in-law hired me, we had a clear understanding."

"So?"

"I told him I never take orders from a woman. All orders come from him."

"*You'll* give *me* orders how to treat my own horses!"

"If necessary, yes."

"I won't tolerate that, not for one minute!"

"And I'll not have horses mistreated."

"Pa Travis did say you know horses," she conceded reluctantly.

"Did he say anything else?"

"Why should he? Horses is why he hired you. Exactly what do you know about thoroughbred horses?"

"Plenty, and then some. Travis knows this is my first full-time job with them. He knows I worked awhile in Kentucky, and quite a bit in California. He's satisfied with me."

"You don't have to boast!"

"Call it what you want. It happens to be fact." He'd never met a girl so infuriating, so high-handed. How had Burr ever put up with her? And how two girls could live in the same house—Susie Drummond had said she lived with Rae-Ellen—one so warm and understanding and the other completely impossible—he couldn't grasp. Just to look at this one made his hackles stand up. And he'd given his word to Travis to tolerate her for six months!

If it weren't for the promise he'd made Burr's father and the ladylike treatment he'd had from Susie, he'd be on the first plane back to California. He'd walk out on this filly, let her get into any trouble she wanted to, let her ruin her horse-breeding farm, drive off her help with that adder's tongue, find out what it was like to be alone.

Chapter Four

POSSESSED by a flash of unreasoning fury, she moved close to him, raging at his arrogance and at the burning which suddenly invaded her loins. If he hadn't been so tall, their noses would have touched. "Just exactly why did you take this job?"

"I consider that my private affair."

"And I consider that, since it's *my* breeding farm, I have the right to know! Or did you scheme with Pa Travis to keep secrets from me?"

Their eyes wrestled.

"Privacy," he said. "No secrets."

"Oh, so that's the way you want it! You know everything about me, and I know nothing about you!"

"You know what any employer needs to know. I'm

single, healthy, and thoroughly familiar with horses. And their ailments. I can do the job I was hired to do—manage your breeding farm, see that it gets off to a solid start."

"It's already off to a solid start! I've got ten fillies and two stallions! I've got two fillies breeding right now! I've—"

"Not good enough. I'll double it in six months."

"Where do you think the money's coming from to buy filly after filly, stallion after stallion?"

"Travis said not to worry about money."

Ha! So Pa meant, in his bossy way, to double the size of her breeding stock, to use that as a bribe! What an underhanded way to get her to marry! She wondered, suddenly, if this California creature knew about the marriage plan.

"What did Pa Travis tell you of his plans—for me and my son?" she demanded.

"Nothing much. Only that he wants you to have a firm start in your breeding program. Wants the best of everything for you. That I'm to manage the purchase of fillies. We agreed that two stallions is enough."

"And if I say they're not enough?"

"Sorry, I can't agree. You need to use other stallions, from everywhere, keep bringing new blood into your line, the best blood. And let your stallions service other fillies in the county, even beyond. Eventually, that will result in stallions you can use, with care, to put strengthened blood into some of your foals."

He'd said "Sorry," but he wasn't sorry, not a bit. Look at his chin. He'd made up his mind she was to have only two stallions, and he hadn't even set foot on the Double T! She clenched her fists, eyes slicing into his, snapping and twisting.

"Susie seemed to think two stallions is enough," he said.

"So! You discussed my private affairs with a stranger!"

"It happens she asked me if I didn't think two stallions are enough and I said yes, at this point they are! Call that discussing your private affairs if you want to!"

The fact that Susie had said the very same thing to Rae-Ellen herself, only made her madder. Not mad at Susie. It was this man. There was something about him besides his beastly handsomeness and arrogance that rubbed her the wrong way. The burning in her loins got worse, and she marveled at that, stunned by it, then tried to think what to say to show him he didn't bother her a bit.

"You'll get so many fillies we can't breed properly!" she cried. "I want a different sire for every foal!"

"Let me worry about that."

She socked her hands onto her hips, knowing she was going too far, but she couldn't stop. Tower now hooked his thumbs into the edge of his pants pockets, still boring into her eyes. His mouth was a stubborn line across his face, and he looked handsome even like that, which was intolerable, and then he narrowed those blue eyes and probed and probed. And clearly didn't like what he saw.

So he was furious, was he? Wonderful! She hurt with wanting to fire him on the spot, but Pa Travis had the upper hand. For the present. And, through Pa, so did this utter lout!

Somehow, she had to send Tower packing. She

47

couldn't stand back and watch him run things. Or . . . wait. She'd let him think he was boss! Sooner or later, he'd do something really wrong and then even Pa Travis would agree he must go. All she need do was wait. If she could endure waiting, since to get rid of him instantly, never to have to look at his arrogant handsomeness again, was what she really wanted.

She couldn't get her eyes loose from his. She trembled, held herself from flying at him, from raking her nails down those hateful, perfect cheeks. She ached to hit him, too, drive her fist into that shapely, angry mouth, to see it split and swell. And how she'd delight in marking up that know-it-all nose!

Jess stood, thumbs hooked into his pockets, taking the unexplained, stabbing rage of blue eyes full-on. Like electricity—or lightning, he thought. He'd seen few, even in Hollywood, who could match her for sheer beauty. Of course, his liking the kind of hair she had, that long, waving wealth of brown curls streaked with red, had something to do with it. With those blazing eyes and that blazing hair, she looked as though she were on fire. Damnation, furious with her though he was, he admired her and wondered what she'd look like if she ever calmed down.

She was tall, too, only six or seven inches shorter than his own six-two. That made for a good couple, height-wise. Her figure, in the snug red shirt and tight jeans set him afire. She had long, supple legs, small, perfectly turned ankles, even in boots. Dainty as those on the highest-bred filly. Her furious stance pushed her breasts against her shirt, pointing right at him.

He felt a slow warmth in his groin, firmed his mouth, fought the warmth. This girl was sex on the hoof. She was dangerous; she didn't have any kindness in her, only a strong, unreasonable will and defiance and a readiness to fight and every other conceivable mark of a spoiled female.

He filled his mind with one thought. He'd like to shake her, shake some sense, some gentleness, into her. In fact, he'd enjoy spanking her. It was plain she'd never been spanked in her life, had always got her own way, even when she was an obnoxious toddler.

He told her one obvious truth, coolly, bluntly: "Your jeans," he said. "They're too damned tight."

Scarlet flashed into her face, was gone, leaving it white with rage under the tan.

"One thing you're *not* hired to do," she hissed, "is to oversee my wardrobe! You've done it now! You're fired! Pack your things, and get back to California!"

"Only Travis can fire me."

"Pah! All I have to do is tell him what you said about my jeans! He's a clean and proper man!"

"He'll agree about the jeans. Any man would. All you can tell him, really, is that you've taken a dislike to me, that you don't care how good a manager I am, you want to get rid of me because I don't lick your boots!"

"Pack. Now. I'll wait until you go."

He looked her over slowly, taking in every alluring, maddening detail. After that, speaking deliberately, he described Susie's visit the day before. Hearing him, despite her outrage, Rae-Ellen remembered

Susie had mentioned seeing him and that he was tremendous in size.

"Susie came to welcome me to Texas," he began, "to say that my quarters at the Double T are ready when I want to move in. She told me how you two are like sisters. Susie's a real lady, as true a one as can be found. She's so different from you, I marvel that you're friends at all."

Fury swept Rae-Ellen. That this movie bum had the nerve to compare her with Susie! The gall of him!

"I was on my way to lunch at the diner," he said, "when she showed up. She was riding, too. Wore fine riding breeches."

"I know the pair! I suppose you approve of the way they fit!"

"Sure thing. She introduced herself, and I asked her to lunch with me and she accepted."

"Susie's a beauty. You'll tell me that next."

"Twenty-one, isn't she?"

Rae-Ellen gave an angry nod.

"That hair is a natural platinum, even lovelier than the coat on that filly you're riding today. I saw her ride up, too, and the sun glinting on the platinum-haired girl and the platinum filly was a real sight."

"Of course she's beautiful!" snapped Rae-Ellen.

"It was her black eyes with that hair that shook me," he continued. "Unbeatable combination. She'd be a star if she set foot in Hollywood."

"If all you think about is Hollywood, why did you ever imagine you could manage a horse-breeding farm?"

He smiled suddenly, maddeningly. "Good question. But the horses won, hands down, years ago."

He told about his lunch with Susie—hamburgers and French fries. But he didn't tell of how hot his neck got, the way it always did when he wanted sex. It was none of this hellcat's business.

Since Susie appealed to him, he had let her see it, wondered if he could handle the yen he felt. She wasn't the easy-lay type. She was a lady, and any advances he made would have to lead to the altar.

He poured her coffee. He loaded his with sugar, took no cream. Susie was generous with the cream, but took no sugar. He commented on the opposite way they drank coffee.

She told him about Drew Knight, a sheepman and some kind of rodeo king, who drank his coffee the way she did. "Or rather," she confessed shyly, "I drink mine the way *he* drinks his. Rae-Ellen and I both do."

"Which means you both have a yen for the guy?"

She'd blushed and not answered. But he knew. His new "employer," Rae-Ellen Travis, and this delectable Susie Drummond both wanted the rodeo king. He wondered if the king wanted either one of them. Then Susie told him she lived with Rae-Ellen and he thought wryly that they could keep an eye on each other about Knight. He wondered who would win.

It wasn't until Rae-Ellen broke in on his thoughts of Susie that he realized he'd been talking a blue streak, then had gone silent. He'd evidently then made some kind of comment, for now Rae-Ellen gave him a sharp, disbelieving look.

"You mean to tell me," she cried, "that Susie

51

invited you to ride in the rodeo, and you said you would—just like that?"

Hell, it'd been automatic. No reason for her to make such a big thing of it. "Sure," he said. "She invited me. Why not?"

"You're not hired to ride in rodeos! You're hired to—"

"I know what I'm hired for. It so happens your father-in-law told me I'm to participate in local events and get acquainted with everybody. Be a regular Texan."

"And you're going to do it?"

"Sure am."

He saw her burn, narrowed his eyes. He'd never dreamed he'd meet a girl—a beauty—he'd hate. He'd never seen one so bullheaded, sassy, hard on the nerves, so infuriating and altogether not to be endured. He was so mad he ached again to grab her and shake her. To at least go to Travis and say he wouldn't work for Rae-Ellen even if he, Jess, *was* boss. But that would be breaking his word; somehow, he had to best this female, get on working terms with her, no matter how strained.

Rae-Ellen could read his mind, and she could read Pa Travis's mind. Tower would never let her fire him; Pa wouldn't fire him. He'd force this damnable oaf down her throat.

He was a sickening, handsome, tremendous, conceited, high-handed, and stupid hunk of man on two legs. He was an old stallion, mean and strong—not even a wild and thoughtless young stallion, but experienced and hateful. She didn't understand why she hated him so, exactly, but hate him she did.

52

Then she saw his eyes go sexy-mad—that was the only way to describe it—and she got madder than ever herself. She went taut, ready for him to dare to make a move.

He saw her do that.

She saw hotness take him.

She didn't give him a chance. She flew at him, fingers arched, reaching for those lust-filled eyes. She'd scratch them out...she'd claw his face to ribbons...she'd...

He caught her wrists, one in each great hand, swung back her arms until she cried out in pain and fury. She had one glimpse of his face. It was twisted with rage, but handsome even so, and his neck was fiery red. He loosened his hold, swooped her into his arms and up, took two steps with her kicking and trying to claw, and threw her on the bed.

She shot right back up. He slammed her down, held her there. She squirmed and twisted and tried to kick, but he was strong beyond belief and she got nowhere. But she kept trying, spitting orders to let go, firing him repeatedly.

"Wait till I tell Pa Travis!" she spat after one heated firing. "He'll kick you out so fast you'll never know what happened!"

He just kept holding her.

"Let me up! I'll scream!"

"Go ahead. Scream. Make a scandal."

Furious, because of course she couldn't scream, couldn't be found by anyone in this situation, she clawed for his eyes again, but he controlled her with maddening ease.

When, exhausted, she stopped struggling, to rest,

he began to unbutton her shirt. She struggled again, but weakly, and somehow he ripped the shirt off her, and she was in bra and jeans. And boots. She had him there—the boots. She tried to kick him.

He flung his body on hers and slammed his mouth over her lips. He'd never tasted sweeter lips and marveled that she could be so poison-mean and have such a wonderful, feminine mouth. He worked his tongue past her lips, and she tried to bite it; he jerked it free and kissed her fiercely.

Even kissing, rage such as he'd never felt came over him and with it uncontrollable desire. When he lifted his mouth, and she began clawing, then hit him with her fists, he got both her wrists in one big hand and kept them. With the other hand, he ripped off the too-tight jeans, yanked them to her knees, something that seemed to be bikini panties sliding down with them. The boots stopped them and, straddling her, he turned back to her face, her pummeling his spine, and tugged off the boots and socks and finally the jeans, until he had her naked.

She almost got away, but one motion and he had her back on the bed. He realized what he was doing, but she had him so worked up, both emotionally and sexually, he couldn't stop.

"Well," she panted, "what are you going to do to me next?" Her hair was fiery and tumbled, and her lips were bloodred and shaking, but she just lay, looking as if she'd thought of some plan of her own.

"I think you've got a pretty good idea," he said. Then, sensing what her hidden plan might be, he added, "And I think you half plan to report this to Travis to get me fired."

She clamped her lips, stared back defiantly.

He looked her over swiftly, saw the rounded breasts with pink, uptilted nipples set in circles of rose. He pulled the flat of one hand over one and it lifted and went hard. She didn't move, but watched him, lips shaking. He stroked one breast and then the other, and she still didn't fight.

He eyed the insweep of waist, the curve of thigh, admired what he could see of her buttocks, noted the perfection of her legs and dainty ankles and narrow feet.

Last he studied the patch of brown red between her thighs. It matched her hair exactly. Wanting her and hating her, he was near to bursting with need, and tore at his clothes to get them off. Then, stripped, he came at her, where she lay suddenly too weak to struggle again.

"You wouldn't dare!" she whispered.

"You want me, too!" he said hoarsely.

Her breath quivered. She couldn't help looking at him while he stared at her. He was better-looking naked than dressed, if that was possible. His body was as handsome as his face—no, handsomer. It seemed to have been chiseled out of sun-bronzed marble by some talented sculptor who then breathed life into it and made the perfect male creature.

His need was tremendous. She caught her breath, just seeing it. There may still be time, she thought. This wasn't what she really wanted. She wanted to choose the man with whom she had sex, not be mauled and ravished by Jess Tower.

Before she could move, he was on her, his great body covering hers. Then he was entering, and it was like a homecoming. Unbelievably, it was. Then he withdrew slowly, teasingly, and she didn't breathe until he entered again.

He moved, very fast in the beginning, then slowly, as if feeling his way, as if waiting for her. When he did that, it seemed natural, even necessary, for her to move, to meet him at every thrust. Her rage seemed to melt; the important thing was to meet him every time.

Their breaths mingled. Their movements grew faster. She was holding her breath finally. Oh, the utter perfection of reaching, reaching for what she knew must be there, had to be. Her arms tightened around him, liking the smooth muscles of his back. She couldn't remember putting her arms there, but that was where they belonged. For now, at least.

Suddenly it was she who went faster, and he who matched her lead. But on the next stroke he regained the lead, and she moved fiercely to meet his assault. All the while, the reaching was deeper, harder, sweeter...and now, at last now, the joy started at the base of her brain, raced down her spine through all her body, and centered where they were joined.

As the silent, shaking explosion reached into her depths, she clung to him, tears wetting her cheeks. "Jess...Jess..." she whispered. "I thought I'd never again feel...oh, Jess!" She thought he was calling her sweetheart but couldn't be sure, because that joy lasted forever, then, slowly, was gone.

She realized what he'd done instantly. She pushed him away and he let her. She sat up, furious. She hated him worse than before. He'd actually raped her. Well, in the beginning it was rape, which was just as bad.

"Rape!" she croaked, trying to hide her breasts and thighs. She stabbed her eyes at his, gasping, determined to make him take the blame.

He was breathing hard. He shook his head.

"No rape, lady. I had your full cooperation, after a certain point."

All at once she wanted to cry. He'd taken her, and she'd let him do it to get some pointers about sex to use on Drew. She really had done it for that reason, and now she couldn't cry because Tower would see and think it was because of him. Him and his conceit!

"I'm not too sorry about what happened," Tower said. "You asked for it. Those jeans alone asked, to say nothing of your behavior. You dare a man—you dared me!"

"I did no such thing! You just—you need to be put in your place!"

"You loved it," he told her.

She sat silent, raging.

"You did love it. I've had— I can tell. You've been married, you have needs, and you love it when they're filled! You'd might as well admit it. It's no big deal. This is the twentieth century."

"I admit nothing!"

"Lie back down," he ordered. "We'll have a second course."

She began to quiver with outrage. She wanted to grab her clothes and run. But there was a core, a heart, to this inner rage. He'd subdued her; now it was her turn to subdue him.

"No, you lie on *your* back!" she flamed. "The way I was! I'll show you what a second course is!"

Amazement made his handsome face blinding in

its perfection, because it was wiped clean of that know-it-all expression. He threw out his hands, stretched on his back, waited. His need was back, urgent and almost exciting. On another man—Drew—it would be thrilling.

She mounted him as she would a horse, only now there was that fullness, that hardness, inside her. He had a scatter of curling brown hair between his breasts and a light strip below his flat belly, which she couldn't see after she was in place.

She rode him in a circular motion, and he let her do it, himself moving in the opposite direction and thrusting. She added a thrust to her attack.

The joy came faster this time and lasted longer. She clung to his shoulders, fingers digging, and felt wave after wave of bliss until, at the last, at the peak of rage, she touched a plateau of raging glory. She forgot she hated him.

Jess, himself carried to heights never before reached, forgot how arrogant she was. His only thought was of the wonder of her, the incomparable passion.

Unwilling for it to end, he rolled, taking her along, and now he was in the dominant position. They burned, fused. And when it ended, they faced each other stiffly, at odds again.

Chapter Five

SHE couldn't think of a thing to say. As for him, he kept his mouth clamped, still handsome, darn him, and started to put on his underwear. Her bikinis and bra were on the floor. She flipped off the bed, and scrambled into the scrap of bikini hastily. She was hell-bent to be dressed first, to leave him still trying to get decent; she wasn't going to let him be the one to walk out, the victor.

Because she had won in sex, she really had. In spite of feeling raped, mauled and then rejected, she had been the winner. She fumbled at her bra, the hook stubborn, but she got it fastened, snatched up her shirt, turned it right-side out, put it on, buttoned it with trembling fingers.

One thing was definite. She'd got control of that

cocky blabbermouth. In her arms he'd become help-less, driven by her allure, melded to her, unable to break the passion which coupled them. Once so joined, she'd been the one in power. He'd been helpless, could only move blindly and fast, surrender his manhood into her body, lost to him forever, hers to cast aside. And he could neither deny it, if she lowered herself to point it out, nor change it.

Yet under her triumph pulsed fury that he had practically raped her, had made her helpless with desire, so helpless she could no longer fight. She'd never forget that; she'd blame him for it as long as she might be forced to know him and even longer, even—all her life. The quicker she got rid of him, the better.

She finished turning her jeans right-side out and stepped hastily into them, hopping for balance. He was putting on his slacks but his shirt and undershirt still lay on the floor—she was still ahead. Both were barefoot. Seeing his haste, the way he snatched up each garment, the intent look he had, her hatred flared anew. How right she'd been from the start! Aversion to his size had come first; deep dislike for his handsomeness and the way he reminded her of Burr—dear, homely Burr—had sprung up next. Dis-gust with his eyes—almost as blue as her own—had filled her at the same time. Probing, stick-the-nose-in eyes. His every move, from saying he'd let no woman boss him, through his enthusiastic descrip-tion of Susie's visit, right up to when he had stripped off her jeans, had increased her first instinctive aver-sion, until now it had become implacable hatred.

She fastened her belt, sat on the floor and put on

her socks. Then she yanked on her boots, sprang to her feet, gave a swipe at her hair, and rushed out of the room and down to Silver Gay, leaving Tower still tying his shoes.

Jess, mumbling curses at his own slowness as she flounced out, was surprised, stunned, and inclined to chuckle. Rae-Ellen Travis was the wildest female he'd ever had. Not that there'd been all that many women. But she was the first who'd matched his passion. No matter how rough he'd been, she was rough right back, full strength.

And that clatter of horse's hooves leaving! She was in a real temper. She'd never report what happened to Travis; her redheaded pride wouldn't let her. Now he did chuckle. She'd even raped him, or thought she had. He chuckled louder.

Abruptly, he sobered. Hell, she'd been the best, sure. But he'd never have touched her if he hadn't clear forgotten, in his wild desire, that she was Burr's widow and, in a way, his employer.

She was as much to blame as he was. She'd stayed on the bed at the end, not fighting him, not trying to get away. And then, the minute he touched her, she'd turned into a firebrand.

He was brushing his hair when he realized how he'd heard her take off on the filly, starting out at a full gallop. His anger smoldered. He had a strong impulse to rent a car, overtake her, yell until she understood she couldn't treat the filly mean, even if she was mad at the world.

But what was the use? The next notion—to go to Travis—struck him and he discarded that. Even if he had been Burr's sidekick, he couldn't go to Burr's father and say, "I give up. You manage that hellcat by yourself. I want no part of her."

No, he'd made an agreement with Travis, and he'd honor it. Still, he'd have to watch her. She'd make some move to get rid of him. She wouldn't just let what happened go; she'd be up to mischief.

He knew how to deal with her. Keep his distance, that was for sure. If she hung around the stable—and she'd do it to heckle him—he'd answer any question she asked, then get the hell away from her. He'd be distant, polite, businesslike, talk to her of horses, only horses and their needs. Stubborn as she was, nature like a wildcat, she could plot to lead him on again, goad him into repeating what happened just now, and someway use it, that time, to get him fired in disgrace.

If only she was a little bit like Susie, everything would be fine. She'd be gentle, with quiet ways, and they wouldn't fight about horses or anything else. He smiled, liking the feeling of being drawn to Susie—she was like cooling water after the searing burn of Rae-Ellen. Her quiet, pure allure was the exact opposite of the angry hunger he'd felt for the other one.

Rae-Ellen was riding Silver Gay homeward at an easy lope. She'd started from the hotel full speed to put Tower in his place. As soon as she'd turned the corner, she'd slowed to a lope.

She wished she'd driven her car. At the wheel, stirred up this way, she'd drive like the wind. If she got a ticket, she got a ticket. She needed to work off this absolute fury. Somehow, loping this way, she had to overcome it. If she didn't, Leah would notice that something was wrong and pry. Susie would notice and worry. Dots would ask questions, and she didn't want to give the answers, dared not.

Her rage cooled, thinking of Drew. He was the reason she'd got mixed up with Tower. Because she'd thrown herself at Drew, begged for marriage, even for sex without marriage, and he'd refused, ever so kindly. And had told her honestly about Susie. Drew, at least, was perfect.

One thing about Tower, almost in his favor. She'd found out with him that Drew wasn't the only man who might bring her to ecstasy. But she'd also learned how much more wonderful lovemaking with Drew would be because him she loved. What Tower had done was to increase her expertise and really awaken her sexually. Just that, nothing more.

She reviewed how it had been with him. He'd been rough, even violent—but under it there'd been some gentleness. There really had been. He'd been indescribably passionate. But he'd also called her an endearing name. If he'd do that all the time, and if he ever came to love a girl, it might—just might—be bearable.

Pah! The idea was ridiculous! He was too self-centered, too spoiled, to be capable of love. The only thing he could feel was lust. And whether this girl or that one would satisfy him at the moment.

Still, she realized, there was *something* to him. He could teach sex tricks to a woman carved from stone. Her loins were beginning to glow, to throb again. She urged Silver Gay into an easy gallop. She'd never go to bed with Tower again, no matter what his attraction. She'd used him once; she knew enough of his tricks to entice Drew when she had the chance. And she knew more: how better to handle the next man—the one she would try out in her quest to win Drew.

By the time she reached home, she was outwardly calm. Being with Leah and Susie and Dots should get her back to normal. She wasn't going to let what Tower had done change a thing; life was to go on, right into the arms of Drew Knight!

Leah met her at the door as Johnny led the filly toward the stable. "Thought you'd never get back," Leah exclaimed. "You got to meet your sister at four. And you missed lunch."

Rae-Ellen explained about the enormous breakfast and later the doughnuts with Drew. She got a knowing look from the housekeeper.

"He propose?" Leah demanded.

Rae-Ellen's face burned. "No. Why should he?"

"He's the one. I made up my mind. Best catch in the county. You been a widow long enough. And your baby needs a pa."

Rae-Ellen managed a laugh. "Of course he didn't propose!" she reiterated. "I've plenty of time to marry—*if* I marry!"

Leah sniffed. "You want some grub?"

"No, I'll wait for supper. I'm going up to see Vic now. Where is he?"

"Asleep in the nursery. Dots went drivin' away in her car, afternoon date at the county line. Says look for her when you see her."

Rae-Ellen smiled, watched Leah turn away, shaking her white head in disapproval. Leah liked Dots, lectured her on morals, warned her to pick a man and marry him before she made a mess of her life.

Rae-Ellen went into the nursery and stood looking tenderly down at Baby Vic. He sprawled fiercely in his crib. He was on his stomach, his hands thrown out to the sides—big, strong hands for a baby. He was going to be a gigantic man, a true Texan.

Next she went into her bedroom, which was large and furnished in walnut. The carpeting was russet, the bedspread and upholstering warm tan, the window drapes bordered with russet. Yellow cushions were scattered about. The bathroom was white with russet towels and rug, the tub large enough to lie down in, the shower curtain—Rae-Ellen hated glass shower doors—russet and yellow.

She stripped, cramming the clothes she'd worn for Jess Tower—never knowing, when she put them on, what would happen—into the hamper. She stood for moments under the shower, soaping and resoaping, washing him off and out of herself. Then she filled the tub with steaming water, soaped again, soaked. When she finished, she felt as cleansed of him as bathing could make her.

She put on fresh blue bikinis and bra, a fresh blue slip and topped them off with a new dress. This was a sheer blue fabric and felt cool. She brushed her hair, let it hang free. She'd washed it only yesterday, and it gleamed, except for tendrils around her face which were still damp from bathing. On her feet she put new blue slippers and was ready to go to meet her sister.

Susie tapped at her door, and came in. She was wearing misty, sheer gray. She was breathtakingly beautiful, her platinum hair moving on the gray dress, her black eyes gleaming softly. Her pink, shapely lips, finely chiseled, were smiling.

"New dress, I see!" she exclaimed. "So's mine!"

"Do you have a date?" Rae-Ellen asked, wondering if Drew was going to be exposed to all this loveliness. And if he was, whether he'd speak of love.

"No date. It's just that the day is hot, and this is new and cool."

Rae-Ellen smiled, relieved that Susie wasn't seeing Drew, but then studied Susie uneasily, wondering if, despite her guilty secret, she meant to marry Drew.

Suddenly, anger over it all—Pa Travis, Drew's rejection, sex with Tower—overwhelmed her, and she cried out to Susie, "Don't let me catch you trying to marry Drew, Susie Drummond! If you try, I'll tell!"

Appalled, Susie stared. "I thought," she managed to say at last, "that you might find Jess Tower attractive. Or didn't you see him when you went into town?"

"Oh, I saw him all right! Don't get the idea I'd ever marry him! Not that arrogant bum!"

"I—I thought he was nice."

"That shows how much you know about men! As you've demonstrated once already!"

"W-what are you talking about, darling? First . . . Drew. Now— Why are you so upset? Please don't be angry with me! You're as dear as the sister I never had! You're so wonderful I want to live with you as long as you'll have me. Unless—"

"Unless one of us marries. Say it out!"

"Well . . . yes . . . that," Susie whispered, ashen.

Rae-Ellen, seeing her pallor, resisted the impulse to comfort her and instead kept talking. Words spilled out, telling Susie she knew what had happened eighteen months ago.

"But how could you possibly know?" Susie wailed. "We kept it a secret!"

"I know. Because Keith was foreman of the Double T, and neither of you wanted scandal! Well, as it happens, I heard you and Keith Belisle talking together once! I was two stalls away, petting Thunder Boy, and the two of you went into a stall for privacy and I couldn't help hearing!"

"Rae-Ellen . . . oh, darling!" moaned Susie.

"I knew you had a terrible crush on Keith, him so good-looking, with that yellow hair and gray eyes that melt a girl! And his build! And his voice, so positive and clear—that'd give any girl confidence in him! To say nothing of the way he's always worked! He'd make any girl a perfect husband, even you! And you wanted him so much!"

"Oh, I did want him," Susie whispered. "So much!"

"I'd already seen that. Then, when I noticed you grow pale and sad and thin, I worried. But it wasn't until that evening in the stable that I heard the truth and understood what was wrong!"

Quickly now, to convince Susie of what she knew, she related the pitiful story. Susie wept quietly throughout.

Keith had turned all his charm on nineteen-year-old Susie, and within days she was besottedly in love with him. They went everywhere together, to dances and movies and rodeos. And they spent stolen, secret hours in a tiny shack at the edge of the Double T.

When Susie knew she was pregnant, the two of them slipped down to the stable to talk. That was when Rae-Ellen overheard accidentally, quivering with concern for Susie, who still lived with her strict parents at the time.

"I really am pregnant, darling," Susie had told Keith. "I went to a doctor in Fort Worth."

"Get rid of it," Keith had said promptly. "That way, nobody will know."

"But you s-said we'd be married!"

"Sure, and we will. Only not right now. I need to get ahead in my job first. And to prove to your dad I can run your ranch when you inherit."

"I'm willing to live on less, darling! And then we can keep our baby! I couldn't... possibly... kill it!"

Keith's voice had tightened: "You had a thing for Drew Knight earlier," he said. "How do I know he didn't use you first? If he did, that makes you used goods, and I can't marry you. For all I know, the kid's Drew's."

"Drew never— There wasn't anything between us, I swear it, Keith! It's your baby, honest and truly!"

"Go to your parents if you don't want an abortion. Get them to send you away. Put the kid out for adoption."

"Keith... you sound so hard!"

"I don't mean to, honey. Just realistic. Forgive me for flying off the handle. Of course the baby's mine. But I can't be saddled with a wife and kid at this point. We have to wait until later. Not much, but anyhow a few months, until my job is set and solid."

"Does your job mean so much to you, Keith?"

"Career. Once I'm really set, say even a year from now, I'll marry you. But for the present, this other mess has got to be cleaned up."

Susie had wept, Keith had murmured comfortingly, and they'd set a wedding date. Susie had looked less forlorn after that, but she rode for hours at a time, and Rae-Ellen knew she was trying to work out her problem, and ached to help her.

But before she could nerve herself to corner Susie, the girl had taken a spill jumping a fence on her horse and miscarried. She was still at the very start of pregnancy, and her mother thought it was only a painful, heavy period, and the problem was solved.

"What you didn't hear," Susie told Rae-Ellen now, in the russet-and-tan bedroom, "is what came later. Keith offered to marry me right away and we'd keep the baby. But I . . . just couldn't. I'd lost all feeling for him, realized it'd just been a tremendous crush, that I'd always, really, loved Drew."

"And you're still in love with him."

"Yes. Oh, I love him so much, darling!"

"You can't marry him. Not without telling him about Keith."

"Of course I can't," Susie replied sadly. "But why are you so intense about it, Rae-Ellen?"

"Because I threw myself at Drew, and he turned me down!"

Susie, stricken, tried to put her arms around Rae-Ellen, who pulled away. "Don't try that!" she cried. "It's no help! You've got all the men! Why, Jess Tower, that you think is so wonderful, as good as told me he means to court you! I'm warning you about Tower! Keith did let you down, yes, but he changed—

69

his warmth and goodness took over! Tower is a man to take a girl, then run. Don't trust him an inch!"

Susie's mouth made an *O* of surprise. "And I hoped maybe you and he—"

"Never! And I'm warning you further: I mean to get Drew if I can!"

"And so am I," Susie said quietly. "What are we to do?"

"We've both got good taste!" sniffed Rae-Ellen. "The field is open. You take your chances, and I'll take mine!"

"And still be like sisters?" she asked doubtfully.

"Sisters often fight over the same man," Rae-Ellen said. "This way, we can keep an eye on each other."

Drew will reconsider, Rae-Ellen thought fiercely, staring at the beautiful, soft Susie, he just will! Now that I know the power of passion, I'll be able to tempt him.

But Susie too knew about temptation.

And had a secret to confess.

Rae-Ellen would never tell him of Susie's past. Because, in spite of everything, she loved Susie as a friend, she simply had to fight, cleanly and fairly, for Drew. And she'd see to it, once she got into his arms again, that her lovemaking was clean and decent. And persuasive.

Susie murmured, dried her tears, left the room, going into her own misty gray blue chamber. It was only then that Rae-Ellen realized Susie hadn't committed herself about either Drew or Tower.

She hadn't stated definitely, that she'd fight for Drew, though of course she would. And she hadn't said whether she'd confess to him about Keith. Also,

II

The Secret

Chapter Six

Dots showed up much sooner than expected.

"Oh, I was so alluring, Wilson took me to the best hotel in Fort Worth!" she exulted. "I know you didn't expect me so soon, but Wilson's got a date with his fiancée tonight, and anyway your sister's coming in and I want to see her. And there's Pa Travis's supper party in her honor! I don't want to miss that!"

With an inward start, Rae-Ellen remembered the supper party. She'd thought, just yesterday, that it was kind of Pa to honor Adah so; now it seemed like another example of his bossiness, and she felt cross.

"Don't frown so, honey," Dots said. "What's wrong?"

"Nothing," Rae-Ellen replied stiffly. "Nothing at all."

"I know better. You need a man, that's what! I've

told you and told you, you need lots of men, like me! You know very well my plan's got a lot of sense to it—go to bed with men until you find the right one, then marry him so fast his ears ring! And have a batch of babies. But he has to be tops in bed, remember, 'cause real love is based on what happens there!"

Rae-Ellen went thoughtful.

"Let me fix you up with a date," Dots pleaded. "I know scads of men, most of 'em real good in bed, too. Try them out. You've been married... you might like it even better the second time around! Ask Adah when she gets here—I'll bet she's happy in bed! Look how fast she had a baby!"

Rae-Ellen shook her head, smiling. Adah's husband, Lance Buford, a wealthy cotton grower in Durham, North Carolina, had struck her as almost stuffily proper when she had first met him, but Adah had confided after the marriage that he was an ardent and inventive lover... and Meggie had come along just nine months after the wedding.

Rae-Ellen got to the airport exactly on time. Both Dots and Susie had offered to ride along, but she had declined.

"You're darlings, both of you, but I want to see Adah alone, first! And I'm selfish enough to want to be first to see little Meggie! Just think, I'm her aunt, and have never laid eyes on her!"

Dots had laughed, motioned to the framed photograph of a tiny, golden-haired, yellow-eyed infant. "At least you know what she looks like!" she teased.

"Nothing like you, with your Italian blood!" Rae-

Ellen teased. "Those ebon eyes and ultra-black hair and the sexiest little behind in Texas!"

Dots giggled, took a little bow. Rae-Ellen was glad all over again she'd let the girl move in to help with Baby Vic. She was tiny, but strong and could handle the sturdy baby with ease. And Vic loved her.

Susie said, "Meggie looks like the photograph you have of Adah. What do you think—are they going to be almost like twins?"

Rae-Ellen had shaken her head. "Meggie's skin is rosy, Adah says. Adah's has a bit of olive to it. Even so, Adah's the family golden girl."

"How come?" Dots had asked.

"Her hair and her golden eyes. And she dresses in nothing but shades of gold and yellow. She's a real beauty. Lance threatens to spank her if she ever dresses in any other color!"

At the airport she spotted Adah coming down the steps first by her gold silk suit, next by her blowing, tawny gold hair. And her graceful move. She carried the baby, wrapped in a white blanket, in her arms.

Rae-Ellen ran to her, hugged, then held her off, feasting her eyes. Adah was just the same—lovelier if anything, as if giving birth had enhanced her beauty.

"Rae-Ellen, darling!" Adah cried in her rich voice. "Here she is... here's Meggie!"

With both debarking and embarking passengers hurrying past, baggage handlers passing and repassing, the roar of planes taking off, the sound of planes landing, the sisters stood on the tarmac, blissfully ignoring all that was going on around them.

Rae-Ellen took Meggie and gazed, entranced, into

Adah's golden eyes repeated. The baby had Lance's patrician features and Adah's dimples.

"She's the most beautiful baby I ever saw!" Rae-Ellen cried. "Wait until you see Vic! He's—well, you can tell from his pictures he's no Adonis."

"He looks like Burr," Adah said gently. "And Burr's looks were so..."

"So ugly he was almost handsome," whispered Rae-Ellen to herself. And then she remembered Jess Tower and his repelling, blatant handsomeness that almost approached being homely in its perfection. Maybe that was why he reminded her somehow of Burr.

"Goodness!" she exclaimed, to get her mind off that bum. "We can't stay here all afternoon! There's a supper party in your honor at Pa Travis's place tonight!"

"That's sweet of him," Adah said. "He's a sweet man."

"I've got a few things to tell that'll show how sweet he is!" Rae-Ellen declared grimly. "But for now, let's get your luggage and make for home!"

Their arrival at the Double T created a flurry. Leah opened the door, smiled at Adah, tried to take charge of Meggie. But Dots came dancing up and kidnapped the baby from the housekeeper, and they all laughed.

"Meggie, you doll baby!" Dots crooned as the others crowded in to admire. "I want a dozen just like you!"

"Best settle down, then," snorted Leah.

Dots ignored her, leaned over and kissed Adah on the cheek. "I'm Dots Romano, you're Adah, and we'll be friends! But only," she added in mock warning, "if you let me rock this baby to sleep sometimes! How old is she now?"

"Three months," Adah said, smiling. "And she loves to be rocked. Her daddy rocks her to sleep every night. She's spoiled about that, and we don't care at all!"

Susie appeared then, hugged Adah and introduced herself. "Your daughter's not like her cousin, then," she laughed. "Baby Vic would have a fit if anyone tried to rock him to sleep. He gets on his stomach in the crib, throws his fists out at the sides and sleeps as if he's fighting some kind of battle. He's his grandfather all over again."

At last the sisters were alone. Adah's room adjoined Rae-Ellen's and they moved back and forth, Rae-Ellen helping unpack, speaking in low voices because both babies were taking a late nap. The nursery adjoined Rae-Ellen's room on the opposite side from Adah's.

"You hinted at the airport," Adah said, "that you don't think Pa Travis is sweet. Is something wrong?"

"Just about everything, that's all! That man—I'd say he's lost his mind, except that he's too bullheaded to lose it!"

"What *has* he done?"

"Called me on the carpet. Ordered me to get married. Within six months."

Adah turned with a soft yellow dress on a hanger. "But *why*? Burr was his son, and it's only been a year! Why would he want you to marry in six months, or at all?"

79

"To give Baby Vic a father! Did you ever hear of anything so ridiculous?"

Adah looked thoughtful. "Maybe it's not ridiculous. For Vic to have a father, I mean. I believe Lance would want Meggie to have one."

"In six months from now?"

"That *is* rushing things. Did you quarrel about it?"

"We certainly did! I'll not marry on his orders, and I told him so!"

"But you haven't said, darling—about whether you think Baby Vic needs a father."

"Oh, someday, certainly. Pa says we're making a sissy out of Vic. Just because he lives in a household of women! But Vic's got Keith Belisle, our foreman and trainer—Keith carries him around, shows him the horses, everything. That's man influence!"

"Does Pa Travis want you to marry Keith?"

"I think he'd like it," Rae-Ellen said crossly.

"What kind of man is Keith?"

"Good-looking, tops with the horses, works like mad. He's kind. Helpful. Courteous."

Adah nodded. "But you can't just turn emotions on and off," she said understandingly.

"Vic likes men," Rae-Ellen said.

"All men?"

"Pretty much. He likes Drew Knight, who happens to be the only man I'd look at twice. The trouble is, Susie's after him, and he seems to prefer her. Baby Vic's crazy about Drew, even pats his cheeks."

"That sounds promising. Give Susie some competition. Concentrate on Drew. Would he satisfy Pa Travis?"

"Never! Drew's a sheepman, and you know how Pa hates sheep! The only reason he tolerates Drew is that Drew's a sort of rodeo king around here, and Pa's crazy about rodeoing."

"Are there other men?"

"A couple."

"Do you intend to consider them?"

"Briefly. But not to marry. I've—well, I've decided to try several men out in bed, learn new techniques and . . . and see to it I get a chance to use them on Drew! To convince him."

"Then you do want to marry?"

"I want to marry Drew. Nobody else."

"And . . . and you think that going to bed with different men will—"

"It's all I can think of to win out over Susie. Dots is using that method to choose a husband. Oh, don't look so shocked, Adah! Modern times call for new methods, especially in courtship."

Adah smiled shakily. "You're in love with Drew?"

"Definitely."

Adah sighed, looked at her sister, and said, "It's not what I'd do, but . . . well, you're you, Rae-Ellen and . . ."

She took Vic along to the supper. Rosita would rage in Spanish the whole evening if she couldn't have the boy in his kitchen playpen, and Pa would be grimly disappointed. Rae-Ellen hadn't the heart to make them unhappy, cross as she felt.

Link Bradley, Rae-Ellen's attorney, who wished to court her and made no secret of it, was already at Pa's when the Double T party arrived. He shook

81

hands with them all, acknowledging the introduction to Adah; then his pale eyes came to Baby Vic and he held out his arms.

Vic scowled and threw himself at Link. Rae-Ellen watched them closely.

Link, stockily built, with smooth brown hair, was thirty-eight and inexperienced with babies. But he held her son carefully, set one fingertip on the end of his nose, and spoke his name. Vic chuckled and, when Link withdrew the finger, threw himself forward, offering his nose again.

This was a ritual with these two, and it pleased Rae-Ellen. She saw the pleasure on Link's full, handsome face and recalled how, when he dealt with legal matters, his manner was cool and sure; he was impossible to beat.

She and her child would be safe in his hands. And she knew she could have him. Though he hadn't spoken of love, she read it in his eyes, which were forever seeking hers out.

While Link was still holding Vic, Clovis Vernon sailed in, smelling of musk. With her was Grant Miller, a widower, who owned the Leaning K Ranch.

Clovis, twenty-three, wore a layered miniskirt. She was a tawny beauty—hair, eyes, skin—all tawny. And she was a manhunter, referring to herself as a swinging schoolteacher. Everybody knew she was looking over the men of the entire county, her aim being to make the best possible marriage.

Clinging to Grant's arm, she greeted everyone in a warm, seductive tone, and told Adah she was delighted to meet her. "This," she warned Adah, smiling, "is Grant Miller, my escort. Hands off!"

Grant shook hands with Adah, smiled and spoke to all the others. He was in his early thirties, six feet tall, and had auburn hair and auburn eyes, darkly red lips and a Texas build. He too always sought out Rae-Ellen when he could.

She now noticed that Bertha Mudd, an attractive older widow who had an eye for Grant Miller, wasn't present. Sometimes Grant took Bertha out; Rae-Ellen had seen them together and knew the woman was in love with Grant. Grant's tender looks, however, were for Rae-Ellen, not Bertha. Clovis, though she now clung to his arm again, got only casual friendliness from him.

Suddenly Rae-Ellen felt very uncomfortable. All the men now present, including Keith Belisle, showed a decided preference for herself, and it made her uneasy. And then Drew Knight arrived, alone, and the situation changed. For Drew preferred Susie.

He made the rounds, greeted everyone, chatted pleasantly with Rae-Ellen, who conducted herself in the most ladylike manner to overcome the way she'd behaved with him over doughnuts. Then Rosita was there, herding them into the dining room where the big table was set with gleaming silver and china.

At table, Rae-Ellen counted the eligible men Pa Travis had assembled—four. And five women. With one vacant place setting which Rosita declared was secret.

"Surprise!" she exclaimed. "Only Pa Travis and Rosita know."

Seething, Rae-Ellen refrained from glowering at her father-in-law. She was aware of his scheme, with his four eligible men, though Drew, being a sheepman, didn't count. He was exposing her to men of his choosing. Well, she'd be double-darned if she'd let that influence her!

Then, with the suddenness of a thunderclap, Jess Tower showed up, complete with that chain around his neck and his slab of watch. Pa, introducing him, announced that Tower was a guest of honor, along with Adah.

"Jess is going to manage the Double T for a spell," he explained. "Get things off to a solid start. It was our lucky day when he agreed to come!"

Rae-Ellen saw Dots spy Jess, then look at her, wink and nod. She flushed. The little minx was signaling for her to make a play for Tower.

He sat down in the vacant chair, Rosita bustling and murmuring Spanish, smiling broadly. All the others began to talk with Tower.

Rae-Ellen glared at him. From his smooth manner now, it was impossible to credit the awful, animal things he had done to her this very day, even making her think she liked them. It was only that she'd been without sex for a year, nothing more.

She'd throw him out of her system immediately, by sleeping with other men. Forget he was alive. Infuriatingly, he and Drew began talking as if they were old-time buddies. She clamped her teeth in exasperation.

All the girls, except Dots and Adah, made a play for him. Susie was quiet and sweet toward him. As for Clovis Vernon, sitting beside Tower, she all but threw herself into his arms, she leaned so close, murmuring as if they already had secrets.

White-lipped, Rae-Ellen ached to pull Clovis's hair out by the roots.

Tower acted entranced. Others noticed, and this further irritated Rae-Ellen. Tower was getting all the attention. She wanted him to be ignored to the point where he'd get disgusted and leave Texas. Instead, he was the star of the evening. Then Drew began to talk about the rodeo, and the others joined in, and Rae-Ellen just nibbled at her food and listened, not speaking one word.

Chapter Seven

AFTER dinner, while the others were setting up card tables and getting ready to play bridge and backgammon, Rae-Ellen managed to get some time alone with Pa Travis. She had to tempt him into the kitchen to see how big Vic looked, sprawled asleep in his playpen. And she had to talk fast, because Rosita was in and out, clearing the table.

"You got something on your mind," Pa said, seeing her wait until Rosita had gone back for more dishes. "Out with it, girl."

"Pa, I want you to fire that Tower!" she blurted. "And I'm saying please!"

"I don't see why. He hasn't even started to work. Just moved into the dogtrot rooms before he came over here—you heard him say that. He hasn't had time to do anything wrong."

Oh, hadn't he just? But nothing she could tell. She could only insist.

"I can't stand him! He . . . he nauseates me! He's stuck-up and plain . . . *mean*! You can't ask me to have him on the place when I hate him so! It's too much! Let Keith be manager—he's already foreman and trainer."

"Good at it, too. He showed me the books and charts you and him keep in the stable office. But there's nothing wrong with Jess. I can't be swayed by some cockeyed female notion. You ain't got one solid gripe against him. You're plain unreasonable."

She made such hard fists she cut her hands with her nails. If only he had the faintest idea of what Tower had done, and that she'd let him do it! He'd see the danger then. But she couldn't tell him. She had to reason with him, and she had no basis on which to reason.

"Cut out that glare," grunted Pa. "I see no call for us to have another fight. Just because I want you to—"

"I know what you want! You don't have to repeat!"

"Now it's Tower you don't like."

"I can't stand anything about him! He's not our kind!"

"You'll get used to him. He's a real horse breeder, knows his thoroughbreds better than any man I've met. You've had my last word. He stays. You'll have to get over your harebrained notions."

Without even glancing at the baby again, he stomped out of the kitchen. Rosita, carrying a tray filled with coffee cups, almost ran into him, barely escaped, came on into the kitchen muttering Spanish imprecations.

Rae-Ellen went back to the living room, played bridge with Link as her partner, snapping her cards down. Drew and Susie played against them. It seemed to Rae-Ellen the very air was thick with things that shouldn't be there—the clear, amused laugh of Tower, and the waves of love that seemed to emanate from Susie to Drew, and Drew's pleasure in Susie. However, to do him justice, he talked to Rae-Ellen when he could steal her attention from Link, and she replied to him as gently and sweetly as Susie herself.

Jess Tower, captured by Clovis, tried to converse with Adah and Grant, who played opposite them. Clovis, however, kept touching him as if accidentally, gazing into his eyes, and smiling meaningfully.

When Rosita came in at the end of the evening with cake and ice cream, Rae-Ellen maneuvered so she sat apart with Keith. The others were at a distance in the large room, and she and Keith could murmur together unheard. She felt she might make some headway with him, because he'd made it clear he was in love with her, though he hadn't yet declared himself.

Now he looked at her keenly. "You've got something on your mind," he said.

"How can you tell?"

"I can tell everything about you, dear. You've had something bothering you all evening. I don't like that."

"It's that Jess Tower," she confided. "I hated him

on sight, can't bear the prospect of having him manage my farm for one day, much less six months! I want him dismissed, gone! And Pa Travis won't fire him!"

Keith looked surprised. "Why, Rae-Ellen, I've never seen you dislike anyone before! Or known that you could be so . . . almost unfair, wanting to fire a guy before he has a chance to prove himself!"

"I'd think you'd resent his being put over you!"

"On the contrary. I mean to learn from him. Become manager for the Double T myself."

"*Keith*—I'm satisfied with you as you are!"

He smiled, letting his affection show. "What has Tower done to you, honey?"

She chewed the inside of her lip to keep from blurting out exactly what Jess Tower had done. She forced her tone to be reasonable when she spoke: "Please, Keith, even if you feel friendly toward him, get him off my farm!"

"How can I?" he asked reasonably. "I'm only the hired help. I've got no power, no right to object to whatever your father-in-law does or doesn't do."

"But you can influence him, Keith! He thinks you're capable, has great respect for your ability and your opinion. If you'd just tell him, in a reasonable manner, that Tower doesn't seem just right, it may set him to reconsidering."

Reluctantly Keith shook his head. "Why don't you ask Jess to leave yourself? After all, you're the owner."

She couldn't confess she'd done that and failed.

"No," she said, "he's too arrogant to listen to a woman. It's going to take a man to budge him. And that man has to be Pa."

"I don't see it."

"Believe me, Keith, I know! I can tell! Please, Keith, try. Just try."

"I wish I could, dear. But Mr. Travis's respect for me comes from the fact that I'm a competent foreman and trainer. One with potential, but still not tops. He'll listen to me about minor things, but when it comes to buying a filly or deciding on artificial insemination, or any important changes such as those, he'll demand the best. Which I can learn from Tower. Right now, Mr. Travis would come near to firing me if I suggested he let Tower go. You think about that, and you'll realize it's the truth."

And it was the truth. Pa had his mind made up. She was stuck. Nobody would fire the bum for her.

Chapter Eight

BEFORE daylight next morning, Rae-Ellen dressed and considered what to do. A frank confrontation with Tower was a long shot, but even long shots hit sometimes.

She tiptoed into the nursery. Both babies were asleep. Adah was asleep, too, and Susie and Dot's doors were shut. Rae-Ellen had the world to herself.

She went along the dogtrot to the rooms at the end. The morning breeze was light and fresh, and it rustled the trees and bushes so their leaves made a little song. In the distance a bird called. Down at the hen house, a rooster crowed.

There was light in the dogtrot rooms. She worked the horseshoe knocker softly, and waited. Footsteps sounded from the far end of the rooms, came right to the door, and a light sprang on.

Jess Tower stood there dressed in jeans and shirt and boots. That sun-streaked hair waved from brow to neck, repulsive in its perfection.

He stared at her. She stared back.

"What can I do for you?" he finally asked.

"The customary thing, when someone comes to your door, is to invite them in!" she snapped. "In Texas, anyhow. Maybe California is different."

He opened the screen, stood aside. She marched in and took a fast look around to see if he'd managed to mess things up in the short time he'd been in residence. The nubby brown sofa had every cushion in place; the chairs were ready to sit in—no discarded jeans draped on them. The ashtrays were shining as they had when she'd placed them around.

"The ashtrays—they're clean!" she exclaimed.

"That they are."

"You don't smoke?"

"Don't smoke anything, even grass, don't chew, don't—"

"Then you drink."

"A cocktail at a party. Odd as it may seem, I don't like the taste of liquor."

Well, she didn't like the taste of it either, but she wouldn't give him the satisfaction of admitting it. Because aside from that, they had nothing, absolutely nothing, in common. Except that raping sex, and it was over and done with and not to be repeated. Let him know the one small thing—that she too disliked liquor—and he'd get ideas about sex. There was no logical reason why he should, but she had yet to see any proof that he was logical.

She smelled coffee.

"You're cooking!" she cried, and it was an accusation.

"I live here, remember? I admit I'm brand-new to the apartment, but I've been assigned to it. I plan to sit in this living room evenings, to sleep in the bedroom, and cook in the kitchen."

"That kitchen's brand-new! It's never been used. You'll ruin it; any man would. It's made for a woman, it's not meant for a man!"

"Want to take a look? See if I've wrecked it, making a pot of coffee?"

"I certainly do! If you let coffee perk real fast—"

"I use drip coffee. Come on. See for yourself."

He turned, and she either had to follow him or stand in the living room alone. He led through the bedroom, and she saw he'd made the bed, neat as a woman would have. For some reason, this made her cross.

The kitchen–breakfast area gleamed and glittered. The towels were hanging straight. The pot lifters were ready to the stove. There was a frying pan on the stove, a pound of bacon beside it, and a bowl with three eggs in it. The table was set for one. With a napkin.

"Now that you're here," he said, "you might as well eat with me. I'll get out three more eggs."

"I eat only one egg!"

"How do you like it?"

"Scrambled, the way you're going to do yours."

He got out another egg. There wasn't so much as a fingermark on the new bronze-colored refrigerator.

Well, give him time. He'd mess up the apartment. Only he wasn't going to be here long enough, she reminded herself, then felt let down and wondered why.

"The reason I was late getting to supper last night," he explained, exhibiting the egg, "was I went grocery shopping first. Then had to rent a car, drive out, and put stuff away. Travis says I'm to use the farm van to get around in."

She wouldn't dignify that with a response. Let him use the van. As long as he was here.

He cooked bacon like an expert, wiped up every dot of grease with a paper towel—irritatingly capable. The smell of the bacon, then the eggs, seeped into her and she was ravenous.

He told her to make the toast, sitting at the table, and she did. They ate in silence. The food was delicious, and she could find no fault with his table manners. She'd noticed them last night. At least someone, sometime, had taught him that much.

Over coffee, he started talking.

"You had a reason to come here," he said. "And I know it wasn't for breakfast. Mind telling me to what I owe this honor?"

"I came here," she said clearly, "to fire you."

"Just like that."

"Exactly like that."

"And if I refuse . . . again?"

"Well, if you can control yourself"—she couldn't keep her eyes from sliding toward the bedroom— "you might listen to my reasons and just possibly agree with them."

"And let myself be fired?"

"Or resign. If you prefer."

"Let's hear your reasons. I'm interested in what they are. Aside from the fact that you purely hate me."

"That heads the list. It alone is enough. When your employer—and I am your employer in spite of Pa Travis—and yourself, hate each other—"

"I don't recall saying I hate you."

"That's beside the point! When two people hate each other that way, it's impossible for them to work together. Each will instinctively oppose any idea the other suggests. This will create strife and turmoil. It will be bad for the horses. They're like children— they sense tension. Besides which, all of this will wash off on my baby. He's a very sensitive child."

He sat nodding.

She felt almost encouraged. "Well," she added when he didn't speak, "it's plain you can't put up one single solitary argument for your side!"

"I can put up a whole slew of them. Even with dislike on both sides—"

"I said hatred!"

"Hatred, then. Even with that, two sensible people can evaluate each other, recognize ability, sit on their tempers and work for the good of the job."

"And that's what you propose to do?"

He nodded.

"Knowing I don't want you here, you'd stay?"

"I *am* staying, as long as Mr. Travis wants me. Up to six months, that is. Even with you wanting me gone, I credit you with being sensible enough not to interfere with my job as manager. You've got the love of horses in you too strong to do anything that might work against them."

97

The fact that his words made so much sense, that he was sitting and talking as if they were friendly enemies, made her feel as if she'd explode. She reminded him hotly of what he'd done to her in the hotel room.

"You asked for it," he said coolly.

"And you didn't even apologize—aren't now!"

Hell, he thought, maybe he had been out of line there in the hotel. But he hadn't been able to stop himself, didn't know whether he could stop himself now, she was getting him so worked up. He felt his neck go fiery.

She saw it, knew what it meant, because she'd seen it before. "And you want to . . . to . . . again!" she accused. "This time, if you so much as lay a finger on me, I'll scream! I dare you to, because then Pa Travis—"

"He'd be obliged to let me go, you raising a scandal," Tower finished. He felt his neck cooling, but his ears were burning, he was so mad. Again he wanted to spank her. Itched. If he could only spank her once, just once, she might be bearable.

She saw his neck fade and knew she'd lost her chance to bed him, revenge herself on him, get him out of her system.

"I don't aim to touch you," he said quietly. "I admit, for a minute there, I was about to make a pass. But now I'm not in the mood. Sorry. Some other time, when—and if—I want it."

She was on the verge of flying at him when Susie called, from the front door, "You two, in there! Want company for breakfast? I'm starving!"

"Come right through," Tower called as if he owned

the place. "Bacon and eggs will be ready on the double!"

He was putting bacon into the pan when Susie came into the kitchen, wearing a lavender dress which was gorgeous with her platinum hair. Rae-Ellen was glad that Drew wasn't here, that he couldn't see how delectable Susie was. With a pang of guilt, still furious at Tower, she smiled at Susie. Drew or no Drew, she was fond of the darned girl, she truly was.

"I really should go to Vic," she said. "He wakes so early."

Susie laughed. "Don't bother! Adah's tending Meggie and Leah's in charge of your son. She's got his playpen in the kitchen. If you change her plans, you'll ruin her day! It'll be bad enough when she finds out we've eaten with Jess, leaving her with only Adah and Vic to serve."

Tower finished his cooking. This time Susie made the toast. Tower watched her admiringly. Rae-Ellen fumed. He must feel like he had a harem in his apartment—herself, whom he'd virtually raped, and Susie, whom he probably had some wild, impossible dream of leading to the altar! For an instant she felt triumphant. Tower would get no place with Susie, whose heart was set on Drew. He might think, this moment, he had a harem, but time would straighten him out.

When they were done eating, Tower wouldn't let them help with the dishes.

"You can make an inspection tour later," he told Rae-Ellen. "I'll leave the door unlocked. You can see for yourself whether I'm a passable housekeeper."

"Keeping house takes time," she countered. "If you devote the necessary time to your job with the stable, you can't polish silver and furniture."

"I thought the knives and forks were stainless steel."

"You know what I mean!" cried Rae-Ellen, furious.

She flounced out, not saying good-bye, though Susie took her leave politely. She came running after Rae-Ellen, caught up with her midway of the dogtrot.

"What's with you and Jess?" she asked.

Rae-Ellen stopped. Staring at her friend, Rae-Ellen realized, like a thunderclap, that Tower really had, somehow, got himself into her system. And that she had to get him out. Fast and furiously.

"I hate that lout!" Rae-Ellen said fiercely. "Pa Travis won't fire him. I've tried to fire him, and he won't go!"

"But why do you hate him, darling?"

"Why do you love Drew?"

"Because he's kind and warm and intelligent and wonderful. Because he's like a piece of Texas itself. But most of all, it's sheer instinct that makes me love him."

"Those are my very reasons for loving him, too. *And* the reasons I hate Tower—because he lacks every attribute Drew has!"

"I thought Jess would make a wonderful—"

"Never! He's arrogant and flashy and lippy and hard! He thinks he's going to have the time of his life bossing me around!"

"I don't see him that way at all," Susie said. "He

100

seems kind to me and intelligent and industrious. Maybe the two of you quarrel— Or do you quarrel?"

"We *fight*!"

"Maybe your personalities don't match."

The two of them, Rae-Ellen thought fiercely, didn't hit it off because Tower was unbearable. Personality might have something to do with it, yes. But that didn't explain his attacking her in the hotel, didn't explain why he'd managed to make her like it while it was going on. Or why she was burning for him this moment.

These things she could never tell Susie. Even knowing Susie's own guilty secret, she couldn't confess to what had happened between herself and Tower. What had come close to happening again, this morning. What Susie would likely have walked in on!

She could think of only one way out of her dilemma—to sleep both with other men and with Tower himself until he was washed out of her for keeps. Which would also teach her arts to use on Drew.

Susie put her arms around Rae-Ellen. "Does my loving Drew spoil your affection for me?" she whispered. "It's so terrible, both of us loving the same man!"

"I'm jealous," Rae-Ellen said. "I resent you, but the affection—it's still there. However, I warn you, I mean to have Drew, so you may as well get used to the idea!"

Chapter Nine

At midnight, with continuing rage in her loins, Rae-Ellen slipped outdoors in her bikini pajamas to cool off. She wandered away from the house, walking through moonlight and shadow, yearning for a breeze.

Her first instinct, felt but not then recognized, had been right. Jess Tower was dangerous. It was he and not Drew, who had roused this vicious burning deep within her. It was a good thing she'd realized it in time. He'd invaded her only once. Once couldn't form a habit. It might lay the foundation for a habit; had done so, perhaps. But she could handle it, get rid of it with the other men. There were men available, and she was going to settle on one without delay. Kill two birds with one stone—put Tower out of herself and absorb the know-how to win Drew. She had time on Drew, for Susie would never bed Drew, and it would take time for her to get the courage to tell him of her affair with Keith.

She wandered on. Ahead was a grove of oak, and she moved toward it. Moonlight showered over the trees, and when she reached them she stood in the open, gazed into the high Texas sky and burned as with a fever.

On impulse, she took off her wisp of pajama top, stepped out of the bikini, flipped off her slides. Now she was naked; a small breeze lifted. It felt wonderful against her hot skin. She should have done this hours ago. She'd stay until the breeze cooled her, then go back to bed and sleep nude, free of the Tower-torture.

Hearing a sound, she whirled.

To her left, himself in moonlight, stood Tower. He was fully clothed.

"What are you doing here?" she hissed.

"Taking a stroll. Couldn't sleep."

"*Stroll*! You've been sneaking around, following me!"

"How come I'd do that?"

"It's clear as day! You couldn't sleep, and you were sitting in your living room. You were looking up along the dogtrot, spying, and you saw me come out! And followed! And *watched*!"

She was so furious at what he'd done that she didn't even think to snatch up her pajamas, but waited for his retort.

He chuckled.

"You're nothing but a . . . a stallion! If you had any decency—"

"You probably knew I was behind you. Did a striptease to get me fired. Or to get *me*. Again. Like in the hotel."

She was so furious she could only sputter.

"Pick up your pajamas," he told her, "or whatever they are. Cover yourself."

Trembling, so enraged her mouth tasted bitter, she grabbed up her top, fumbled it on, then rushed into the bottom as fast as her trembling hands and unsteady feet would allow.

Then she just stood, shaking, trying to think of something—anything—scathing enough to say. He beat her to it.

"Know what you are?" he drawled, almost like a Texan. "You're a tease, the worst kind. One who gives in once or, if it suits her, just often enough to keep a man on the string. Let me make it clear that Jess Tower is not about to be kept on any female's string. If he chooses to be on one, he'll pick it out, and he'll control it."

"You're a beast . . . and a liar!"

"You saying it isn't so, about the string?"

"I certainly am!"

"That'd be hard to prove, way you just stood there naked and let me look. You didn't make a move to cover yourself until I told you to. That fact by itself proves my point. So you're wrong, calling me a liar."

"I don't have a string!" she hissed. "And if I did, believe me, you'd be at the bottom! You'd be scraped off, because I'd drag it along the ground!"

Almost, he grabbed her. Almost, he stripped off that flimsy thing she wore, so he could have her on the grass in the moonlight. Then the idea took him

105

that it would be some kind of victory for her, and he managed to control himself.

"Get back into the house," he muttered, "where you belong. Back to your kid. Don't go gallavanting in the night, looking for a man."

His accusation left her breathless. Speechless. She was still sputtering, trying for words, when he turned on his heel and went tromping back toward his rooms.

She stood, trembling with outrage, until she heard his screen door bang softly shut. And then she tried to run but had to walk instead on suddenly rubber legs. It was worse than she'd realized. Now he was twice as dangerous. One time with him *had* been habit-forming. Because, this minute, she wanted him, only him, in her bed. And she couldn't understand it.

In her room, she fell into bed exhausted, lacking strength even to take off her pajamas so she could be cooler. Her whole being was on fire. She had to find a way out of this.

She tossed the rest of the night. At dawn, she had the solution. She'd have sex with him one more time, a purely therapeutic measure. Somehow, he'd got into her blood. One more bout with him, with her knowing its purpose, and she'd be rid of this unholy desire. After that, free of him, she'd bed a couple of other men as she'd planned, then approach Drew again. Only this time, she'd be soft and alluring. She'd glow with shy charm. And if she was good enough at it, Drew himself would make the advances and he'd be hers because, in lovemaking, she'd win him with her own deep, true love.

* * *

Jess Tower turned and twisted, pounded his pillows. He couldn't doze off. He should have subdued her with sex when he had the chance, and he wouldn't be feeling this way now. Naked, he flopped over again. He tried to think of any girl he'd ever disliked more than Rae-Ellen Travis, and couldn't. It was dawn when he realized she was the only girl he'd ever hated, and that somehow shocked him. But it didn't change the way he felt.

Chapter Ten

RIGHT after breakfast, Rae-Ellen and Adah took their babies to the nursery to bathe and dress them. Baby Vic had graduated to the bathtub, but Meggie still required the Bathinette.

Dots and Susie tagged along but, when their assistance was laughingly refused, drifted away. Before she left, Dots whispered to Rae-Ellen, "I'm keeping hands off that gorgeous Californian! He's your territory!"

"You're welcome to him," muttered Rae-Ellen, then felt gratitude to Dots, which was followed by crossness. If only Dots knew! Well, she'd be delighted, think it was wonderful. She watched the girl leave, Susie following.

"Let's trade babies for the bath," Adah suggested.

"That way the two aunties can get better acquainted with them."

"Fine," agreed Rae-Ellen. "But I'm warning you . . . Vic splashes like mad. Sometimes I feel like getting right into the tub with him."

Gently she lifted Meggie from the crib, laid her on the closed lid of the Bathinette. With practiced hands, she took off the tiny nightgown, the wet diaper. Meggie lay kicking and laughing, hair true gold, skin rosy.

Rae-Ellen dropped a kiss on the bridge of her little nose, lifted her, laid back the cover of the Bathinette, and lowered her into the water, supporting her carefully, and began to bathe her. From the bathroom came Vic's shouts of glee and a tremendous splashing.

When the babies were in the kitchen playpens with their bottles, Leah clucking and cooing, Adah said she had some more unpacking to do. "If you need to go to the stable," she added, "run along."

Rae-Ellen said she might just do that, to see what the new manager was up to.

First she hurried along the dogtrot to see if Tower was still in his rooms. He'd been up so late last night, spying on her, he might have overslept. Deliberately. It would be like him to consider that his due, to catch up on sleep and go to the stable and take over when it darned-well pleased him.

He should have been at the stable early, looking it over, getting acquainted with the horses, inspecting the feed supply, the saddles, all the tack. If he wasn't, she really had grounds to fire him. He was hired to work, not play around in the moonlight.

Sure enough, he was in the apartment! The door

110

was open, and there were voices. So. He had someone with him. Not only was he loafing on the job,
but he was entertaining!

She lifted the horseshoe knocker and banged it,
hard. Right away footsteps sounded, getting louder
as they neared the door.

At least he was dressed for work. He had on jeans
and a blue shirt. But they were spoiled by the chain
and the watch.

Before she could light into him, he lit into her.

"I thought you'd be at the stable," he said
belligerently. "The horses were awake at dawn.
Compton and Johnny and Keith were all there,
feeding the horses. How come you weren't there—or
don't you come see with your own eyes that they're
properly fed?"

"No, I do not!" she flared. "Keith Belisle has seen
to that for months! You forget I have a baby to look
after! And if you've taken the time to inspect the
horses, you've seen that they're in perfect condition!"

"They're fine; you'll get no argument from me
about that," he said. He opened the screen. "You
coming in, or going to stand there and yammer? If
you're upset about whether I'm doing my job, put
your mind at rest. Susie came down to the stable to
pet the horses and suggested we have a coffee break.
I've got store-bought cookies, too, if you want some."

So Susie was here. Rae-Ellen wondered if Susie
was trying to find out, in her ladylike way, whether
Tower had a crush on her. She wished she'd never
told Susie about the Californian, then shrugged it off.
It was the only fair thing to do. Susie was her friend,
despite the situation with Drew. She shouldn't be

exposed to a clever rapist-type without warning. Susie was still an innocent, in spite of her youthful affair with Keith.

Susie was putting an extra place at the table when Rae-Ellen and Tower got to the kitchen. She looked a little embarrassed, a little excited, and . . . guilty?

Rae-Ellen gave her a piercing look. No, Tower hadn't laid his paws on Susie yet, but if Rae-Ellen hadn't turned up when she did, no telling what could have happened. Tower was just animal enough to bed Susie, and Susie was so upset about Drew, she just might turn to this animal for solace.

Susie chattered about the horses as they sat at the table. She was too excited, too worked-up. At the very least she was aware of Tower's sex appeal.

An intense feeling pierced Rae-Ellen. At first she didn't recognize it, and when she did, rejected it. Of course she wasn't jealous! Not of Susie and Tower. If she wasn't jealous of Susie and Drew—and Drew she was determined to marry—how could she be jealous of this stand-in? Anger burned away the jealousy. The whole thing proved what he was, a sex-crazed bum who took pride in bedding any girl he fancied.

She wondered, fuming, if he kept a notebook of his conquests and, if so, how many names were in it. Or just pencil marks, one for each girl. With his ego, he'd not take the trouble to write out names. He'd not give a girl he'd mauled even that much courtesy.

Sheer hatred swept her, and she took sips of coffee. He and Susie were discussing oats. Seemed the oats at the Double T didn't suit Tower. When the present supply was gone, he meant to order a different strain.

"There's nothing wrong with our oats!" Rae-Ellen cut in. "Pa feeds the same kind to his cattle! And—" She paused for effect. "I suppose the kind you want costs more!"

"Undoubtedly," he said, his mouth stubborn. "And worth every cent."

"I forbid it!"

"Feed is in my jurisdiction," he said coldly. "But since you feel so strongly, I'll mention it to Mr. Travis."

"He'll side with you!"

"Likely. You'll see the improvement. In fact, I may just have our supply of oats carted over to Mr. Travis for his cattle and get the horses started on the new strain right away. I don't believe in fooling around. If I'm going to do a thing, I do it and get it over with."

She began to feel electricity in the air. Tension. Because she and Tower had locked horns over the oats . . . because Susie had come to have coffee alone with him.

Susie was wearing the lavender dress again. Rae-Ellen wondered if she meant to drive over to see Drew.

Now, pushing her cup away, Susie stood. "I'm going in to the Forks to do some shopping," she told Rae-Ellen. "Odds and ends. Want to drive along?"

Rae-Ellen shook her head. "Not this time. I've plenty to do right here."

She had to keep her eye on Tower. See what trouble, besides changing oats, he'd stir up. She didn't know exactly what the trouble would be, but if any was possible, he'd make it. That was a certainty.

He escorted Susie to the front door. When he

came back, Rae-Ellen was stacking cups in the sink and turning on the water. She poured detergent in, watched the suds form.

"What the hell you doing?" he demanded.

"I think that's obvious!"

"They're my dishes, I'll wash them!"

She turned off the water. "Be my guest." Her seething temper shot off flames. "So," she cried, "I got here just in time!"

"In time for what?"

"You told me yourself you have a yen for Susie! You brought her here to ply her with coffee and sweet talk and . . . do what you did in the hotel! And don't try to lie out of it! I know what you're like, know what you'll do, right down to the last move!"

He stared, his anger plain to see. Before she could claw him, he had her in his arms and she didn't fight, not really. This was what she'd come here for, what she'd been wanting last night, and he'd walked away from it. Well, this time he didn't want to walk.

As if they were both magnetized, they moved together into the bedroom. She gave no resistance when he pushed her onto the neatly made bed and then dropped down beside her and began to undress her. Well, she thought, my plan is working. In a few minutes I'll be rid of him.

Then, abruptly, she realized what she was actually doing, and began to struggle and kick. He held her down with ease, continued to take off her shirt, her bra. And then he was at her jeans and bikini.

She kicked at his shins, but didn't even make a dent on his boots. She drew in her breath to scream, then swallowed it and choked. If she screamed,

114

everybody would come running. She twisted and squirmed and tried to rake his cheeks with her fingernails, but he had her under control.

She went limp, let him strip her. She lay quiet while he undressed himself. He looked madder by the moment, and she couldn't keep a smile from trembling onto her lips.

He saw the smile.

It made him madder than hell. Somehow, she was using him. For some female reason, she was laying it all out for him to take. Hell, he didn't give a damn. She'd been married, she'd met him movement for movement the other time; she must like it.

He looked her over, waiting there so quiet, though with a shaking she couldn't hide. She was as lovely as before—more so. Because now he knew what it'd be like with her.

"You want this!" he accused.

"What are you waiting for?" she taunted. "Lost your nerve?"

He couldn't figure out what she was up to, but it didn't matter. There she lay, naked to her toes, arms out at her sides. Still waiting. He couldn't stand it another second.

This time she moved before he did, and harder than he did. He remedied that immediately. He got the lead, held it; she wound her legs around him and moaned, speaking his name, and once he thought she sobbed. As for him, he was in such a wild frenzy that when they finally peaked, he felt like he'd been blown apart. She seemed to feel the same way.

They lay still, touching.

Without warning, she was mad again. "You're a beast, a brute!" she cried.

She jumped off the bed, ran into the bathroom, turned the water on full force, got into the tub, grabbed the soap and began to rub it all over herself. He saw this, because he chased after her, and then just stood and stared.

"What the hell you doing?" he demanded.

"Washing you off myself!" Her eyes were raging, her voice shaking.

He laughed, she looked so comical, even cute, sitting in his tub and covering herself with lather. Already she had lather for breasts, and now she was working on her belly, and lower.

He stepped into the tub and sat down with her, the two of them crammed together so close they could hardly breathe. He grabbed the soap away from her and used it on himself; she grabbed it back, but before she'd made a swipe with it, he knocked it out of her hand and it fell into the water.

He grabbed her to take her right in the tub, with the water running. Hissing, she scrambled out and went for the bedroom, him after her. She ran hither and yon, soap suds dropping onto the floor, and he chased her, suds falling off him too, and when he caught her, they were both so slippery they fell down twice before he finally captured her and flung her onto the bed.

This time they really went wild, slipping and sliding, her hissing and spitting like a wildcat, him laughing and having the time of his life. At the end, mad as she was, she went into that same whispering routine, and they clung for a long, long moment, drinking in ecstasy.

Then, before she had time to get scrappy again, he entered her the third time. This was more leisurely, but just as thrilling at the end, and he chuckled. "That," he said, "was to dry ourselves off."

"The floors!" she exclaimed. "You've ruined them— all soapy and wet! I *said* you'd ruin the apartment!"

"I'll wax the damned floors," he promised. "Don't worry. But now I have a thing to say."

"Say it, then." She'd won. The burning for him was gone.

"A thing to ask you, actually. Matter of curiosity."

"Well? What is it?"

She sat up, nude and cross-legged on the damp spread. He sat the same way, facing her.

"Just what have you got against me?"

"You . . . you're . . . a drifter, a woman-crazy bum, going where you want, doing what you want. No . . . foundation—just a cocksure, arrogant, irresponsible—"

"I took a responsible job here, remember."

"For six months only! It shows you can't stay put!"

"You're not an example of perfection yourself," he said, from between his teeth.

She started for him with her nails. Then, knowing what that would lead to, she kept her hands quiet and breathed deeply. "You have a right to point out my faults?" she asked, from between her own teeth.

"After what's happened, yes. You've got the shortest fuse I ever saw on a woman, and a temper to do it justice. You came here wanting a man, and now that you've had him, you don't want him!"

"I did *not* want a man! I wanted—"

117

"You put on a good show, then. Your body betrayed you. On top of everything else, you're spoiled. I don't know who spoiled you, but you mean to have your own way, and if you don't get it, you throw a fit—like now!"

"It's your fault! Because you...ravaged me...upset me—"

"You mean to say you do have some feelings? You can get hurt?"

"After what you've done to me—"

"You cooperated, even asked, in a female manner."

"*Oh!* If you had one iota of decency, you'd never treat your employer the way you've treated me! And I *am* your employer!"

"In a way, yes. And we do both like horses. And sex. You can't deny it. I was there, I know."

"That means nothing! What you need is a purpose in life!"

"I've got one. To breed horses. Like you. Only better."

She gasped. The insult! And was his ambition real, or just talk? From footloose temporary ranch manager to owner and breeder? Ridiculous!

His handsome mouth was in its straight line. "Between us," he said, "we have got what the experts call the basic ingredients for marriage. Both of us like the same things: horses...and this." He patted the bed.

"I'd die first!" she cried.

"Doubtless. I neglected to mention that you're also stubborn. No man with a brain would marry you—Burr must have gone off his rocker. Or else you've changed."

118

She was too mad to get off the bed and dress. She tried to glare a hole through him.

"Burr knew what he was doing! And now there's another man, one who's known me ever since I came to Texas, and I'm going to marry him if it's the last thing I do!"

"Just who is this lucky guy?"

"Drew Knight, that's who!"

He grinned; it was a mocking grin. "You've got your wires crossed," he told her. "Because Drew almost proposed to Susie during the cardplaying preparations, only Mr. Travis came up and interrupted. She told me this morning. She hasn't made up her mind, for some reason. I predict she'll accept."

"*You!* To gossip about a thing like that! Something Susie told you in confidence!"

Even as she spoke she wondered, stricken, why Susie hadn't confided in her. Was she, after all, devious? Or only so disturbed and mixed-up she hadn't yet got up the courage to tell?

"She didn't ask me to be quiet about it," he said. "Even said she might discuss it with you and Adah. So, when you announced your intentions toward Drew, I did you a favor, gave you fair warning."

"If you had a spark of decency—"

"If this guy wants Susie, you need to know, so you won't—" He indicated their nudity, the rumpled bed, the soapy patches on the floor, the small puddles.

"You . . . *fiend!*" she whispered.

"Don't blame me for those two, along with everything else," he said. "The guy spoke to Susie of his own volition. He knows what he wants. The sooner you swallow that down, the better. He's not the only man in the world."

Trembling, she whispered, "I'll nip it in the bud! I can, easy as anything!"

"How you can is beyond me."

"All I have to do is tell him what happened!"

"That being?"

"That Susie had an affair with Keith, got pregnant, and had a miscarriage! That she's not the pure, innocent virgin Drew thinks she is!"

Tower's lips parted, went back into their line. His face was like marble.

Abruptly, tears sprang into her eyes. She had betrayed Susie, and she'd never planned to. It was all Tower's fault, like what had gone on between the two of them, even the soapsuds. Of course she'd never tell Drew about Susie. Susie would do that herself; she'd never deceive him.

She realized Tower had been quiet for a time. She looked at his face and it was more like marble than ever. His neck too, with that chain.

"I've thought about you," he said now. "Tried to understand why you're so spoiled and stubborn and downright mean, with a she-devil temper, all that. And now I find there's more. You're a sneak, too."

"If you mean about Susie, I tried to help her, am helping her. I've kept her secret—"

"Until now, when you're hell-bent to use it against her. Good thing I got at the truth about you. At first I thought the way sparks flew between you and me might be natural attraction. And I couldn't decide which one of you, Rae-Ellen or Susie, to court."

"Of all the colossal—"

120

"I was drawn strongly to you, understand, but to Susie too. In opposite ways. You I itched to—well, wrestle into common sense. Susie was a lady, and the only way with her was a wedding ring. Now I can decide. Have decided, more or less. After what you told me, I may just give Knight a good dose of California competition."

"You *are* crazy as those actors, always changing partners! If you believe that a girl like Susie, so sweet and gentle, would ever submit to your—your stallion sex—"

"Any time I'd marry Susie," Tower said, his tone maddening, "I'd be the gentlest lover in the world. But strong. She'd know what love is. But she'd not be violated."

"And I suppose I wasn't violated?"

He shook his head. "You got what you wanted. My mistake was to think you might like the other kind too."

She jumped off the bed. He let her. She threw on her clothes. He let her do that, too. He put on his own clothes as if he had all the time in the world.

Before she flounced away, furious, knowing that he wasn't washed out of her yet at all, he said, "Everybody's coming to the stable to see the horses this afternoon. Susie too. Maybe you'd better come to protect her from me."

Chapter Eleven

JESS, after she stamped out, took his time about getting dressed. After that, he smoothed his hair as flat as it would go, using two brushes vigorously.

Mad, was she? Spitting mad? Well, her rage couldn't match his. He wasn't used to this treatment. When a girl spread herself for him, he gave full satisfaction and she was grateful, often loving. So loving that he had to break off with her gradually, so as not to hurt her. But this one!

She'd begged for what she got, had given it back to him full measure. Even enjoyed their soap chase around the room, he'd bet his last dollar. Then, after the last bout, when by rights she should have been purring, she had turned on him.

It was a good thing he'd found out about her in

time. Before she really got under his skin. She could do that, too, give her credit. But knowing what he did, he was in no danger. He'd have sport with her if she invited it, but he was forewarned; it wouldn't get to him. He could brush any soft feeling aside the way he'd deal with a mosquito.

He set his brushes in place with a thunk and made for the stables. He'd wax the floors later, at his convenience.

Rae-Ellen went into her rooms and took another bath. This time she put on a dress that was even more electric blue than the one he hadn't liked. She stood back, satisfied with what she saw in the mirror, the soft material of the dress falling gracefully, nylons shimmering, sandals high-heeled.

"Where are you going?" Adah asked, wandering into the room. She wore dark gold jeans and a matching shirt with brown stitching.

"Noplace special," Rae-Ellen replied, keeping impatience at Tower out of her voice. "To the stable later, when everybody goes."

She'd not risk coming face-to-face alone with him. Not today. It wasn't that she was afraid of him, but that she didn't trust herself not to be hot-headed—he drew out the worst in her—and be overheard by Keith and his helpers.

Besides, that would give him real satisfaction. He'd gloat that he could upset her. What she had to do was show him he had no effect on her whatsoever. Then, when she decided to bed him again—one more time should get this unholy yen out of her system—he'd know he was being used, couldn't possibly get the idea that she had tender feelings toward him.

She grew aware that Adah had said something, and she didn't know what it was. "What did you say, dear?" she asked. "I was thinking about . . . oats."

"Nothing important," Adah replied. "Only that it looks unusual for you to wear a dress and high heels to the stable."

"No reason why I should wear pants," Rae-Ellen replied airily, "when I don't plan to ride. All I'm going to do is look at the horses, pet them, talk to them. I wear a dress sometimes, want them to get used to the fluttering, not to be skittish."

Adah took up Meggie then, who cried suddenly. This woke Baby Vic, who roared his displeasure. Rae-Ellen tended him, laughing at his small, furious rage, soothing him. But he wouldn't be soothed. Not until she took him to Leah in the kitchen, who produced a cookie. This he grabbed and began to chew on, smearing his wet face with crumbs.

Watching him there on Leah's arm, Rae-Ellen wondered if Pa Travis could be right, that being raised by women would ruin the boy. She shrugged off the thought. Vic wasn't going to be raised by women. He was going to be raised by Drew Knight.

They were all home for noon dinner—Rae-Ellen, Adah, Susie, Dots, Baby Vic in his high chair, and Meggie in Vic's carriage. Leah served them, stopping once to put a finger under Vic's chin. He growled, jerked away.

"Still cranky," Leah said. "It's that tooth, and him wakin' up too early from his nap."

125

"He should drop off right after his dinner," Adah said. "Then he'll be fine when he wakes up."

Once he was asleep, Rae-Ellen changed her mind and set out for the stable alone. Dots wanted to do her nails, Susie had a letter to write, and Adah wanted to call Lance long-distance and chat.

At the stable, Rae-Ellen found Keith grooming Thunder Boy, the stallion she had once raced in Florida. Keith was murmuring to the stallion the way he'd learned from Burr, and Thunder Boy stood fairly quiet for him. She stood and watched. Thunder Boy nuzzled at Keith's pocket, and she guessed the foreman had some lump sugar there to be given later as a reward.

She smiled. Keith was so kind. To everybody. He'd been kind to Susie, back when they'd had their ill-fated affair. He'd always been kind to Rae-Ellen too. She couldn't recall a cool word they'd ever exchanged.

"I see you there, Rae-Ellen," he singsonged, drawing the currycomb along Thunder Boy's withers, using the tone he used to the stallion. "How come you're alone? Where is everybody?"

She admired his yellow hair before she answered. Waited until he finished with Thunder Boy, gave him sugar, came to stand with her, gray eyes admiring. "You look too lovely for the stable," he said. "Where's Vic . . . where's my boy?"

"Sleeping off his bad temper, I hope," laughed Rae-Ellen. "He didn't get his morning nap out, and has been cranky ever since."

"He's cutting a tooth, isn't he?"

"One definitely, and two maybe."

"What can you do for him?"

126

"We rub paregoric on his gums, but that doesn't last. When it's gone, he seems to hurt. The only way to quiet him is to give him a cookie to chew on, and I'm afraid they'll make him sick, though Leah grumbles that her cookies won't make anybody sick, baby or grown-up. I'll be glad when this tooth business is over if it's going to make Leah cross, too."

She didn't mind Vic and his tooth. Or Leah and her cookies. What she minded was this turmoil Jess Tower had her in. The faster she got him out of her system—and bed was the only way she could think of to do it, make herself sick of him—the sooner she'd be back to normal.

She studied Keith. She wondered what he'd be like, and determined to find out. Could be that his lovemaking would free her of this awful burning.

She stood while he went to a filly, already groomed, and gave her sugar, which she lipped up eagerly. She wondered where Tower was, but didn't care. He'd be in evidence sooner or later. She smiled back at Keith when he smiled at her, and his kindness and warmth coiled into her, almost making her content.

Suddenly she longed to go rushing to Drew off on his sheep farm, and throw herself into his arms. But Drew's arms weren't ready for her. She watched Keith. His arms would be warm; they'd hold her close. She could lie against his wide chest and sob out her hurt and unhappiness, and Keith would comfort her.

Soberly, she followed along the stalls, each of which held a horse. They were all eating oats. Farther down the long line of stalls, Compton was grooming and now, at the far end, she spotted Tower, working on the pregnant filly, Silver Girl.

To show him that he didn't have her bested in the least, she moved quietly down to that stall, stood outside the manger, looking across it. He went right on with his grooming, as if she didn't exist.

He knew she was there. Grimly he curried, keeping the comb both firm and light on the filly. He murmured to her when she stepped about, and she quieted. He wondered if the hellcat had sense enough to recognize how cooperative the sensitive filly was, and temper her own actions accordingly. He doubted it. Doubted it seriously.

He held his mouth in a straight line and curried. He couldn't understand himself. It seemed like he had only to glimpse her and he wanted sex.

He set his mouth firmer, then remembered the filly and started to sweet-talk her. She quieted, busy with her oats. Now he could curry and stroke all he liked. He even worked her mane and tail, knowing the hellcat was watching. He increased the sweet talk.

"Groom her tail some more," Rae-Ellen said softly—softly because of the filly, not him. "It's a beautiful tail."

"Ought to be," he grunted, not missing how softly she'd spoken, realizing she did, after all, have a great deal of consideration for her horses. He worked at the tail, which was already perfect. He wasn't going to let her rile him into a fight. The tail could use more attention, anyway.

"This will be her first foal," Rae-Ellen said.

She didn't want to talk to him. But she couldn't

128

just ignore him, because Keith and the others would notice and wonder. No matter how she despised him, regardless of her opinion of his nature and morals, she was obliged to maintain a surface employer –employee relationship.

"Hope she doesn't have trouble when the time comes for her to drop the foal," he said.

"Why should she? She's in great shape, comes from the best bloodlines. There's no history of trouble in her whole ancestry! She's a perfect filly... she'll foal easily. She'll be a wonderful mare!"

"I'm sure she will be," he said grimly. But he had a fleeting doubt. He'd studied the filly's chart last night, and her history was perfect. Still, he'd seen fillies, even fine mares, in trouble when they foaled. It could strike the highest-bred, difficulty in foaling. Sometimes he thought it could strike them more surely than, say, a dray horse. But he couldn't mention that to hellcat. She'd go into one of her fits.

It came to him that she needed as careful handling as the thoroughbreds, that he'd been rough with her. Then he got mad all over again. She was too mean to tame, the way you could a skittish filly. She'd had the bit in her teeth too long, had grabbed it and run way back there. No man could ever tame her, and he wasn't about to try.

When he finished the tail, he and Keith turned the horses into the corral. There were twenty lovely silver thoroughbreds. Inside the long stable, they slept and ate in stalls that lined each side of the great building, fifteen to the side, the extra stalls being for new horses.

Rae-Ellen's heart lifted as she watched all the

129

silver loveliness. Keith was grinning at the horses, proud as if they were his own. Even Tower smiled. She saw him pat a silver flank, go right up to one filly and stroke her withers, still smiling.

Well, naturally he would have some good qualities. Since he was such a top-notch manager, he'd love the animals. Horses were very sensitive creatures; they knew when people hated them. So he loved horses. So what? It didn't change anything else.

She turned her gaze away from him. Anything was better to look at than Jess Tower. It was then she saw the rest of her group coming.

Susie led, carrying Baby Vic, who was gnawing on a cookie. He'd been crying, but now, with the cookie, he grinned when Rae-Ellen dropped a kiss on his hair. But he wouldn't come to her when she held out her arms.

This delighted Susie. "Your son has a mind of his own!" she laughed. "He knows who gave him the cookie!"

Rae-Ellen smiled, but she was a bit worried. They couldn't go on bribing Vic with cookies. He had regular meals to eat, milk to drink. She couldn't permit him to take over, cookie in hand, and rule the roost.

Dots was carrying Meggie, Adah walking beside her. Meggie was making cooing noises that increased as Rae-Ellen leaned over her. Vic had never been like this, she thought. He'd always been fire and spirit, like Burr, like Pa Travis. She sighed. She had some coping to do with her son in the future. And Drew simply had to be the one to help her cope.

Keith came right up to the group, was introduced

to Meggie by Adah. He touched her little hand, smiled. "She's a beauty," he said. "Next time she comes to visit, I'll put her on a gentle mare and hold her there for a ride, the way I do with Vic."

Susie called to Jess Tower, who was standing apart. "Come over and meet the real bosses!" she cried.

He came long-legging it. Dots displayed Meggie; he leaned over the infant, spoke her name, using his singsong horse manner, and Meggie cooed and kicked. It was a loud coo. Then she laughed and gurgled, and Tower put his finger in reach of one of her waving hands; she grasped it and gurgled some more.

He looked like an idiot, prostrating himself before an infant who couldn't even sit up alone! She knew why he was doing it. To impress everybody, to show how perfect he was with babies as well as with horses.

She'd no sooner had this thought than Susie went right up to him, Vic on her arm. "Here's a Travis you haven't met!" she exclaimed. "He woke up early from his nap again—he's cutting a tooth—but one day he'll be boss of the Double T! Isn't he the image of Burr?"

Deliberately, Tower looked the baby over. This made Rae-Ellen extremely cross. What right did he have to examine her child as if he were a foal?

Vic stared into Tower's blue eyes. He scowled. He threw his cookie on the ground.

"Why, fellow!" Tower said, in his singsong voice guaranteed to soothe any horse, but Baby Vic was no horse. "You lost your cookie!" Tower went on. "Well, that's all right...there'll be more. I'm Jess...Jess..."

He put out his finger, as he'd done with Meggie, poked it gently against Baby Vic's fist.

The boy grabbed the finger, pulled it to his mouth, clamped his few teeth shut on it, held. Consternation sprang out on Tower's face. With his free hand, he pried Baby Vic's jaw open and freed his finger. It was bleeding.

"You stop manhandling my baby!" screamed Rae-Ellen.

"Oh, my goodness!" squealed Dots. "Everybody knows a human bite's the worst kind! You'll have to get a shot, Jess! You could have tetanus or something! You've been handling horses!"

Rae-Ellen snorted, then her heart jerked. Dot was right. There were tetanus germs around stables, and Tower had had his hands all over the filly and hadn't washed them since.

But Jess Tower, true to form, was bullheaded. "No year-old kid is going to give me lockjaw!" he declared. "All I need is a Band-Aid."

"You need more than that," said Keith, who had come over to see what was happening. "Dots is right. Whether you think there's danger or not, play it safe. I'll take you to the Forks in the van and you can get a shot."

Tower looked as bullheaded as ever. He glowered at Rae-Ellen. She glared right back, one fact crystal-clear.

This monster could never be a father to her baby!

But neither could she have him die in agony because her son had bitten him. Alarm sliced through her because he looked so bullheaded. She couldn't bear it if he were to die—he was good with horses,

132

he was a human being. He had—face it—an inborn talent for making a woman find glory in bed. That she wasn't the right woman was beside the point. He shouldn't be wasted.

She started to order him to get the shot, stopped just in time. An order he would defy. And she wouldn't try to reason with him because he was too bullheaded to listen to reason.

What would work, then?

Swiftly, she had the inspiration. "Please, Jess," she said softly. "Have the shot. Otherwise, we'll worry about you, all of us."

His bullheaded look turned to sheer surprise. Even shock. He felt it do that. And for some reason that he couldn't understand, he heard himself give in to her, to all of them. And rode to town with everybody in the van, even the babies, went to the doctor, and had the shot.

And still couldn't figure out why he'd gone soft. His mouth drew into its line. It wouldn't happen again, the going soft. Nothing the least bit like it would happen. Rae-Ellen Travis could bank on that!

Chapter Twelve

LATE that afternoon, Drew Knight drove over from the K-Bell. They were all in the living room having coffee—Tower too, since Rae-Ellen couldn't be obvious and not invite him when Keith, the foreman under him, was coming. Tower'd won a point about his thumb, after all. Though he'd had the injection, he wore only a Band-Aid.

Rae-Ellen wondered how he'd talked the doctor into that, but wouldn't ask. She just hoped he wouldn't get germs in it and start some other kind of infection.

Before she knew she was going to speak, she mentioned it, said it right out. It was Drew who put her mind at ease, and she noted that he was staying close to Susie and that Susie was glowing.

"Doctors today give an overall immunity injection," Drew said. "Not just for tetanus. Even if you hurt yourself now, Jess, you're protected against infection for the time being."

"That's right," Tower said, and shot Rae-Ellen a look. The look told her to keep her mouth shut. She seethed. Then, deliberately gentle and ladylike, she told Drew how happy they all were to have him here.

They were seven: Drew, Keith and Tower; Rae-Ellen, Susie, Dots, and Adah. Leah's plate of cookies was going down fast, as was her pot of coffee.

"What I actually came for," Drew explained, russet eyes glowing, "was to suggest we take Jess and Adah on a short tour tomorrow morning, if that suits everybody. To see a couple of ranches and rodeo practice. I've already mentioned it to Grant and Link. They're all for making a thing of it."

"Ooh, exciting!" squealed Dots.

Drew smiled, half-embarrassed. "I should have asked here first," he said. "I went at it backwards. It's no big deal. Just a couple of ranches interested in rodeoing, anxious to give our newcomers some idea of rodeos."

"Sounds good to me," Tower said. Rae-Ellen was almost shocked to hear him converse in a normal, friendly tone. "How about you, Adah?"

"I'd love it!" Adah exclaimed. "I've heard about rodeos, seen bits on TV, but never have been to one! I don't think they have them in North Carolina."

"I've asked Bertha Mudd too," Drew added.

"And *not* Clovis?" cried Dots. "They're both crazy about Grant Miller. I do believe Clovis would *attack* Bertha if she got Grant for her partner!"

Drew half smiled. "It's Saturday, no school. They're both coming."

They needn't be concerned about that triangle, Rae-Ellen thought crossly. Clovis would latch onto Tower; she'd made it clear at Pa Travis's supper that she was after him. That would leave the field clear for Bertha, in her forties, tiny and dovelike, to be with Grant.

He was always polite to Bertha, but Rae-Ellen doubted he'd marry a widow older than himself the second time. He was too attractive not to seek beauty in a wife now, and he could afford to marry, having inherited his first wife's ranch.

She mused on his looks—that auburn hair and eyes to match, his handsomeness. She'd take special note as to how he and Baby Vic got along. In the unthinkable event that she failed to win Drew, she meant to have studied the field of eligibles. And to have slept with them. Guiltily, she felt that Bertha Mudd wouldn't stand a chance if she, Rae-Ellen, wanted Grant. Nor would Clovis.

Next morning, after the horses had been turned out to pasture, the sightseeing party gathered at the Double T. Leah, delighted, was to be in charge of both babies while they were gone, and asked Adah if she could give Meggie her first taste of cookie.

"Just a crumb!" she pleaded. "Not big enough for her to choke on, nothing like that! And I'll have her bottle ready to wash it down with milk!"

Adah laughed, hugging Leah. "I wouldn't have her *not* know your cookies!" she exclaimed. "Next time I bring her, she'll be walking, trailing you, *begging*! You don't know what you're letting yourself in for!"

Rae-Ellen in electric blue skintight slacks and shirt, had threaded a blue ribbon through her hair. And she hoped her eyes were blazing as hotly as her clothes.

Which, undoubtedly, they were, because after all had gathered—Bertha Mudd staying close to Grant, and Clovis permitting it because she had her eye on the door—Tower came in. His look flew to Rae-Ellen, and she could see his eyes sparkle, he was so mad.

"Jess, you gorgeous man!" Clovis purred, but the purr was loud enough for all to hear. "I thought you'd never show up! I choose you for my partner, okay?"

Well, give him credit; he had to say yes, couldn't refuse with everybody listening. But he didn't have to . . . sort of sparkle when he consented!

Link Bradley arrived, all his attention for Rae-Ellen after he'd nodded at the others. "I'm playing hookey from a special brief to be with you," he murmured, capturing Rae-Ellen's hand. "Be my partner?"

She nodded, smiling. She could have hugged him. All wool and a yard wide, that was Link. Not for the first time, she admired his broad, almost stocky build, his brown hair and eyes. She even approved of his age, which was thirty-eight. If any man promised solidity, it was Link.

They piled into cars, Grant at the wheel of one, Bertha beside him. Tower and Clovis took the backseat. Rae-Ellen rode with Link, Keith and Dots and Adah in the back.

"Ten seconds!" Drew called out, stopwatch in hand. "Hope you make it that good at my place!"

Rae-Ellen knew that Slim, the rider, would do even better in real competition. He was the best calf-roper in the area. She smelled the dust from the brief event and felt, as she had before, the strange attraction rodeo competition had.

Next they drove to Grant's spread, the Leaning K. His ranch house was redwood, not as large as some ranch houses, but sturdy, homelike and attractive. Grant had arranged a steer-wrestling demonstration for them, and again they stood back from the corral and watched.

The steer was an ugly brute, a longhorn. He was black, and he pawed the ground and moved his head from side to side, nostrils wide, blowing audibly. A couple of times he made a run for the side of the corral, pawed the earth, raising dust, his nose at the ground, eyes rolling.

"He'd like to kill us!" wailed Clovis, and clung to Tower's arm.

"He can't get at us, don't worry," said Tower.

"It's the rider who's going to tackle him he'll try to kill," Keith said. "Watch!"

The cowboy pitted against the steer was on a bay quarter horse. Now, two other cowhands opened the corral gate and he rode for the angry steer at easily twenty-five miles an hour. The steer lifted his head, wheeled, and looked red-eyed at the oncoming enemy.

"He weighs seven hundred pounds, that steer," Grant said.

Bertha shuddered, tucked her hands into his arm, looking more than a little frightened.

"Don't be afraid," Rae-Ellen heard Grant say. "Chester knows how to handle himself."

The steer charged. Chester spurred his quarter horse, got in behind the furious animal, and began to chase him. The steer, with no time to turn and charge, ran wildly. Chester pursued, ready in the saddle.

As the quarter horse came even with the steer, Chester sprang onto the animal's back, grabbed a big horn with each hand, and started to wrestle. The quarter horse ran to the side of the corral and was led away.

With Chester on his back like a burr, an unrelenting grip on the horns, the steer twisted and went into a spinning motion. Chester's hips lifted, slammed down. The steer whirled.

Chester hung on to the wide horns and bore the head powerfully to the right. The steer's neck turned under the pressure. His hind quarters hit dirt and he lunged, bellowing, to his feet.

Chester hung on, wrenching the powerful neck. The steer jerked and jumped straight up, but Chester kept bulldogging. He stayed on the steer's shoulders, behind his horns, and then, as the animal was about to tear free, lowered himself, still hanging on and twisting; quickly, he sank his teeth into the steer's lower lip and, holding his teeth clamped, wrestled it to the ground.

Two other cowboys ran out with ropes. Chester tied the steer and the three of them fought him out of the corral and into a small pen.

Adah was distressed for the animal. "His mouth— won't that kill him?" she asked.

"Not at all," Drew assured her. "Grant's got salves and disinfectants. This happens all the time. It's within the rules. That steer will be ready for our rodeo, may get another bite then."

"You don't know about the clowns, do you?" Grant asked Adah.

She stared questioningly, wide-eyed.

"They're used in bull riding. They dress like regular circus clowns and act as a moving target for the bull so the rider can get away after he's thrown. Some clowns are barrel men, lug a reinforced barrel around the arena and let the bull maul the barrel around with the clown inside. Clowns usually take a beating, but they never quit. It's in their blood, too."

Bertha, at Grant's suggestion, asked if any of the men in the party wanted to tackle some rodeo event. To Rae-Ellen's surprise and anger, Tower spoke up.

"I'd like to try saddle-bronc," he said. "Just for the hell of it."

"Your legs are too long!" Rae-Ellen snapped. "You have to ride with your spurs raking back and forth on the bronc's shoulders!"

"I can manage my legs," he snapped.

"Go on, do it!" urged Clovis. "Make me proud of you!"

Rae-Ellen glanced around. No one was on her side. They were all rodeo-crazy. Even Adah said nothing. Well, if Tower wanted to break his neck, let him! She frowned, watching Grant and Keith and Link go with Tower to saddle the bronc.

In a very short time, almost as soon as Jess had obtained and fastened on the dull spurs that prodded but did not cut a horse, the bronc was led out. He was kicking his heels, walleyed. The men who had gone to watch him be saddled, followed along, keeping their distance.

Jess long-legged for the corral. Three cowboys were fighting the bronc into a small pen. When he was inside, they dropped the gate and stepped away.

Jess, following Grant's directions, vaulted onto the pen, crouched with a knee on each side of it. He waited a second, then dropped into the saddle, grabbed rein in his right hand, slid his spurred boots into the stirrups, then up along the shoulders of the bronc.

A cowboy raised the gate.

With a tremendous jerk that snapped Jess's head in a whiplash, the bronc was out of the pen. He jumped straight up, all four feet bunched, and came down with a jolt that made Jess bite his tongue. He managed, long legs and all, to run his spurs along those brown, moving shoulders, held rein in his right hand, left arm out from his body, and took what the enraged bronc could give.

The bronc went into a rocking-chair motion, legs stiff. Jess clamped his teeth to keep from biting his tongue again, took every jolt, fighting to stay in the saddle. Unbelieving, he felt the saddle loosen, felt it slide, let go the rein and went in a flying dive for the ground.

He landed on his hands and knees, sprang up and loped for the side of the corral, the bronc bucking and kicking at him. He was quickly over the rail and safe.

Rae-Ellen, whose heart had almost stopped, ran to him. "What'd you break?" she cried angrily.

"Not a damn thing! Busted the knees out of my jeans is all, bit my tongue."

Shaking, enraged that he was such a fool as to try the most dangerous type of riding, she paid scant attention to the fact that the cowboys had caught the bronc. Gradually, she became aware that they were examining the saddle, and all the gear.

"It was the girth strap," Drew reported when he came back. "Somehow, it wore through and broke. If it hadn't been for that, Jess, you might have set a record for saddle-bronc your first try! Hope it doesn't scare you off!"

"Hell, no," muttered Tower. "It could happen to anybody."

"But not on my spread," Grant said grimly. "My apologies, Jess. I'm going over all my gear personally. Today. I don't understand how that girth— I keep a close eye on everything."

All but Tower he kept a close eye on, Rae-Ellen thought, knowing it wasn't logical and not caring. Well, he'd had his lesson, the crazy fool. He'd stay off broncs now. That much she was certain Pa Travis would agree with.

She glared at Tower. He was letting Clovis wipe a dot of blood from the corner of his mouth. Clovis said something to him, and he grinned.

Suddenly furious, Rae-Ellen was glad Baby Vic had bitten his finger.

III

The Rodeo

Chapter Thirteen

The tour was cut short after Tower's fall, leaving out Drew's sheep ranch on the tour; he said they'd see it the day of the rodeo.

Dots phoned one of her boyfriends, told him the morning had gone flat, offered to spend the afternoon with him. "If we can do something excitin'!" she laughed, but there was an arch threat beneath the laugh.

He came up with a plan she liked, because she didn't eat lunch at home, but went spinning away with a young man who had bright red hair. His white sports car was built for speed and they were out of sight in no time.

After lunch, Adah went to take a nap, and Rae-

Ellen was finally able to get Susie alone. "What's wrong, darling?" Susie asked. "You seem so disturbed."

"I've just got too much on my mind, that's what! Drew, and the situation with the three of us. And now Tower has to try to break his neck!"

"It wasn't his fault, darling. The girth—"

"I wouldn't put anything past him! He'd sue the Double T if he got a *scratch*!"

"No he wouldn't. Not Jess. Besides, he couldn't sue the Double T for what happened at the Leaning K!"

"Well, maybe not. And maybe he wouldn't."

She couldn't, somehow, see him battling over money, despite his faults. Then she wondered if he'd marry for money, and got mad all over again.

"I told that Tower about you!" she blurted.

Susie paled. "I ... don't quite understand."

"About you! And Keith! I didn't mean to, but I had to shut him up, don't you see? He was unbearable. Also, he had the nerve to insinuate that he's attracted to you and he may try—oh, no telling what! But he's no good, never forget that, no matter how g-gallant he acts! Never trust him!"

She ached to tell what the bum had done to her. But for some reason—pride, rage—she couldn't. Susie would just have to take her word for it that Tower was no good.

"I ... don't know what to say."

"Tower—"

"I don't mean that. Your telling him about Keith. Do you think he'll tell anyone else?"

"I don't think so. He pretended to be shocked

because I told *him*! I just can't understand that hombre!"

"Rae-Ellen, oh, Rae-Ellen, I wish you hadn't told!"

"Maybe you don't think *I* wish it! There's no way to explain why I did it, no excuse. I don't even dare ask you to forgive me!"

Susie came to her, embraced her.

"I know how you are," she said. "There's not a spark of badness in you. It just came out, was said before you knew it, isn't that true?"

Miserable, Rae-Ellen nodded.

"Then forget it, dear. When I get my courage up— Want to listen to some Brahms with me?"

"No," Rae-Ellen said, "music won't soothe me. I'll stay here in the library, try to read. And not about rodeos!"

When Susie was gone, she tried to settle down with a new mystery novel, but couldn't. Susie hadn't said one word about what she'd do, now that someone else knew her secret. She didn't say whether she would tell Drew at once. And she'd made no comment about Tower's avowed intention of perhaps courting her.

She put the book back on the shelf.

Secretive. Susie was always secretive!

Well, so be it! Rae-Ellen clung to her plan to win Drew for herself. If only Jess Tower weren't in the way! He'd sullied her, not once but twice—well, more than that, but on two *occasions*, anyway—and she had to rid herself of the lust he'd planted in her before she could make another, definite move to get Drew. And meanwhile, there was Susie. Her only consolation was that Susie would delay her confession as long as possible. Meanwhile, she had to work like mad on her Tower problem.

The rodeo was two weeks off. Cowboys were practicing for the events. Rae-Ellen told Pa Travis of how Tower had ridden the saddle bronc, but Pa knew already. Then she demanded that Pa order Tower to stay off saddle broncs, and he refused.

"He's his own man," he said. "I'll not interfere with what he does in his free time."

Fortunately, Tower had enough to do at the Double T. He had no free time. He was remaking Rae-Ellen's careful charts, drawing up beautiful family trees for all the thoroughbreds. When he wasn't actually with the horses, he was in the stable office at his paperwork. He didn't practice any riding tricks. They didn't discuss it.

She spent her days with the horses, Adah, and Vic. She noted that Tower limped, but since they barely spoke to each other, she didn't mention it to him. Susie began to take long horseback rides and, when Rae-Ellen asked if she'd seen Drew, replied in the negative. That must mean she was pondering and suffering, trying to decide what to do. Dots spent all her time with redheaded Sammy Soose.

Once she told Rae-Ellen, "He may turn out to be *the* one! He's a blast in bed, he's swell company, we like the same things, he's fairly rich, and he wants as many babies as I do! Don't be surprised if we elope to one of those states where there's no waiting period!"

On the third night, Clovis gave a housewarming party, inviting everyone except Pa Travis and Bertha Mudd. "Just our intimate, *young* group," she told

Rae-Ellen over the phone. "Dots is bringing her Sammy. Link insisted that he bring you and I said I'd ask, but he said he'd do his own asking." She laughed. "Only I'm doing the asking!"

Rae-Ellen wondered if Clovis would come right out and ask Tower to marry her. She said, "I'd love to have Link for my date! He's wonderful company!"

"And dress up! This is my first house—small, but my own! And no roommate."

That makes it convenient, Rae-Ellen thought, feeling catty. No roommate. She can let Tower stay all night every night!

The girls at the Double T went to great lengths to dress for the occasion. Rae-Ellen got out a new, off-the-shoulder white silk that clung to her breasts, hugged her waist and fell to the floor in graceful folds. Her hair she braided and wound around her head, with a diamond clip at the front. The matching clip she fastened at the bottom of the plunging neckline of the dress. Her fingers and arms were naked of jewelry, as were her neck and ears.

In fact, looking herself over in the mirror, she decided she looked all but naked in this outfit. Even her high-heeled sandals were tiny strips of white silk, her rosy toenails showing through nude nylons. She dusted powder on her lips to subdue their redness, picked up her small white evening bag, and was complete.

Adah, of course, was all gold. Her gown was sleeveless and made of sequins that glittered with every move. It was a slim dress, cut up the sides almost to the knee, her slippers high-heeled and gold. She wore a topaz at her throat, a topaz on her right hand, and her heavy gold wedding band set with yellow diamonds.

Susie, coming in on them while they were admiring and exclaiming over each other, was equally lovely. Her gown was a filmy, floating gray. She'd left her platinum hair free and it floated down her back, moving when she moved. She wore a jet pendant as black as her eyes, and that was her only jewel. Now she was included in the compliments.

It was then Dots burst in on them. She wore ankle-length, fire red chiffon. It was gathered and tucked on the bodice, and the skirt was composed of tiny, sharp pleats. Rubies, only a shade darker than the dress, sparkled on her arms in twin bracelets.

Now the others exclaimed over her. "It's a surprise for my Sammy!" she declared. "I'm dressed to go with his red hair!"

Their escorts arrived. They got into cars, one couple to each car, and took off for Travis Forks. The van was missing; so was Tower. Well, naturally, Clovis would have snagged him for her date, and he'd gone on ahead, Rae-Ellen thought crossly.

Clovis, Tower indeed at her side, greeted them as they entered the five-room house, which was beautifully decorated in tawny shades running from chocolate-brown through deep gold to dark orange. Tawny-haired, tawny-eyed Clovis herself wore a stunning gown that combined all the shades of the décor of the little house. It was so fashioned that it displayed all but the nipples of her generous breasts.

Rae-Ellen burned. Clovis's dress made her own daring gown look almost demure! She tried, but never caught Tower looking at either dress, though the other men looked smilingly and complimented every gown on every girl.

"We're having dinner here, not at a restaurant!" Clovis trilled. "Cooked every bit of it myself, got a maid in to serve!"

They all laughed, protested she shouldn't have, and there was much gaiety. She served cocktails. Rae-Ellen set hers down unobtrusively, keeping a secret eye on Susie and Drew.

They behaved as usual. Obviously, Susie had made no confession yet. Rae-Ellen's spirits lifted. Then she caught Tower giving a cold look at her near-topless gown, and got ready to bless him out if he said a word about it.

He looked past her, as if she didn't exist, and she went hot all over. While she was still looking, Clovis wrapped her naked arms through his, stroking his coat sleeve.

Dinner talk was rodeo. There was much about a black bronc Drew had just bought, which was to be delivered in time for the rodeo.

"I believe he'll be the star bronc," Drew said. "Certainly hope so."

"He should be!" Susie exclaimed. "Drew's paying five thousand dollars for him!"

All were amazed at this. Drew defended himself: "He's a good investment. A really good bronc is very hard to find, and he's one of the best. 'Diablo,' I'm going to call him. I expect to put him at stud and make back my investment."

Of course, Rae-Ellen thought warmly. Drew would

never do anything to show off. He was the direct opposite of Jess Tower.

Later, they danced. Clovis asked Tower to stack records on the player, and they paired off and moved about the bare, polished floor gracefully. Clovis danced with her head on Tower's shoulder; he didn't seem to mind. Link held Rae-Ellen a trifle close, and she let him. She wondered how he'd be in bed.

Finally Tower presented himself for a dance. Rae-Ellen ached to slap him when he stepped up and said he was free for this one, but went into his arms stiffly.

Once stepping to the music, the stiffness vanished. He held her properly, and they danced as if they'd been born to do so. This infuriated her. It maddened her that he looked so handsome that he was almost homely. He should be one way or the other, not change back and forth.

They didn't even speak. From her, he went to Susie, and her he held closer. He murmured to Susie and she murmured, and they smiled, and once Tower threw back his head and laughed.

So. He was making good his threat. He was courting Susie. And he let Clovis practically hang around his neck. Dots had eyes for him, too, but with her it was hands off, because she maintained he was for Rae-Ellen. Even Adah seemed to like Tower, danced with him, and they talked and smiled as they danced.

Rae-Ellen could scarcely bear to see him dancing. Each girl he held in his arms, it looked as if he wanted to get into bed with her. And not a female present, she'd bet, would fail to get a thrill if he did!

Finally the evening ended. Long after the house

was dark, Rae-Ellen tossed in bed, her mind on Tower. To heck with it! She'd decided to have sex with him until she was fed up, and she'd decided to try out other men. She'd start immediately. No time like the present.

In her shortie pajamas, she stole along the dogtrot. She tapped at Tower's door. Right away, he was there. He hadn't been asleep, either. What girl had he been thinking about,—Susie? She almost asked him, but did not.

"I've been waiting for you," he said.

Her pulse jumped, raced. She should be angry, but she wasn't. At least he hadn't been thinking about Susie.

He put his arm around her, led her to the bedroom, everything dark. In darkness, he drew off her shorties. He was already nude; she could tell when her fingers accidentally touched him.

In darkness, he laid her on the bed, entered, and they moved as they had on the dance floor, in perfect accord. And when they had soared to the top and then leveled off, they lay not talking, not fighting. This was it, this was the way. She was satisfied. He had cured her of himself.

Still not speaking, she put on her shorties, stole to her room.

Adah was there, wide awake. And Adah knew. Her knowledge was on her lovely, hurt face. "Darling," she whispered, "things will work out without your—"

"How do you know what I've done?"

"I've seen you with Jess Tower, saw you dance with

him tonight. You'll find a husband without..." She gestured, tears in her eyes.

It was then, at the word "husband," that Rae-Ellen knew Tower wasn't out of her, after all. Not yet. It was going to take more. More of him, and all the other men she could get. She crushed back tears of her own.

"I can't find a husband with Tower around!" she whispered fiercely. "He's... he's a thorn in my side!"

"The way he looks at you—forgive me, darling—reminds me of Burr. Before you married him."

"And he reminds me of a bum and nothing else!"

"It's only that it's so soon," Adah comforted. "Relax, dear sister. Be friends with all men. The right one will come along. Someday, he will!"

"Ha! Maybe at Pa Travis's dance, tomorrow night? *Big* chance! He's asking the whole countryside, but I already know all of them. No shot at even seeing a new man!"

Not that she needed to. Drew would be there.

Tomorrow night she'd wear her brown gold gingham. It had streaks of auburn in it, too, and was demurely made. She'd wear no jewelry. She'd package herself especially for Drew.

Chapter Fourteen

THEY all met at the Double T to go to Pa Travis's in a body, those who had gone on the tour. Bertha Mudd had got Grant to drive over after her, and she looked years younger than usual, wearing a checked blue gingham that hit her very good legs midway. She'd got a permanent; her brown eyes were shining. Rae-Ellen felt sorry for her because she didn't think Grant would marry her, pleasant and well-fixed though she was.

Tower, surprisingly, showed up alone.

Clovis appeared with a handsome blond blue-eyed man whom she introduced possessively. "Clifford Dixon, everybody," she said. "Partner in one of the biggest law firms in Fort Worth! Hands off, girls...he's mine!"

Dixon acknowledge each introduction without taking his eyes off Clovis. Obviously, he was smitten. Rae-Ellen purred inwardly. Now, with a rich and handsome attorney dancing attendance, Clovis would drop Tower. Dixon, being an attorney, could give her the sort of future to which she aspired. We'll see no more of Clovis after this night, Rae-Ellen thought contentedly.

They got ready to drive to the Star-Bar. All the girls wore gingham and the men wore jeans. Rae-Ellen rode with Keith, chatting gaily with him, wondering what Tower, who had paired off with Adah, v·~s thinking.

Was he feeling triumphant about her coming to him last night? Did he want her to return? Was he waiting impatiently for her, or did he consider her as low as the dust beneath his feet?

Pa Travis, the ranchhouse already filled with gingham- and jeans-clad guests, was waiting at the open door. He boomed a welcome. Rae-Ellen had rarely seen him look so happy, so contented. She knew the reason, too. He reasoned that he was exposing her to men, lots of men; that she was so lacking in spirit she'd fall in love with one acceptable to him; and that Baby Vic would have a father again. She set her teeth, glanced at Drew, who was playing close attention to Susie. Dots had her redheaded Sammy in tow.

"Didn't bring the boy, did you?" Pa demanded of Rae-Ellen, even as he shook hands enthusiastically with Keith. So. He'd accept Keith, then.

"He'd just get cross," Rae-Ellen said. "Leah's delighted to be in charge."

Rosita pushed in to say hello. "I heard that!" she snorted. "Why not Rosita watch over both little ones?"

Rae-Ellen hugged Rosita. "I have to give Leah a fair share of time alone with them," she said. "Next time is yours, I promise!"

There were so many guests that they ate supper all over the place. Most of the talk was about horses. Rae-Ellen spoke at length about her silver beauties; Tower said nothing unless he was asked a question, then replied with authority. This both pleased Rae-Ellen and made her cross. She wouldn't want a manager who didn't know his job; however, she resented Tower's portrayal of a quiet and courteous man when she knew him to be the exact opposite. Oh, he was a consummate actor!

After dinner, the host of guests flocked into the purple living and dining rooms. They set the furniture against the walls and put the throw rugs aside, leaving the polished oak floor ready for dancing. Rosita deserted her hated dishwasher and presided over the stereo, keeping it stacked with lively dance records.

The square-dance sets lined up, two sets in the living room, two sets in the dining room, one set in the wide entrance hall. Pa Travis stood in a central spot and called the dances, his voice booming and throbbing. The beat was lively and loud; for Rae-Ellen, Pa's words flowed into it, becoming an almost indistinguishable part of the merrymaking.

"Swing your pardner!" he sang into the music and the stamping of feet, and Keith and Rae-Ellen merrily obeyed and danced on, hands clasping and unclasping on order.

"Swing her right!" intoned Pa. "Swing her left! Sashay...down the middle...and back...and swing your pardner!"

Rae-Ellen clasped hands with Keith, above their heads, and they danced in a circle, then went dancing back to their places in the set. When it came time for her to dance to meet Tower, they merely touched fingers and circled. He didn't say a word, nor did she. They didn't smile, just got away from each other as fast as they could.

For the next sets, Rae-Ellen had county men for partners. Tower wasn't even in her set, but Drew was. When they danced to the middle to circle, they smiled at each other, danced back to place. Rae-Ellen glowed. Drew still liked and respected her! She would continue to be the lady for him right up to and during the time she made her final, desperate play for him. It would all be ladylike, every bit of it.

For the third set, much to her joy, Drew asked to be her partner. She had the satisfaction of seeing Tower look at them and scowl. What the scowl meant, she wasn't sure. It did mean he disapproved of her dancing with Drew, whatever the reason, and that was a small triumph. She ignored the itch even his glance had set up in her. Drew would charm it away.

And he did. For she was so happy to be partner to smiling, courteous, friendly Drew, she forgot everything else. Her next partner was Link, and she enjoyed dancing with him, and the next was Clovis's handsome attorney. She began to have fun.

Then Pa shouted that they'd danced enough and would play pinochle, and all the guests helped set up card tables and chairs. Rae-Ellen found herself paired off with Keith, opposite Bertha Mudd and Link.

Before the first hand was dealt, she realized that Susie and Drew had disappeared. Pa Travis said nothing about their absence, which meant they'd told him they were leaving. No one else mentioned them and Rae-Ellen decided she was the only one who didn't know where they were; and she wouldn't ask, not if she died.

Her pulse throbbed. Where were they? What were they talking about? She looked at her cards, played automatically, smiled at Keith and chatted as if she were having fun. Keith was good to be with after the roughness and neglect of Jess Tower. She began to enjoy Keith. She glanced at Tower, but he was engrossed in a flashy blond and never looked her way, so she couldn't tell whether he knew she was having fun in spite of him.

They played on and on. Susie and Drew were still missing. Rosita served coffee, and promised ice cream and cake for later.

Upset by the absence of Susie and Drew, chagrined because Tower never glanced at her, Rae-Ellen deliberately responded to Keith's warmth. When he murmured how beautiful she was tonight, she smiled into his eyes, grateful that at least one attractive man was treating her intimately.

Thus, upset over the turn the evening had taken, when Keith suggested they slip away for a drive, she consented eagerly. This was her chance! Keith would certainly try to make love to her, and she wasn't

163

going to hold him off. It was an opportunity to learn whether she might, in future, choose Keith for husband, but most of all a chance to get Jess Tower out of her blood.

They slipped, undetected, into the night.

In the car, Keith pulled her close to him. "Come over here, where you belong," he said, and then he moved to kiss her, and she raised her lips to him.

His kiss was warm and gentle; she kissed him back the same way. Surprisingly, she liked it. His tongue edged into her mouth, and she met it with the tip of her tongue, and they kissed that way.

He spoke breathlessly. "You *know* I'm crazy about you! That I can hardly keep my hands off you! Ever."

She didn't know what to say. His words pleased her, made her feel wanted, not used and rejected. They kissed again.

He started the car, drove with one arm around her. "I've wanted you for a long time," he said gently. "I believe I'm good enough for you and can prove it."

"You're good enough for any girl," she murmured. "You don't have to prove it."

"Need to, then. If you're willing."

"You mean . . . a motel?"

"There's no place else. Leah's at the Double T."

"All right," Rae-Ellen said recklessly. "You pick the motel."

It was a new place, set back in a grove. There were lights; it was visible from the highway, but not garish. And their room was almost homelike, decorated in muted green and blue and orange. There was a wide bed, a big dresser with a vast mirror, and two armchairs flanking a low, round table. Lamps gave off soft light. Off to one end was the gleam of the bathroom.

When he'd locked the door, Keith came to her and held her in his arms for a long moment. Presently he stroked her hair, lowered his cheek, laid it against hers.

"My doll . . . my sweetheart," he whispered. "How would you like for me to undress you?"

She laughed softly, lightheartedly and safe. "Let's do a double striptease," she said. "Garment for garment."

First he kissed her deeply, then he let her go and began to unbutton his shirt. She worked at the buttons of her gingham dress. He removed his shirt and she stepped out of the dress at the same second.

Now she felt excited, but a bit frightened, too. His gray eyes never left her, roved over her as she moved, and all of his warmth was in them. She felt an answering warmth.

When he took off his boots, she kicked off her slippers, pulled away her nylons. When he stepped out of his jeans, she got out of her slip. When he took off his T-shirt, she threw her bra aside, breasts springing free. And when he got out of his briefs, she discarded her bikini.

They stood gazing at each other. He was so excited at the smooth beauty of her body that his passion surged. She saw that he had a scatter of yellow hair on his chest, that a line of yellow ran down his belly to his crotch. He was strongly built, smoothly muscled.

"You're handsome, Keith. More so . . . this way."

He moved to her, and she went into his arms, skin to skin. She still felt shy-bold and it seemed, almost, that this was her first time with any man. They kissed; he lifted her and carried her to the bed, his tongue entwined with hers.

He came into her without further preliminary; she liked the sensation of fullness and smoothness, waited for him to take the lead, to show her how to move. He started a circular motion and she matched it, in the opposite direction.

His breath fanned her cheek, and hers struck his face and came back to her own skin. His breath was sweet and made no sound. He moved ardently and fast, but in silence, and she sank gratefully into that silence and herself moved, waiting, reaching for the moment of bliss which was sure to come.

She was holding her breath when ecstasy struck. Her hips rose from the bed, lifting his body, and they hung, melded, for seconds, breaths mingling. Then they dropped back and she lay in his arms.

"You're wonderful!" he breathed. "You're a dream!"

She sighed happily; her breath quivered.

"Was it good for you?" he asked.

"It was perfect," she said, and then she remembered other times, remembered Tower. "Perfect," she repeated, and with honesty, because it had been. Tender and sweet and silent. Soothing. And, at this moment at least, all desire for Tower was gone.

As Keith cuddled her, contentment and hope mingled in him. He'd wanted this girl for so long, for so many reasons; now, it seemed, she might be his.

"I want to love you again, right now," he murmured, "but there are things to be said first. I love you, darling, want you for my wife."

"But," she protested instinctively, "it's... well, we

166

can't get married just because of making love one time. It was wonderful, but marriage—"

"There's Vic. There's your son. He should have a father. And he's fond of me. I like him because of his own little personality, not just because he's a part of you, though that does make him dearer. I'll love him as much as I'll love our own sons, you can depend on that."

She ran her hands down his hard back, and he joined himself to her again, and this time it was even better. Rae-Ellen glowed. She was freed, at last, of Jess Tower.

But she was unable to give in to Keith's plea for marriage, though he kept urging while they dressed. Because there was Drew.

She felt a pang of guilt. She had learned from Keith, learned gentleness and sweetness and silence in the love act. She'd learned from him whom she did not love the meaning of love, which she must convey to Drew.

"No," she told Keith. "I can't promise marriage."

"I'm afraid you're half in love with Drew, that you're bewitched by Tower," Keith said unhappily. "Just say that I can keep trying to win you—give me that much hope, sweetheart."

"All right," she agreed reluctantly. "But please don't expect too much!"

At this moment Drew and Susie were in a small cocktail lounge, the curtains of their tiny booth closed. They sat close together on one side of the minuscule table.

"We'll be in disgrace, cutting out on the party," he said, smiling.

"We told him we wanted to go for a long drive, Drew. We had his blessing."

"He sensed that we need to be alone," Drew said. "And outside of going to my place—"

"I couldn't do that! I just couldn't!"

"So we're here. The sweetest, most beautiful girl in Texas and, I hope, the most irresistible sheepman," he said in a half-teasing tone.

"As far as I'm concerned, you're the most attractive man in the world," Susie said softly, then blushed. She began to tremble.

He took her hand. "You must know I'm in love with you, Susie." He tapped her marriage finger with the tip of his forefinger. "I want to put a platinum and diamond ring there. To make you mine for keeps. If you can bring yourself to say the vows with a sheepman."

Her heart was in her throat, fluttering. The moment of which she had dreamed was here, and she was no more ready to deal with it than she'd been months ago. She couldn't, simply could not tell him about Keith—not yet!

"Love me?" he whispered, his lips against her hair.

"Yes . . . oh, yes!"

"Then we get married. It's simple as that. We go back to the party and announce our engagement!"

She had to give him a reason why not, and the reason had to be true without betraying the secret until she could think of the right way to tell him. "I can't be engaged . . . not yet!" she whispered.

"Why not?"

"I . . . there's a confession I have to make first, and I'm not ready."

"There's nothing you can 'confess' that will change me, darling. Out with it!" He put his arm around her, drew her close.

Tears were stinging her nose. Now they crept out of her eyes and down her cheeks, but he couldn't see them in the dimness.

"Please, Drew," she begged. "I'm just not ready! Could you wait? Not long. But give me time enough to get my courage up!"

He was silent for a moment, then kissed her cheek, tasted the salt. There was salt on her lips, too. No matter what she believed she had to confess, he thought, kissing still, she was forgiven. This girl, this wondrous, sweet and lovable woman, was good to the core.

"You can have the time," he promised. "Take as long as you need. All that matters is that I get you for my wife."

Chapter Fifteen

SUSIE and Drew were still out together when Rae-Ellen got home from the party. Abed, she couldn't sleep. She was free of Tower—not a trace of that burning was left—and she felt grateful to Keith.

She tossed, tried to get her mind off Drew and Susie; couldn't. What had gone on between them tonight? Where were they now? Had he declared his love? Had Susie admitted her love for him? Most important, had Susie confessed her affair with Keith?

And if she had, what had Drew's reaction been? Would he be hurt and disappointed, reluctant to marry a girl who had, unmarried, got herself pregnant? Would he forgive? Would he, being Drew, say that what happened between Keith and Susie was in the past, that only the future counted?

Over and over these questions marched through her. And there were no answers. She was nude, and a certain amount of hotness glowed in her body. She'd be glad when August ended and cooler nights arrived. The burning couldn't be for Tower, even if it was creeping into her, because Keith had banished it. She found herself almost loving Keith for that.

It was three o'clock and still she hadn't slept. She punched her pillows, stacked one on top of the other, plopped her head down.

It was then she heard the sound of horses neighing. She sat bolt upright, listening. The neighing continued; there was a distant splintering noise. It came from the stable.

She jumped off the bed, snatched up her white robe, stepped into slides. Voices called from the other girls' rooms . . . so Susie had sneaked in. But Rae-E.'len fled for the door, not answering, and ran for the stable, losing her slides before she'd gone ten steps.

Barefoot, she raced on. There was confusion and movement ahead. As she neared the stable, she heard the sound of hooves, many hooves, and knew that her horses were loose and running. Racing, panting, she was aware of others on the move, and of the shouting of men.

The pounding of hooves continued, farther away now. Lights were on in the stable. She glimpsed Compton and Johnny, and the stableboy, seeing her, screamed, "All the thoroughbreds . . . loose! We got to get them!"

She sped down the center of the empty stable, into one big corral, across it, the way the horses had gone. At the big gate she stopped, clung to a post, her breath hurting and tearing through her chest. The big gate was broken, splintered! That was the sound she'd heard! Had her horses done that, cut and injured themselves?

Keith appeared, bridle in hand. He was running, didn't so much as glance at her. "What happened?" she screamed.

Another figure with a bridle pounded past. It was Tower. "Somebody spooked the horses!" he yelled.

She raced after him, barefoot, poured on every ounce of speed. The bridle was streaming behind him as he pounded toward a corral, and she grabbed it and hung on.

"Let go!" he roared. He yanked the bridle loose and charged into the corral. She ran to its fence and saw that a few cow ponies were penned there and that Keith and Tower were throwing the bridles onto them. Each grabbed a coil of rope and sprang astride a bareback pony, and then went thundering through the gate Johnny opened, twirling their ropes, ready to lasso the first runaways they found.

Rae-Ellen streaked out of the corral and into the pasture land, the better to watch. They were riding furiously, rope loops standing in the air, seeming to gain on the fleeing herd. Her breath snagged.

Oh, they had to stop her horses, her beauties, had to get them back into the stable, into their stalls, go over them for injuries. Had to let them know that they were safe and loved and treasured. Later, they'd find out why the silver herd had run, but not now. The only thing that mattered was to get them back.

Now Susie and Dots and Adah, all in robes, came

panting through the corral, through the open, broken gate to her. "What happened? What's going on?"

"The horses," Rae-Ellen said. "They spooked."

"Where are the men?" Susie cried.

"Keith and Tower rode cow ponies bareback after them. I don't know where Compton and Johnny are—riding, too or waiting out there someplace with lassos."

"How could it happen?" Dots asked. "How could anything or anybody frighten the whole herd? Don't three men sleep back here in the stable?"

"Keith has an apartment at the house," Rae-Ellen said stiffly. "Compton and Johnny and Keith have efficiencies near the stable office. They even take turns making rounds during the night. Tower instituted the rounds... for all the good it's done," she added bitterly.

"What about your pregnant filly?" Susie asked. "Is she loose, too?"

"I suppose... only, maybe... let's go look!"

The four girls ran back across the corral and into the stable. Silver Girl wasn't in her stall. Every stall was empty.

"But the stalls aren't damaged," said Rae-Ellen, looking in closely as she passed each one. "Somebody has opened each stall and then, when the horses were in the corral, spooked them, leaving the corral gate ajar so they splintered it breaking through."

They were examining the corral gate by lantern light when Compton and Johnny came trotting up. "Keith and Jess'll round 'em up, Rae-Ellen," Compton assured her. "It ain't a stampede, just a straight run. All we got to do is wait."

*   *   *

They waited. An hour dragged past. Then, distantly, came the sound of hoofs. The sound grew. Rae-Ellen strained her ears, peered through the far darkness, trying to see.

After forever, she glimpsed the silver herd, starlight making the horses glisten. They were coming at an easy lope, and were followed by two mounted figures. Rae-Ellen felt weak with relief.

The riders would be Keith and Tower, bareback. She felt a surge of gratitude toward Keith. The only thing she felt for Tower was irritation.

Sure, he'd gone riding to the rescue. Just like a movie cowboy, bareback and all. And where had he been while someone was tampering with her priceless herd? Asleep in his bed, that was where.

Grimly, she waited until every horse was in its stall. Tower examined Silver Girl first, and reported that she didn't have a scratch on her. He singsonged her until she stopped her restless movements and began to eat the extra ration of oats he'd ordered for all the horses.

Then he and Keith, with Compton and Johnny trailing, slowly walked the length of the stalls and examined every horse. They found no wounds, only nervousness, which they soothed away with singsonging, sweet-talking, and oats. Somehow Tower was better at the soothing routine than the others, and this irritated Rae-Ellen.

Tower's singsong got into her blood. She listened fiercely for Keith's singsong, took it into herself and tried to banish the unwanted burning. It didn't succeed. What *was* it about that bareback show-off that

175

could get to her so, keep her stirred up? Keith was the better man by far.

It was Keith who came to her and said, "It must have been kids, teenagers. Turned the herd out for pure devilment."

Tower, who had also come up, was quiet for a space. Then he half agreed with Keith, saying, "Rae-Ellen has no enemies—it must have been something like that. Unless some horse thieves have moved into the territory." With that, he went back to Silver Girl.

It was almost five o'clock, dawn near, when Susie and Adah and Dots went back to the house. Rae-Ellen told them she'd be along later, that she wanted to keep her own eye on Silver Girl, make certain she wasn't going to foal too soon as a result of tonight's run.

Tower ambled over to the departing girls, assured them all the horses were in top shape. He even laughed over something Dots said about maybe a mouse scaring the horses.

Later, when they were gone and Compton and Johnny had gone to eat breakfast, Tower strode toward the house. Rae-Ellen followed and, when he went into his apartment, followed him inside. Everything about him, from the day he raped her in the hotel through his show-off rescue of the herd this morning, had her at a slow boil. And that burning deep inside was at top heat, which made her maddest of all. A sudden conviction came to her. At one level, she knew it was unjust, almost insane—but her temper was out of control, and she was prepared to believe anything bad about Jess Tower.

"You louse!" she hissed. "You absolute louse!"

176

Chapter Sixteen

HE wheeled. He was in the middle of the living room, she was just inside the door. Her fingers went into claws, but she kept them rigid at her sides.

His face was handsome-mean. "What's eating on you now?" he demanded.

"I have things to say to you!"

"Spit them out. I've got work to do."

"You did the whole thing!" she yelled.

"I hope you know what you're talking about. I sure-hell don't."

"Stop swearing at me!"

"Then don't make me do it!"

"Don't try to change the subject!"

"Just what is the subject?"

"My horses! You did it... you spooked them!"

"Doubtless you know why I did it." His voice dripped sarcasm.

"So you could ride bareback and round them up! Be the big hero!" As she spoke, the stupidity of what she was saying overwhelmed her. And that was his fault, too, leading her into making a fool of herself.

"I suppose that's why Keith rode, too?"

"He has no need to show off—he's had his job a long time!"

Tower threw back his head and laughed.

She clenched her fists and held her breath, searching wildly for another accusation to throw at him.

He quit laughing, gave her a keen look. Then he whispered, "Get to your own room, right now!"

"You also hang around Susie and Clovis and . . . others!" she cried. "Talk about *my* having a string of men! What about you with your women?"

"You going to your own room or not?"

He itched to get his hands on her. But whether to shake the meanness out or to get her on the bed, he didn't know.

She settled it herself. She shot an electric glare at him, spun about to pass him and rushed into his bedroom. By the time he'd followed her, she'd thrown off the white robe and was facing him, a naked bundle of fury.

"You want a fight?" he demanded, so mad he couldn't think. "Well, I'm here to give it to you!"

He tore off his clothes and came at her, neck redder than she'd ever seen it, that face handsome even in rage, and caught her nude body to his own.

She clawed, but only halfheartedly, because this was what she wanted. To bed him until she was sick

178

of him and would never again feel that horrible, flaming desire. Still—no, she didn't, not really... want this! She didn't know what she wanted. She began to kick and pound in earnest to get free.

He had only one objective: to subdue her, once and for all. Between fending off her claws and kicks, he swooped her up and threw her onto the bed, where she landed on her back. Before she could pop back up, he was over her, and they entered into a wordless, loud-breathing sex-fight that left them limp.

Thoughts flared through her. He'd both transported her—as usual—and ruined what Keith had accomplished. She hated him more than ever.

As for Jess, he was madder than he'd been the other times. Mad at her, mad at himself. Why did he want to make violent love to his little filly when he couldn't bear the sight of her, when he realized that Susie would make a perfect wife?

Now she was trying to get off the bed, pretending that he'd try to hold her there by force. He leaped off himself, made an exaggerated bow, a film of sweat on his naked skin, and gestured that she was free to leave. She scooted off the bed, threw on her robe, and went running barefoot out of the apartment.

After breakfast, she went directly to the stable. All the horses, including Silver Girl, were in the pasture, browsing, trotting a bit, as if they'd never gone on a rampage.

Tower was repairing the broken corral gate. He had some lumber and a saw, hammer, and nails. He was pounding on a length of board when she walked up to the gate and stood watching.

"Those teenagers," he said as coolly as if he'd

179

never laid a hand on her, "saw to it that the horses did a job on this gate—or did it themselves."

"Why not put up a new gate?" she asked snippily. She couldn't help the snippiness; he brought out the worst in her. You'd think he'd at least apologize for what he'd done to her this morning.

But there was no apology.

"Would put up a new gate if the damage was worse," he said.

He set a nail, drove the hammer against its head; the nail sank into the wood. Clear to the head. Like . . . like in the bedroom. Her cheeks burned at the comparison. She sniffed so he could hear her disdain, since he wouldn't look at her. He drove her insane, that's what he did, finding time, after he brought the horses back, to laugh with Susie. She couldn't bear him!

Jess, setting another nail, driving it in with one blow, unwillingly realized she was deeply interested in her farm. How many other girls would watch a gate being repaired? He had to give her that—she was all out for horses.

Crazily, Rae-Ellen found herself jealous of the wood as he drove another nail into it. That gate was absolutely unfeeling, incapable of response! Suddenly, out of nowhere, she knew he wasn't a bum.

"You've not told me your complete background!" she snapped. "Is it a secret?"

"No secret," he said, going on with his work. Now he had another short length he was nailing in place. "Grew up in California on a farm, loved horses from the time I could walk. Before that even, I'd guess. Went to college in Austin with Burr, made my way

180

back to California, working on farms. Always with horses. When I got there, I kept working with horses. Just horses. And now I'm here, as manager."

He shot her a look, let his eyes remain.

"You're staring at me!" she accused. "You do the same with Susie! Why—that's what I want to know. Why? By what right?"

"Habit," he said. "I look things over—farms, horses, women. As I should have looked over that girth strap before I rode."

"You do it to find out if things are good enough for you!"

He kept staring, deeper and deeper.

"See, you're comparing me to Susie this minute! I've seen the way you treat her! Like she's a great lady! It seems you don't care that she's not a virgin!"

"I don't. I look for other qualities: what's inside a woman, underneath any impulsive, foolish thing she may have done. I look to see if she's good, if she's solid at the core. And if she is, that's all that counts."

"You're taking digs at me! You're—"

He dropped his hammer, took a quick look around. Compton and Johnny were at the far end of the pasture, putting out fresh rock salt.

He gripped Rae-Ellen's arm and marched her to the house. She walked stiffly, speechless. She'd never been treated like this in her life! She started to scream at him, to demand where he was taking her and why, then clamped her lips. She wouldn't give him that satisfaction. Or have the girls and Leah hear. She'd simply bide her time, and when she found out what he was up to, foil him. Yes, that was the word—foil!

181

He walked her into his apartment, straight to the bedroom.

"Undress," he ordered.

Furious, rebelling against his orders, driven by the need to rid herself forever of this awful burning, she yanked off her clothes.

He pushed her onto the bed and she let him. She opened to him, impatient to free herself. They had long, feverish, savage sex. Not purely sex, she realized as she clung to him, but almost a lovemaking that might be harder to get rid of than just plain passion.

Jess ground at her, driving hard, and wondered if he might hurt her. But he didn't, because she gave as hard as she got. Her breath was stabbing in and out; he could hear it. This time, for sure, he was going to cure that itch he had for this girl. And never think of her again. She was nothing but trouble; he wanted no part of her.

Exhausted, they lay flat, not touching, catching their breath. There was a kind of peace until she spoke.

"You've had women. Have you ever been in love?"

"I don't see that's any of your business."

"It is my business . . . you've made it my business!"

"Just how the hell do you figure that?"

She ignored the question and went on. "The times you've . . . we've . . . Have you . . . with Susie?"

"Susie hasn't got round heels."

"And I have, I suppose?"

"Going by the way you've been with me, I wouldn't call them exactly square."

"Always the gentleman, aren't you! You still haven't answered my question—have you ever been in love?"

"Like I told you, it's none of your business."

"Then I know!"

"Tell me. I'm interested to find out."

"You can't leave sex alone! You won't 'sully' Susie because you r-respect her!"

"So?"

"So you don't know what you want! The great Tower is trying to make up his mind between two women—Susie and me!"

He laughed. "Your premise is that I aim to marry at all."

"Most men do. Whether they plan it or not. Look around you."

"I'm looking. And in these parts I see bachelors— Miller and Belisle and Bradley. And Sammy Soose, that Dot's got hooked. And oh yes, Drew Knight. Seems I'm in good company. Though it's my guess that any one of them, except Soose and Knight, would marry you tomorrow."

"And you!"

"That's right. Count me out, too."

"Who *will* you marry, what kind of girl?"

"A Susie-type, way I feel now. But if I ever do marry, I'll not have any trouble making up my mind. It'll come over me like a thunderclap."

"What if the girl says no?"

"She won't. It'll come over her like a thunderclap, too."

"And love? You haven't answered me yet!"

"That," he said grimly, "will take care of itself."

And then he marched her to the door and out.

Chapter Seventeen

RODEO practice was under way on all the ranches except the Double T. There Rae-Ellen's crew tended the horses, coddled the pregnant Silver Girl, put Thunder Boy out for stud.

Grant Miller, who had been dropping in every day to chat, invited Rae-Ellen to drive with him to the Leaning K for lunch. She consented readily. She was cordial with him, smiling softly, because she meant to try him out in bed. She'd learned from Keith; she might learn much from Grant that would please Drew. And he might cool her heat for Tower.

Grant, who had been half in love with Rae-Ellen from the time she married Burr Travis, looked forward to being alone with her in his house. His mind went to Lorna, the homely widow whom he'd married to acquire the Leaning K.

There had been no courtship. He was Lorna's foreman, and she said he was the best the Leaning K had ever had. After her husband died, she gave Grant more and more responsibility and he discharged it all faithfully, hoping for a raise.

Then came the night she invited him to supper. After the meal, they sat in the parlor and drank coffee. He tried not to look at her too much. She was so very homely, horse-faced, a big wart on her chin and a tooth missing, hair a graying straggle; he was afraid his near aversion would show.

"I've got a proposition for you," she said. "Are you willing to hear me through?"

"Of course, Mrs. Fish."

"I told you to call me Lorna."

"Lorna. Sorry."

"I'm no beauty, and I'm twenty years older than you," she began. "But I've got the Leaning K, three thousand acres of pastureland stocked with cattle. That you know, and that everything is in top condition, because you keep it so."

He nodded, waited.

"I want you to marry me, Grant."

He blinked.

"If you marry me and are a husband to me—no outside women—I'll leave the Leaning K to you when I die. And the investments Hiram made, which are sizable."

Now it was her turn to wait.

"I'm ... astounded," he said at last. "Why me?"

"I find you attractive. Yes, even at my age. And

186

I'm lonely. I need your companionship. It seems a fair trade to me. I don't know how it seems to you. You're a young man, and I'm an old woman. But you'd have the ranch, and the investments. You'd be prosperous when other young men are struggling. I'd give you a half-interest the day we married. As a binder."

"And what would my binder to you be?"

"Your name with mine on a marriage certificate. A gold ring on my wedding finger."

She'd given him a week to think it over. He'd discussed it with Keith Belisle. Keith thought it was the chance of a lifetime. "Take it," he'd said.

So he'd married Lorna. The marriage hadn't been bad; she was even adequate in bed. And the marriage had been short. Lorna had died of a heart attack in seven months and Grant, briefly saddened, buried her and was once again a free man.

Then Bertha Mudd began to cast warm looks at him. She'd been widowed at the time Grant married Lorna, but seemed content to live alone on her X-M with only her hired hands on the place. She was much more attractive than Lorna had been; in fact, Grant rather fancied her dovelike appearance.

Also, she had four thousand acres of rangeland, well-stocked, and he knew her deceased husband had invested in oil. Further, though she too was older than himself, it was by only ten years.

He pondered whether to court her. He took her to a program at the school, and she was pleasant to be with. He liked the admiration in her eyes when she looked at him. He took her to supper when Old Vic

Travis invited people in. But he didn't take her to church; that would have put too serious an aspect on their dates.

He waited, and wondered if she'd speak up, as Lorna had. He wasn't sure he wanted her to. Actually, he was well enough fixed to marry a young woman, to have a family.

So he let it drift, fully aware that Bertha's affection for him was growing. One thing was certain; he meant to give himself time to make a decision.

Then Burr Travis got killed in a rodeo and there was a new widow, Rae-Ellen. Who could win her was the question. She was a lively woman, a beauty, and obviously passionate. Also she was young. He and Keith discussed her thoughtfully. Time passed. Grant waited; when Jess Tower came to manage the Double T, Grant saw the sparks between him and Rae-Ellen right away. It was then he began to bring himself to Rae-Ellen's notice as often as he could. He made a point of being at every gathering to which Rae-Ellen went. She was the most attractive woman he'd ever seen, he was drawn to her, and if he didn't make a move soon, somebody else would. She had too much beauty, too much spirit, too much potential wealth not to be snapped up by the first man who appealed to her.

He spent no time in formal courtship; he didn't ask for dates, sensing this wasn't the way to win her. Lorna could have tried to court him and he would never have done a thing. She'd had to make her proposition. Likewise, if he wanted Rae-Ellen, he had to make a definite, unexpected move. Make her notice him, shock her into awareness, sweep her off her feet.

Today, at lunch, could be the day.

He escorted her into his house—Lorna's house— with its comfortable rooms and white, thin, starched curtains. He took her into the kitchen and began to prepare the food.

"Where's Molly?" Rae-Ellen asked.

"I gave her and Bart the day off. They're driving to Fort Worth, won't be back until late. Besides, lunch is easy . . . it's just my Texas chili."

"The best in the world!" she said. "And cheddar cheese to eat with it?"

"And crackers, and boiled coffee. Deep-dish apple pie for dessert. Molly baked it last night, to tide me over."

Rae-Ellen set the table, insisting that they eat in the kitchen. She sliced the cheese and ladled thick cream into a pitcher for the coffee.

Grant kept telling funny stories about the cow- boys, about the falls they took practicing for the rodeo. Rae-Ellen laughed, wouldn't let herself think of how Burr had been killed at the last big rodeo, gave herself completely to Grant's merry mood.

They chatted and laughed and ate. They washed dishes. And then they went into the parlor to talk rodeo.

Rae-Ellen sat on the sofa, watching Grant. During the meal, he had grown more intimate by the mo- ment. His voice had gentled until now it had a stroking quality. He moved to the sofa, sat close to Rae-Ellen, and she didn't move away.

Her pulse went faster. As they talked on, their

voices a murmur, he slid his arm around her shoulders, and she let it stay. It felt good. Kind, warm, gentle ... safe.

He was going to make a pass, for sure he was. He had invited her to lunch, the two of them alone in the house, and he meant to make his play. And she was going to let him. He was offering himself, and she meant to receive what he offered, and measure, oh so carefully, what it could mean to her. Maybe it wasn't quite fair to Grant, but she was doing it for Drew, to learn more of gentleness for him, to become what he wanted.

Grant kissed her brow with many warm, light kisses, and this she permitted, too. She liked the kisses, felt a small thrill run down her spine. It seemed to her that it wasn't impossible that she might, in the long run, choose Grant for her mate if she failed with Drew.

He trailed kisses along her cheeks and onto her lips. Tiny, warm, just-touching kisses. And now his hand came under her breast and held it as if it were precious, and the thrill touched her loins.

She quivered.

"Rae-Ellen," he whispered, "I want you so!"

"I ... too," she whispered back and, in that moment, she did want him. This thrill he gave her; it might free her from Tower. She nestled to Grant, let him draw her to her feet, up the stairs and into a walnut-furnished bedroom.

He wanted to undress her, and she let him. As he drew off garment after garment, his fingers trailed along her skin, increasing the warmth in her depths.

Warmth, blessed, comfortable warmth, not a rage of fire.

When she was nude, he whispered, "Perfect! I knew you'd be perfect!"

He got out of his own clothes fast, urged her onto the bed. She opened to him, and it seemed natural and right. Natural and right, too, when he came into her.

Though it was their first time, they began to move as if they'd known each other's ways forever. The warmth grew and swelled and broke and blossomed, and all of Rae-Ellen sang with the absolute beauty of it.

Grant, holding his breath, felt he was being carried through the air. It had been so long since he'd had a young woman the delight was nearly unbearable.

After they'd reached the crest the second time, he held her tenderly. "You're wonderful," he told her. "Absolutely wonderful!"

"And you," she murmured.

She felt fed and satisfied. Grant had proved to her that she had a healthy appetite for sex. Not for sex-battle, but for natural, thrilling lovemaking. She could imagine being married to him, she really could. Only, there was Drew. Bed with him would be like this.

"I want you to know," Grant said, "that I planned this today."

"I . . . felt it coming."

"And didn't try to prevent it?"

"No. I wanted to . . . explore my feelings."

"I'm in love with you," he said. "Can you, possibly, be in love with me?"

To be fair, she considered. Grant could be very dear. But there was Drew, already dear. As for Tower, Grant's superb performance—which was lovemaking, not sex—had at last rid her of the yen for him.

"Rae-Ellen?"

"I'm fond of you, Grant. It might grow into love. I honestly don't know."

"I'm a patient man," Grant said. "I'll wait. But I have to tell you now I want to marry you. My marriage to Lorna . . . well, it was . . ."

"I understand. You made a bargain and kept it."

"Since you do understand," he said, "there's no need to wait. We can be married at once, let your love grow. What do you say, sweetheart?"

"I'm not ready to marry yet," she told him.

"Is it the other men? Drew, Jess Tower?"

She shook her head. Drew had rejected her, Tower hated her and she hated him.

"We need to think of Vic," Grant argued gently. "The younger he is when another man becomes his father, the better. I'll be a good father, sweetheart. He likes me now; let me live in the same house with him, and he'll love me. I've wanted a family, but Lorna was past childbearing, past adopting. I'd hope to have a son with you, but if not, there's Vic. He can be my heir. What's it going to be, dear heart . . . yes?"

As he spoke, the uncertainty, the feeling that what she felt for Grant might grow and change, vanished. "It can't be," she said slowly. "Now or ever. Even after . . ." She motioned at their nude bodies. "You're worthy and good and I'm fond of you, but I've got to feel deep love when I marry. And it won't be that way, on my part, toward you."

She kissed his sober, disappointed face.

And yearned for Drew.

Chapter Eighteen

THAT evening, Rae-Ellen pondered still another bed partner, Link Bradley, for whom she held deep, trusting regard. Often, after her outbursts at Tower, a fleeting thought of Link came to her. She had taken comfort thinking of his strong, stocky build, his brown hair and full-toned voice. And his patience as her attorney.

At least if a girl married Link, she'd win a mature man, one she could trust. His lovemaking would also be mature, smooth and satisfying. If she went to bed with him, having good sex with two solid men would eradicate forever her hunger for Tower. Yes, she decided, Grant and Link on the same day. Scandalous, maybe, but she needed them; they were like balm spread on a burned spot that otherwise wouldn't quit tormenting her. She had to admit it, she still hadn't made herself sick enough of Tower; she needed help, and it was available.

She closed herself into the library, went to the telephone, and dialed Link's office.

"Rae-Ellen!" he exclaimed. "Is everything all right?"

"Just fine," she said lightly. "I didn't call on legal business. Social only." She laughed. "I don't suppose your evenings are lonely, you an eligible bachelor with a tremendous law practice!"

He laughed too, the sound full and low. "I don't need to ask if you're lonely," he bantered. "A beautiful, young, rich widow can have her pick of the state. If she wants it."

"That's one of my troubles," she confessed. "When you find yourself in that position, there's no peace, no way to make up your mind. So I do have lonely evenings. Which is why I called you."

He took her right up on it. "Tonight? Dinner? At your place or mine? Or at a restaurant?"

"Restaurant," she said gaily.

"Deal. If you'll let me have a minute with Vic. I don't want that little guy to forget me."

"Deal!" she agreed. "Pick me up at eight?"

"Fine."

Rae-Ellen went at once to her room to select what she'd wear. She wanted to look her most ladylike, yet entice Link into taking her to bed. She studied the closet in which she kept evening wear.

She decided on an ankle-length, slim dress of blue sequins. The fitted skirt was slit halfway to the knees on one side. The bodice was like a bra in front, then rose to a high, tiny, sequined collar. There was no back to the gown, none at all above the waist. She'd never worn it before, but when she'd had the fittings, she had seen that it gave her the naked look she liked to achieve.

The three other girls came in when she was winding her braided hair around her head. They stared at her.

Dots broke the silence. "Wow! Who's the lucky guy?"

"I don't know how lucky he is," Rae-Ellen said, smiling, "but I'm going out with Link."

She caught Susie's speculative look, caught Adah's worried expression. "I won't *hurt* the man, Adah!" she said. "He's a grown attorney; he can take care of himself."

"He can take care of you, too!" laughed Dots. "Oh, do let him, honey! You might find out that a solid lawyer is just what you and Baby Vic need!"

"You're a goose!" Rae-Ellen retorted lightly. Then, to change the subject, "what do you think, Susie . . . should I wear a diamond clip in my hair?"

"No!" cried all three girls.

"That dress with you in it is jewel enough," Adah added.

"You sparkle like a Christmas tree!" breathed Dots. "Don't change a thing!"

The front-door knocker sounded, and they heard Leah sing out she'd get it; then there was the rumble of a man's voice, and the girls scattered, leaving the field clear for Rae-Ellen. She went into the nursery, caught Vic wide-eyed and sucking his thumb, took him up.

"You have a caller," she told him. "Now be good."

Link was in the living room sitting on one of the great sofas. He sprang up when Rae-Ellen entered with the baby. She'd never seen Link so handsome. They'd make a striking couple at dinner and later, in bed . . .

He came to her, smiling. The smile lent his full features a handsomeness she hadn't noticed before, because she'd had her mind on Drew. And her anger on Tower.

"Vic," she said to the baby, who was still sucking his thumb, "this is Link. You know Link."

Link put a hand gently on the baby's shoulder. Vic continued to gnaw his thumb and stared solemnly at Link. With a slow, easy gesture, Link took the child onto his own arm, and the baby permitted this. Telling him what a fine boy he was, Link gently pulled the thumb out of the little mouth and this too was permitted. Suddenly Vic laughed, drooled, patted Link's chin with his wet hand, and Link laughed with him.

Rae-Ellen, watching, saw how good they looked together. Vic had never allowed anyone else to pull his thumb out of his mouth without screaming, not even Rae-Ellen.

The thumb returned to the mouth, and Link didn't interfere.

"It's a tooth," Rae-Ellen explained.

He nodded. "That's what I thought. Well. We've cemented our relationship. Shall we leave him with Leah or Dots and be on our way?"

In the car, a new, economical compact of which he was proud, Link rolled up the windows. "The breeze is cool," he explained. "We can't have you getting chilled."

"I should have brought a wrap," she said.

"It won't be needed," he said, and she liked the quiet way in which he took charge. "We're going to a new place, the Golden Room. They say it's all sequins, even the walls and ceiling."

Rae-Ellen caught her breath when she saw the inside of the restaurant. The lighting was soft, but the sequined walls and ceiling snatched the light and twinkled it and kept it on the move. The all-girl orchestra members wore gold satin with sequins glittering on them, and the waiters' black satin suits glittered at cuff and collar. Even the golden tablecloths had a band of glitter around the bottom.

Link seated Rae-Ellen with pride. This was the first real date he'd had with her, and he was excited and hopeful. From the time she'd married Burr Travis, she'd ruined all other women for him. When he noticed an attractive girl he immediately compared her to Rae-Ellen Travis and forgot the new girl. Ever since Rae-Ellen had been a widow, he'd quietly and persistently kept himself in the close-knit group around her, but it was only now he'd been able to get her to himself socially. The hours they'd spent over legal matters had made them friends, but there had been no chance for courtship then.

The cuisine was French, and she asked him to order. As they sipped cocktails—Rae-Ellen barely tasting hers because she disliked liquor—they talked of everything. Even politics. They differed slightly on President Reagan. Rae-Ellen was afraid Vic might someday be taken into the army. Link said that was a long time off, that there would be more presidents before then.

She told a couple of bright things Vic had done. Link laughed, marveled at the child's precocity. He was really interested in her baby, Rae-Ellen thought. After they went to bed tonight, if Link met her expectations, maybe she should give him serious consideration. She sighed. No. It had to be Drew. Dear, likable Link could serve only two purposes: to finish off the job of flushing Tower out of her system and teach her more about ladylike seduction.

The music throbbed, sparkled. They danced, cheek to cheek. She felt Link's strong body pressed to hers, anticipated how it would be, later, if he asked. And he was going to ask, she knew, because his manner became softer, more seductive, and when he looked at her, his heart was in his eyes. This both thrilled her and made her feel guilty. Dear Link. Whatever happened, she mustn't hurt him.

When they'd finished dinner, it wasn't quite eleven. "It's too early to end such a wonderful evening," Link said. "Or do you want to end it?"

"Of course I don't!" she exclaimed. "I wish it could go on forever!"

One thing she was certain of: the absence of Jess Tower was enough in itself to make it pleasant. But the intimacy with Link, the closeness to him which she anticipated, made it thrilling.

"Want to go dancing?" he asked. "Try all the new places, and some of the old?"

"Not really, Link. What I'd like is to just sit alone and . . . well, talk. But we can't do that at the Double T. Too many people."

"My apartment is deserted," he said. "I have just a daily woman. She leaves right after dinner when I eat at home. We could talk our hearts out there. I like the idea as much as you do, maybe more." His voice softened. "My dearest wish is to get you alone. To hold you in my arms, to . . . Shall we go?"

The apartment was all white with touches of silver. The carpeting was white plush; sofas and chairs were white velvet. Tables and a fine desk were painted white. There were silver bud vases, each with a single white rose; the drapes were white bordered with silver, and there were silver cushions everywhere, and small white tables with silver ashtrays.

Rae-Ellen frankly stared. She wondered what woman had decorated this place for Link. She asked him that.

"A woman did it, not for me, but for herself," he replied. "She was transferred to New Orleans. She was a client; she knew I wanted a larger place—the kitchen I had at the time was a cubbyhole—and I took this apartment, glad to get it."

He displayed the white decor of the dining alcove, the white and stainless-steel kitchen, which was roomy and immaculate. He showed her the white and chrome bath, which opened both into a hallway and the bedroom.

"I saved the bedroom for last," he said. "I hope it'll be your favorite. I have a reason, you see," he added and placed vibrant hands on her naked shoulders.

This was white and silver too, the spread on the

201

wide bed a glitter of silver. Rae-Ellen touched the spread carefully.

"Exquisite! I hope you don't *dare* sit on it!"

He chuckled. "I handle it like eggs. But I use the apartment; it's my home. If, in time, the whiteness gets to be too much, it can be redecorated. If I keep it, that is."

His pale eyes locked with her blue ones. Her pulse warmed, as it had done before this evening. He took her slowly into his arms, stroked one hand down her bare back.

"I'm in love with you," he murmured, "so in love! I'm full man, and you're full woman, and I know you're drawn to me. Shall we find out, darling?"

"F-find out what?" she stammered, knowing what he meant, but suddenly embarrassed.

"I want us undressed and in that fancy bed, Rae-Ellen. I want to make man's love to you, show you how it would be if we were married, and then I want to ask you to be my wife."

Suddenly, she couldn't. Couldn't go through with what she'd cold-bloodedly planned. Link was too fine. He didn't deserve to be used.

She pushed away, and he let her go. Kind, gentlemanly Link. He who had seen her through all the difficult legal matters following her widowhood. Now she must repay him with a slap in the face.

"I can't, Link," she said. And continued honestly, "I thought I could, but now . . . There's someone else. If I can't have him, I don't believe I'll accept a substitute. And that's what you'd be, Link, dear."

He was thoughtful for a moment. "And if I accept

substitute status? Will you marry me then? If the other . . . falls through?"

She shook her head, tears in her eyes. He drew her into his arms and comforted her, assured her he'd be standing by should she change, and then he took her home.

Chapter Nineteen

By late the next afternoon, Rae-Ellen, after hours of thought, had come to a decision: it was time for her to take the initiative.

She was hurrying it, yes. But Susie and Drew were at a stalemate, and Rae-Ellen had been freed of that burning for Tower, and was less upset than she'd been in days. Also, she had acquired skills from Keith and Grant. She knew now how to lure and tempt, not come right out and tell what she was after.

She put on her electric blue midcalf dress, braided her front hair with an electric blue ribbon and tied it in a bow, letting the back waves ripple almost to her waist. She hoped to bring Drew to the point where he'd run his fingers through her hair.

When she was ready, with a drop of perfume behind each knee, she drove to the K-Bell. She parked quietly, went to the front door and knocked.

Drew appeared, switched on the front gallery light. She caught the gleam of admiration in his russet eyes before they veiled over. So. The way she looked had registered.

"What gives me the honor of a visit?" he asked.

"Didn't you know?" she teased. "There's a new fad."

"Which is . . . ?"

"Trading meals. I had chili with Grant . . . alone."

"This means you've come for dinner?" he asked.

"Exactly! Aren't you going to ask me in? I'm hungry, too!"

He opened the door and they went into the living room. "I'm the cook tonight," he explained, "so it'll be potluck. Vinnie and Shep drove to Fort Worth to celebrate their wedding anniversary. She left a pot of stew and a cherry cobbler."

"That's pretty heavy food!" Rae-Ellen exclaimed, in slight dismay—an overfed man might not be in much of a mood for lovemaking.

"Vinnie believes in good plain cooking," he said.

"Yes, indeed! Okay, let's eat in the dining room with one soft light! I'll set the table with your best china and silver, while you heat the stew."

"Fine," he agreed. "Everything you'll need is in the dining room."

"I know where things are," she assured him, heart beating fast. And she did, because she'd taken note, daydreamed about what changes she'd make if she came here to live with him. She set the table excitedly. Everything was going just fine, so far!

He was in and out as she worked. Because rodeo was what he was most interested in, she started the subject. He spoke of the new bronc, Diablo, due tomorrow, of the various rodeo events, of the fact that the Double T crew wouldn't ride.

"I hope you don't mind," she said. "It's just that with this new manager underfoot, and Silver Girl going to foal, they need to spend all their time with the horses. Also, I want to buy two more fillies when I can find them."

"Sure, I understand. You don't know how much I admire you, Rae-Ellen, tackling the job of raising thoroughbred horses on your own!"

"Well, it's what I want," she replied, and blushed. This was the first real compliment he'd paid her except for that look in his eyes when he first saw her tonight.

When the stew was on the table, she went to the liquor cabinet. "Can't we open a bottle?" she asked. "To celebrate?"

"To celebrate what?"

"Your new bronc. Isn't he worth it?"

"Sure he is. But you don't like liquor, and I don't either. Why can't we use milk? We both like that."

She laughed, took a fifth of whiskey from the shelf, brought it to him. "Open it!" she ordered gaily. "Milk! Who ever heard of toasting a five-thousand-dollar bronc with *milk*? Why, I'll drink a whole big glass of whiskey in his honor if I have to hold my nose!"

He laughed, too, took the bottle to the kitchen,

brought it back open. She'd already put big glasses on the table, and now she filled them.

"That's too much booze!" he objected.

"Don't be silly! And don't sit down yet! Lift your glass! To Diablo, your new bronc! Drink up... to the bottom!"

They clicked glasses, drank. The whiskey took her breath, but she gulped on and on. At the end, a coughing fit threatened, but she got by with clearing her throat. She noted, with satisfaction, that he cleared his throat, too, and that his glass was empty.

"Let's eat," he said. "A full glass on an empty stomach... don't want to get you tipsy!"

"I don't want to get tipsy!" she laughed. "I'll eat loads of stew to counteract the booze!"

She watched him eat. His hand was steady. Not a drop of stew escaped his spoon. She felt slightly far off herself, but after she ate some stew, she came part of the way back.

When his bowl was half-empty, she insisted on pouring a second glass each. He protested, but she poured, nontheless.

"We've got to toast the rodeo!" she urged. "Come on, now... glasses up... to the rodeo! Drink every drop!"

Again they drained their glasses. This time she coughed and cleared her throat. He shot her a puzzled, sidewise look. His eyes didn't seem quite normal. That was fine. Drew wasn't a drinking man. But she didn't want him drunk, just freewheeling.

Her own head felt thick, and she worked at clearing it. She had to stay in charge, whiskey or no whiskey.

"What's come over you?" he asked. "You hate liquor. And now you're downing it, one glass after another." His voice sounded thicker than normal, and this encouraged her.

"There's so much to toast!" she evaded. "It's just that it's all come at once! Tell me more about Diablo's blood lines!"

While he did, speaking with obvious care, she listened carefully, watched him closely. When she got up to go after the cherry cobbler, she was careful to walk straight. Not that she really needed to, but she had to put her plan through tonight or never.

She served the cobbler, filled the glasses again.

"Now what you going to toast?" he asked, voice slurred.

"Silver Girl and her foal . . . bottoms up!"

He hesitated. At first she thought he was going to balk, then he drank. After that, his eyes were really clouded. Her head felt stuffed with cotton, but she had the one idea, and clung to it.

"Look at me, darling," she coaxed.

Heavily, he lifted those russet eyes.

"You haven't said a word about my dress! And I wore it 'specially for you!"

"Saw the dress first thing," he muttered. "Color of your eyes. Ex-actly. Gives a man ideas."

"What kind of ideas?"

"Wrong kind. Don't want to . . . discuss them."

She was so pleased, through all the cotton in her head, she could have squealed. She dared not talk much. Her tongue was very thick and so was her brain. However, she was confident. Her plan was so firmly set that no amount of whiskey could shake it loose.

He ate his cherry cobbler.

She wondered if she dared propose a toast to the two silver fillies she was going to buy when she found them. She decided against that. Maybe he hadn't had just quite the right amount of whiskey, but she'd had more than enough, and she still had much to accomplish.

They decided to leave the dishes on the table till morning. "I can wash 'em then," Drew said, "in no time."

"Then let's sit in the living room," Rae-Ellen suggested.

"Won't they be missing you at home?"

"I told them to look for me when they see me. Now I want to talk. Besides, I shouldn't drive this soon. I'll need coffee before I leave, too, and I couldn't hold coffee now. Not after that cobbler."

He agreed that she was right, and they wove into the living room. On the way, Rae-Ellen deliberately cracked her ankle against a chair leg, bent over and gripped it. It really did hurt. She hadn't meant to hit it so hard; she blamed that on the whiskey. Also, it made her dizzy to bend over this way.

Drew made her sit on the sofa, and took her ankle into his hands, feeling it over, sort of fumbling. "That hurt?" he asked. She shook her head, he pressed on a different place, and she yelped.

"It hurts!" she confessed. Then, hewing fuzzily to her plan, looking into his now definitely befuddled eyes, she said, "If I could soak it. Then lie on the bed awhile and you bring cold cloths or hot, which-ever is right, maybe I'll be able to drive home."

He had to get his arm around her to help her to the bathroom. She pulled off her sandals and nylons and sat with her feet in the tub.

He closed the drain, turned on almost hot water, let it splash and leap in the tub. He said he didn't know which was proper—hot or cold. She said the hot felt good, and when it covered her ankles he turned it off. He produced some Epsom salts and dumped them into the water.

They didn't talk except for his asking if the pain was wearing off. Finally she said it was, and if he'd help her dry her feet and support her to the bed, she'd lie there and rest. "And you bring cloths for the ankle," she reminded.

While he was getting things ready, she stepped out of bed on her good foot—the injured one felt normal now—and took off her clothes. When he came back with a hot towel, she was stretched on her back, arms out at her sides. He stopped, stared in the light from the lamp.

"Why'd you do that?" he asked.

"To get comfortable. Put the towel on my ankle."

He did, and when he straightened, she cast discretion to the winds. Which was easy, with all that cotton in her brain. "Take off your clothes," she said fuzzily.

"That wouldn't be right," he said. He swayed slightly.

"It would be ex-exactly right. You having to deal with hot cloths. I'm your guest, and I've got like this because of my ankle and you should, too."

That somehow didn't sound as sensible as she intended, but luckily it meant something to his clouded mind, because he unbuttoned his shirt. It took him a long time.

It took him forever to undress, the whiskey had made his fingers so clumsy, but she was willing to wait. She seemed to be floating into and out of consciousness anyway, but she had the one objective that pulled her back, every time.

"Now," she said, when he was at last naked, and she could see the wonders of his body, six-foot and Texas-built, like so many of the men here. He had little russet curls on the chest and down his belly. On his legs, too.

She held her arms up to him. He turned slowly, looked behind himself as if to see if someone had entered. And then he turned back to her.

She did have one clear thought. That it was a shame she had to ply him with whiskey to entice him, that her own allure wouldn't do the job. But once she'd succeeded *with* the whiskey, everything would be all right. He'd come to his senses, know that she was the wife for him.

"Come!" she urged, arms still up.

His manhood surged. He groaned, came onto the bed and into her with one swift, smooth motion. He began to move, and she returned his movements, matched them.

Warmth filled her, flooding along her veins. The warmth began to throb, was delicious, and the more she moved the more it throbbed. When he groaned and stiffened, when her body lifted so that the hips didn't touch the bed, the warmth and throbbing burst and there was all of glory. No wild, angry passion, no crazy, impossible peaks. Just warmth and satisfaction. The way love was meant to be.

They lay still connected, and she thought fuzzily into the years to come. For, of course, he now felt as she did. There would be utter, lifelong content. Like this. For her, and for Drew.

Drew, still linked to her, experienced one last sweet instant of bliss. Forbidden bliss, stolen. Lying so, he felt that fuzziness leave his brain, realized with a sobering shock what he had done.

Completely sober, he sat up. She sat up. Neither reached for clothes.

"Drew . . . oh, Drew!" she whispered. She was sobering; she fully appreciated the glory of what they'd done.

He shattered her joy flatly. "I did wrong to make love to you."

"Oh, but you didn't! You used the magic word—*love*! We made *love*, darling!"

"We had sex," he countered. "I can never marry you, my dear."

"Why can't you marry me, *why*?"

"You know the answer to that, Rae-Ellen. It's Susie or nobody. As for what we did, you and I, the blame is mine. I apologize from my depths. You have my friendly affection and true respect. I regret I can't offer more."

She flew into her clothes, brain miraculously clear. She had his respect, but Susie had his love. He was being very gentle, very sweet, but her heart seemed to break, then suddenly to harden toward Tower because he was so . . . different. So rough and overbearing. Not listening to Drew's apologies further, she ran out the door and to her car, boiling mad.

She drove home like the wind, her anger scalding. Jess Tower wasn't out of her at all. Not even after Drew. Her course of action was still clear—to bed Tower until she was sick and tired of him. Only so would she be free of torture. It was being forced on her.

She drove faster. Her body screamed for Jess Tower; she ached to claw his eyes out.

Chapter Twenty

TOWARD dawn, when she'd finally begun to doze, even then starving for Tower's horrid, degrading sex, head afire with a mighty hangover, he came slipping into her room. The first she knew of his presence was when he settled on the edge of her bed and whispered her name.

"Rae-Ellen . . . you awake?"

Her head gave an enormous throb. She realized she was nude, started to order him out, then, crazily, was glad she'd not put on pajamas. Her head ached miserably.

"How can I sleep," she hissed, "with you shouting?"

"I didn't shout," he whispered. "You know that damn well."

"What are you doing here? What do you want?"

"Couldn't sleep. Thought if we . . . well, got friendly for a spell . . . we could both drop off. Get some rest."

"Ha! Now you want me for a sleeping pill!"

"No such thing."

"Then why—"

"Can you tell me, truthfully, that our nights together didn't help you sleep? They sure-hell eased me off."

"You'd like to trick me into admitting a thing like that! You'd just love it!"

"Oh, shut up," he murmured, grabbed her into his arms and held her cradled there.

At first she was going to fight him, then changed her mind. There was her headache. And her plan. To be with him until she was sick of his very touch. To free herself so she could proceed with life. So she let him hold her.

She could feel his beating heart under her right ear. Stroke, stroke, it went. Strong. Steady. Her own heart was racing. She wondered what he'd do if he discovered she meant to use him. That she'd already used him. She had to be very careful, because he was so bullheaded he'd never touch her again if he did find out, and she might be in turmoil for years.

His arms tightened, and his face bent above hers. His lips put kisses, hard, strong kisses, along first one eyebrow and then the other. They jabbed kisses the length of her nose, deposited more than she could count on her chin. She rested in his arms, headache fading, and let him kiss. It wasn't too bad actually. And it would lead to what she must have.

His whole mouth covered her lips. His tongue

probed, and she parted her teeth. He tongue-kissed her, and she felt her own tongue respond. He withdrew and kissed her lips, long, lingeringly, and so hard it hurt. She kissed back. It was part of the game, even though she felt herself being carried away by it, being lured into the very path she had plotted for him. If he only knew what her objective was!

Jess found himself both soothed and stimulated by the feel of her. She'd never kissed this way before—with warmth and strength. Even ardor. In the back of his mind, he wondered why she was being so sweet. She wasn't really sweet, that he knew. Anything but. She had a reason for letting him kiss her, for letting him hold first one breast, then the other.

He took a nipple between his lips. It hardened. Yes indeed, she had a reason. She was being carried away by passion, but that wasn't the whole thing. He couldn't figure it out, didn't want to, not right now. What he wanted was pure, unadorned sex for his own reason, which was to get her out from under his skin. No girl had ever riled him like this one, and she wasn't going to be allowed to continue. He'd conquer her sexually, go his way, and let her go hers.

Rae-Ellen caught her breath when at last he came into her. Smoothly. No roughness. Not until he moved, and then she gave him roughness back. As they struggled, each seeking to subdue the other, one aching thought took her: why, oh why, couldn't Tower be ardent, intense, perfect? Why did he have to be flawed?

Together they climbed, reached for completion, found it, and she drank of his passion and he of hers.

When it dwindled, her hatred for him returned, and it made her so angry that she wept.

He watched her, dazed. He couldn't see her face by the night light, but he knew she was crying. He couldn't understand it. She sure-hell had given him prod for prod, had clung to him, moaning in delight there at the end. Now she was crying.

"What's the matter?" he demanded. "Have you got some crazy notion I did something wrong? What the hell is it?"

"That's r-right, curse!" she sobbed. "Wrong, you said! Well, everything in the whole world is wrong, and it's all your fault!"

"What did I do wrong?" he demanded. "Bedding you? You wanted it as much as I did! No married couple could have enjoyed it more!"

"That's just it!"

"I don't know what you're talking about!"

"M-marriage!"

He sucked in his breath so hard she heard it. "What the hell is it now? You want me to *marry* you? After the way you—"

"I'm p-perfectly aware that you think I'm loose! But who made me that way? Besides, I wouldn't marry you if you got down on your knees and begged! And on top of that, Baby Vic hates you! That alone would settle the question!"

"I'm not about to get on my kneees to any woman!"

"Let's hope not! She might be f-fooled by your looks and say yes and ruin her life!"

"Your life's not going to be ruined," he snapped. "Not by me. Your own hell-hot temper'll do that for you!"

218

She began to cry so angrily she choked on her tears. And then she got hiccups and choked worse. Her head ached some more. He said he smelled liquor on her, that she was drunk. She choked again, gasped for breath, and he pounded her on the back. The way she was carrying on, she'd die right in his arms and he certainly didn't want that. Mean as she was, she didn't exactly deserve to die.

He held her close after she'd coughed. She continued to weep bitterly, and it seemed she cuddled. After a time she quit sobbing and lay quiet, and he found himself holding her carefully, so relieved she'd quieted that he almost liked what he was doing.

Rae-Ellen lay with her nose along his chest. It was stuffed up from crying, but gradually it cleared after she blew it on his handkerchief, and she got the clean man-smell of him. Wonderingly, she realized that she liked it. It must be the soap he used. She tried to remember what kind of soap they'd used the time they bathed together, and couldn't, because she hadn't been paying attention when it happened.

Jess almost began to enjoy her lying against him. When she wasn't spitting mad, but quiet, her body was softly firm. In fact, this was a pleasure. Except, say one word to her and she'd go tight as a fiddle string and the pleasure would be gone. Inwardly he sighed. What a waste.

He remembered how she looked holding that kid of hers, thought how she'd look with others, three or four, clustered at her knee, her the heart of a flower, them the tender petals.

A painting of that would look good in a person's

home. Impossible. With a girl like Susie, yes. With fire-eating Rae-Ellen, never.

Still, the idea lingered, and a sudden thought came to him. "If I've got you pregnant, what'll you do?"

"Not marry you, that's a cinch!"

He reared up on one elbow. "No one's aborting my kid!"

"I didn't say that. If I'm pregnant, and I happen to know I'm not unless— Well, I'm just not. Then I'd raise the baby with Vic. They'd be brother and sister."

"Or brothers."

"Sister. Girls run in my family. Vic took after the Travis line and was a boy."

He got off the bed feeling rejected, not relieved. "Looks like you'd want a father for such a baby," he said.

"I'd get him a father. I'll get Vic one. It only takes one man, you know. And it won't be you, so you're safe."

He started to speak again, could find no words, padded out of the room, carrying his pajamas. Her decision was best, he supposed. Tied to each other, they'd battle; this way they were both free to find a more suitable mate.

For some reason, he didn't even think of Susie.

Chapter Twenty-one

KEITH Belisle and Grant Miller were having a conference in the parlor of the Leaning K. They'd had supper, discussing the rodeo, planning to ride over and see Drew's new bronc, while the housekeeper served the meal and cleaned up the kitchen.

When they got down to business, they were alone in the house. They often had confabs and enjoyed them, their thoughts being in accord. They could speak openly, knowing no word of what they said would be repeated to anyone else.

"You've seen Rae-Ellen lately," Keith said. "She seem to favor you?"

"No. She turned me down."

"Hmm," Keith murmured. He studied Grant and was glad, as always, that no one would ever suspect they were half brothers, not if the two of them kept their mouths shut.

Grant was thinking along the same lines. "It's odd," he said, "my being older than you."

"How do you mean, odd?"

"For me to be the illegitimate son. Usually, it's the other way around. A man wants a change from his wife, doesn't let the fact that he's got a son by her hold him back, and plays around. Which makes the illegitimate son younger."

Keith gave a chuckle. "Never thought of it that way. In our case, the old man had his fun first, left you with your mother, and put the ring on my mother's hand."

They fell quiet. Grant's thoughts went back to when he lived with his mother. He'd been only three when he was put in the orphanage, so all he remembered of her was the smell of starch and flyaway auburn hair. He supposed he must look like her.

When Grant was five, three-year-old Keith Belisle was brought to the Home by a pale, coughing woman with yellow hair. Grant, standing unnoticed in a corner, had listened to her sobs.

"My h-husband died of consumption," she'd wept, "and I'm dying of it. I have no family. Keithie has no blood kin, only that boy named Grant. He was my husband's son by a pretty girl who left him here and ran away. If the boys could be adopted into the same family, please! Then each of them would have a brother!"

But it was not to be, though Grant tried. When Keith was seven and he was nine, he confided that they were half brothers. "I'm illegitimate," he explained.

"What's that?" Keith asked, gray-eyed and wondering.

"Means my mother wasn't married to our papa and yours was."

"We had a papa?"

"He died. And your mother died. Mine ran away."

Keith, wide-eyed, listened. Grant tried to explain better, but couldn't find the right words.

"They want to adopt us into the same family," he explained.

"That means we'll be brothers?"

"Yes. But we're brothers whether we get adopted that way or not. We've got to stick to each other, no matter what. If you get adopted by one family and I get adopted by another, we still have to keep track. We're all the blood kin each other's got. We've got to fight for it."

They paired off at the orphanage, played together. They had their cots side by side in the dorm. Each one preferred the other to any other boy in the Home.

But nobody ever adopted them, either together or separately. When folks looking over the orphans found out they wanted to be together, they turned away. Most of the people who adopted at all took the little ones, babies.

Grant heard one lady say, "The younger the better. Then the child won't forever be remembering the past and upset our home. If you get a baby two or three days old, that's what my husband and I want. You can call us immediately."

As they grew, Grant and Keith were taught to work. The orphanage acquired a farm, and the boys learned to do chores, curry horses, and milk cows, even to ride. They cleaned stalls and put down fresh straw for bedding, even tended chickens.

"Both of you can get work as farmhands when the time comes," the matron told them when Grant was fourteen and Keith was twelve. "In a way, it's good that you're growing up at the Home, because you're together. When you reach the age of sixteen, you can get work on nearby farms, maybe even on the same farm, and still keep in touch."

Grant had to leave first, being sixteen, while Keith was only fourteen. They seriously discussed the idea of Keith, who was large for his age, running away and getting a job near the farm where Grant was to work.

That had been their first conference.

"I'm almost as big as you are," Keith said. "I can do the work."

"Sure you can," Grant said, thinking hard. "But the Home."

"What about the Home?"

"The matron'll report a runaway. Report that you'll look for farm work."

"They won't know what farm."

"Police can find what farm."

"Police?"

"You've got to watch out for police, always. They'd bring you back and you'd have to stay until you're sixteen. And you'd have a mark against your record. Whatever we do, we don't want marks against us. We've got enough work ahead, just making our way.

Getting to be somebody. We don't need trouble. I vote you stay at the Home."

"You'll forget me on your farm."

"I won't forget. I'll come to see you all I can. Then, in two years, maybe I can talk my farmer into hiring you too. And when we've saved money we can go west, deeper into Texas, and get jobs on a ranch! And get rich!"

Keith's eyes had glowed at this. The idea of his becoming a cowboy changed his mind. He agreed to stay at the orphanage the required time, and he practiced riding horses all they'd let him.

Grant kept his word. He visited Keith at the orphanage farm as often as he could. Between his own duties and set visiting hours, he didn't get there more than once a month, but it was enough. It kept Keith content and working hard to be a cowboy.

The half brothers became fast, firm friends. They didn't exactly love each other, but there was genuine liking. And they planned, deeply, cleverly.

"Since we've got different last names," Grant said just before Keith was sixteen, "when we go west, let's pretend to meet there for the first time."

"You mean, never tell we're brothers?"

"That's right. It would make people wonder, talk."

"You mean, we can do better apart?"

"Apart in name only, with our kinship secret. We can even work on the same ranch. We can be side-kicks. Settle out west, buy ranches of our own, be friends all our lives. Stick together."

"But why the secret? Really?"

"What I said—to avoid gossip. Besides, I don't like the idea of people finding out I'm illegitimate."

That Keith understood, even at sixteen. "Sure," he agreed. "We'll do it your way. And we'll have our private talks, plan what to do, all our lives."

They stuck to their boyhood agreement, and they prospered. When Lorna made her proposition to Grant, Keith more than approved. He was enthusiastic.

"Lucky guy!" was his first comment.

"She's so old," Grant had said.

"But she's rich, and will leave you everything. I don't think you'd be able to play around, the way our father did. She's old enough to be on the lookout; she'd catch on, and you'd be the loser."

"She's promised me half the ranch when we marry."

Keith had nodded, triumphant. "You've got it made, brother. It's sure enough a sound financial deal."

So Grant had married Lorna, never regretted it. And then she passed on and he became sole owner of all her assets, which made him moderately rich.

Keith, in the meanwhile, had worked for old Vic Travis, then become foreman of the Double T when Burr Travis married. He'd been bowled over by Travis's bride, had envied him, but kept his eyes to himself. He worked very hard, accepted more and more responsibility; then he got involved with Susie Drummond, who would inherit a ranch some day, and almost married her. He'd felt let down when she'd said no, finally, but now, the way things had worked out, he was relieved to be footloose.

So tonight, in Grant's parlor, they were embarked on still another of their talk sessions. "Yes," Grant repeated, "I even got Rae-Ellen in bed, but she still turned me down. I don't know who she wants for a husband, but it isn't me."

"You've got another prospect who'll inherit," Keith said.

"Susie Drummond? She's involved with Drew Knight."

"And she's not a prime heiress."

"No. The home ranch goes to her brother. She'll get money, stocks and bonds. Maybe an oil well."

"There's always Bertha Mudd," Keith reminded.

Grant nodded.

"Which leaves me loose," Keith said with a half-smile. "I made it with Rae-Ellen myself, and I know she likes me, but she said no to marriage. I mean to keep working on it."

"She's the real prize," Grant mused. "I'd like to see one of us get her, preferably me."

They laughed, without humor. Their situation was similar to the one when Grant had been old enough to leave the orphanage and Keith was still fourteen. "You've got one big advantage," Grant put in thoughtfully. "Rae-Ellen's kid is nuts about you, and that's very important to her."

Keith inclined his head. "We're at a turning point again, brother. The kid's liking me is a big plus. Rae-Ellen likes me, but she also likes you."

"You've got the inside track. You've been around as long as she has, and you're foreman. She depends on you. I'm a neighbor she doesn't exactly hate."

"What are we going to do?" Keith asked.

They fell into a thoughtful silence.

"There's Tower," Grant said.

"He's only a newcomer. Can't be a real threat."

"That's right, he can't. We're established and solid in the whole community."

"So what move do we make?" Keith asked quietly.

"It's almost for-sure I can marry Bertha Mudd," Grant said. "She's got all those acres, and there's oil on them for the drilling. I'd be a really rich man— nothing like Travis, but rich beyond the dreams we had as kids. Bertha's not so bad-looking, and she doesn't look her age."

"No, she doesn't."

"Then let's see where that leaves you," Grant speculated. "You've got no land, no wife, modest-to-substantial invested savings. I vote you don't give up on Rae-Ellen. Get that kid of hers following you wherever you go, minute he learns to walk. Treat her good, keep her aware you want her for your wife. See her every day; work on her. I'd say you can bring it off."

"You make it sound like a solid, sure thing."

"It is, it is."

"It's settled!" Keith declared. "Ever since we were kids, these talks have always worked out for our good. I had to wait two years to get out of the Home. If I have to wait for Rae-Ellen, I'll do it."

"I'll help," Grant promised. "We'll work together on it, do what's needed. I can put in a word now and then to Rae-Ellen about what a good foreman you are. Maybe even ask if she'd consider letting you come work for me."

"That's stretching our luck!" Keith protested. "She might just do it."

"No, she won't. She likes your work. Nothing we do will be going too far. It never has been, and it won't be now. We'll not quit. We'll both end up rich men."

Chapter Twenty-two

RAE-ELLEN had been thinking about what Tower said about pregnancy. She was angry at him, but angrier at herself. The thought of getting pregnant had never entered her mind. Now she could think of nothing else, considered going to the doctor for an examination; delayed. Then one morning she found she wasn't pregnant, and relief made her almost weak.

Yet, in a way, she was disappointed. This she couldn't understand. Did she want to use a baby against Tower? Certainly she didn't want to marry him; she'd die a widow of ninety before she'd be his wife. She blocked such speculation. She wasn't pregnant; she'd not cause him a moment's worry, though he deserved to worry.

At ten she drove to Travis Forks to the doctor, reluctant to make the request, but she steeled herself and spoke. "It's . . . I want birth control pills," she said.

The doctor gave her a keen look. "You getting married?"

He was a good friend of Pa Travis. She shouldn't have come to him. Still, doctors never told about their patients. She wished her face weren't so hot.

"It's a possibility," she admitted, and it was. Though Drew had rejected her completely, she wasn't giving up.

The doctor wrote the prescription, she had it filled and drove homeward, furious. She blamed Tower for the embarrassment she'd suffered with the doctor. If Tower hadn't started this burning, she wouldn't be forced to keep on having sex with him to get rid of it, and she wouldn't have to humiliate herself by going to the doctor for pills. Sure, she'd use them if she bedded other men, but it was still Tower's fault.

While Rae-Ellen was driving above the speed limit, Grant Miller was inviting Bertha Mudd out for the evening along with Keith Belisle and Rae-Ellen Travis. At the same time, Keith was waiting impatiently for Rae-Ellen to get home from wherever she'd gone so he could invite her himself.

Bertha lifted her eyes—pretty brown composed eyes—to Grant when he mentioned the double date. "I'd love to go," she told him softly. "Is it to be a dress-up affair? I'm afraid my wardrobe can't compete with Rae-Ellen's."

"You always look fine to me," Grant said. "In fact, you remind me of a dove, the pretty kind."

He watched her blush. This wiped at least ten years off her face, with that smile trembling on her lips. She looked thirty-four, easy. Why, she might even be able to have a kid! He liked the idea of a kid, probably because he and Keith were loners. If they both started families, they'd be patriarchs, given time.

"What time do we leave?" Bertha asked.

"Eight o'clock tonight. In case Rae-Ellen's tied up—Keith has to ask her yet—you and I will make it a twosome. Okay?"

"Okay," Bertha said, and he saw the trace of a dimple. This pleased him, too. The courtship wasn't going to be bad at all. He said he'd be seeing her at eight, mounted his horse, lifted his hand in farewell, and cantered away toward his own ranch.

Rae-Ellen found Keith waiting for her. Tower wasn't in sight. She stopped her car, started to glare at Keith, saw that he was smiling, realized she had no reason to be mad at him, and tried to smile back. She did a halfway good job, because his smile broadened.

"What's up?" she asked.

"Just me waiting for you." He came to the car, leaned his arm along the window ledge beside her. She moved her arm a bit, then let it stay, their arms touching.

"Waiting for what, Keith?"

"To ask for a date. To make amends for what I did, for what happened between us. To show my respect, soft-pedal the love bit until you're ready. I want to be close friends. Grant Miller's developed a yen for

233

Bertha Mudd, it seems, and we got to talking and decided to ask you two ladies for a double date tonight. Dinner and dancing, maybe a drive. I'd be honored and feel forgiven if you'd go, Rae-Ellen."

Well, why not? she thought. Keith was in love with her, sure, and she had no present intention of marrying him—but friends . . . yes. She looked into his steady gray eyes, saw the honesty of his intentions.

Besides, if she dated him, it would put Tower in his place. If she decided to go steady with Keith, maybe it would take fewer bed sessions to smother the flame she had for Tower. So she told Keith she'd go, and that Bertha would probably enjoy that new place with all the sequins.

The four of them sat at table in the glittering restaurant. Rae-Ellen, at Keith's request, wore the sequin dress in which he'd once seen her, and he hardly took his eyes off her.

Bertha wore soft brown chiffon, the bodice of which was beaded. Though they didn't sparkle like Rae-Ellen's sequins, they glittered. Bertha had bought the dress that afternoon, and she'd been to a hairdresser, for her brown hair had lost its drabness and curled softly about her face.

"You look like a girl tonight, Bertha," Keith said, over cocktails. "Why didn't you pretty yourself up before?"

She glanced at Grant, blushed. The dimple showed.

Grant took her hand, lifted it to his lips. "Salute to a beautiful lady," he murmured. "She's been sitting at home too much. From now on, she's circulating. Is

234

it a deal, Bertha? We make the night spots, go to parties?"

She nodded, deeply pink, unable to meet his eyes. "I—if you want it," she faltered.

"I want it," he declared. He indicated the others. "And I have two friends present—they heard you say we'll be a twosome!" He smiled deeply at her. "Shall we dance?"

They got up and danced away, seeming to float. Bertha, as it turned out, was a magnificent dancer; she followed Grant's lead as if they were professionals.

Keith watched them. It seemed Grant was off to a good start. And judging by Bertha's new look, the difference in age didn't matter. It was highly probable they'd have a good, even happy, marriage.

If Bertha said yes. Keith couldn't imagine her saying no. Yes was in her blush, in the trembling smiles she gave Grant, in the way, at this moment, she melted close and they began to dance slowly, intimately.

"Why, they're perfect!" Rae-Ellen exclaimed. "The way they look tonight, it's a wonder they didn't discover each other before!"

Then she remembered how recently Grant had made love to her, remembered his proposal. She flushed. Still watching the pair, seeing the grace with which they moved among the other dancers, the way their very steps seemed to throb with the music, she realized that Grant had taken her refusal as final, and was relieved. Actually, she decided, what he wanted was a wife, a companion.

If only he'd marry Bertha! She'd make him a charming, perfect mate.

"Dance?" Keith asked now.

The beat of the music rode her blood. Her mood was good because Bertha was so happy. She looked at Keith, smiled.

"Of course!" she told him.

He held her intimately but properly as they glided to the music, bodies very close but not touching. He began to hum softly to the tune, and she joined in, blending.

She was aware of the warmth of him, of the respect with which he held her. It was as if they'd never known each other sexually, as if they were simply old, close friends. She liked the feeling. It made her know she was cherished. And safe.

Keith would never again try to make love unless her actions invited it. She could trust him. He wouldn't pick a fight with her over nothing, either. He wouldn't be rough, no matter what they did. If they did anything, which they wouldn't.

But if, someday, she were to decide that Keith was what she needed in a husband, she'd never have to endure quarrels and accusations. Everything would be as smooth as their dancing. She closed her eyes, gave herself up to the pleasure of dancing... safe ... secure.

The way it would be with Drew.

She sighed, nestled to Keith, dreamed of Drew.

Dots was now dating her redheaded Sammy exclusively, dropping hints about marriage to the other girls. Clovis they never saw, for she was concentrating on her millionaire Fort Worth attorney.

The double dates—Rae-Ellen and Keith, Bertha and Grant—continued. Twice Drew saw them together and Rae-Ellen willed him to be jealous, but he showed no sign of it.

Every time she saw Tower now, they fought. But always out in the open; never in privacy where they could get at each other and she could grind him out of herself. Even when he went to the Leaning K to practice bronc riding and she objected because she was afraid he'd be hurt, they fought. But he went.

He was limping one day when he came back and she waylaid him on the dogtrot. "Trying to break a leg?" she flared. "Then how'll you do your work?"

"I've ridden saddle bronc before," he said stiffly. "I never got anything worse than a bruise or two. So set your mind at rest. I'll do my work. There's no need for you to worry over me. I don't mean that much to you."

She seized on that. "You've never spoken of . . . of affection or love to me!" she cried. "All you've done is use me for s-sex!"

"Any man dared to offer you love," he growled, "you'd give him a kick in the pants! I have good eyes. The last thing you want is love!"

"That's not true! That's—"

"Hush up. I'm going to tell you what's wrong with you."

"What's wrong with *me*? Why, you—"

"You had a husband, all right, the world's best, and you lost him, and like hundreds of fool widows, you shut your eyes to the qualities of other men!"

"I understood *your* qualities fast enough! Bossy, know-it-all, rough—"

"The world," he continued as if she hadn't spoken,

237

"is full of husbands fit for widows. Even you, if you stop being a hellcat!"

Nearly choking with rage, she swallowed back words. Right out here on the dogtrot in full sight she could hardly fly at him, wrestle with him, on a bed or off. Well, let him rave! She'd found her man, though she still had to work to get him. Drew, only Drew!

Jess Tower was nothing but sex on the hoof and though she burned for him at this very damned moment, she'd not give in to it. She'd not follow to his apartment.

Without a word, he turned and made for his door.

She let him go. For once they parted without ending up in bed. And it didn't make her feel one bit better.

Chapter Twenty-three

SUDDENLY it was rodeo day, Drew's big day. Rae-Ellen's also, because it meant so much to Drew. Their group, including Pa Travis, met at the Double T to go together. Clovis and her attorney didn't show up. The last time Rae-Ellen had seen the swinging schoolteacher she was wearing a three-carat diamond on her engagement finger. She'd found her niche; she wouldn't be hanging around the ranches now.

Rae-Ellen had decided to take Baby Vic along, and had dressed him in a short, bright red jump suit. She watched Pa swoop the boy up, saw Vic's whole face open in a grin, and said nothing as the old man made for his purple car with her son.

She watched them drive off, herself getting into a car with Keith and Grant and Bertha. She was a little cross that she'd let Pa take Vic, then relented. That strong old man, that loving grandfather, was a good man. Then she hardened. He was also interfering in her life. True, he'd done little openly—just hired a manager—but she knew he was making secret, stubborn plans. The only way she could defeat him was to get Tower out of her blood and Drew into her arms.

Drew's rodeo arena was a half mile from his ranch house. When Rae-Ellen's party arrived, cars were parked thick and close and spectators were milling about. Children scrambled up and down the seats in the grandstand, teenagers whistled and whooped it up, and the young marrieds laughed and called back and forth, while the older people chatted in groups, and were first to make their way to grandstand seats.

Going into this merry crowd, Rae-Ellen felt a shiver race down her back. There was an air of danger about any arena, even this small one, and it never failed to touch her. She scanned faces in the crowd; most were smiling broadly, but a few looked a bit sober and even uneasy over the daredevil events to come.

She gazed all about. The arena had two chute gates at each end, with a tower for the judges and other officials. Behind the chutes were open areas filled with cowboys waiting for the events to begin. At the sides of the chutes were pens already filled with the horses and stock to be used today—calves for the roping, steers, bulls, the various bucking horses, each kind of animal in a separate pen. She spotted Diablo, Drew's new bronc. He was the wildest animal Rae-Ellen had ever seen, and the meanest.

The men in Rae-Ellen's party wandered off to the pens to talk to the cowboys and get a close-up look at the animals. The girls stayed in a cluster.

Pa Travis came to stand with Rae-Ellen, Vic on his arm. The boy, wide-eyed, was staring all around and looked very solemn. The noise now was tremendous; it covered the area like a lid—people screaming back and forth at one another, children yelling and playing, babies crying, the animals in the pens bawling, horses neighing and rearing.

"I'll take him now, if you want," Rae-Ellen said, reaching for Vic.

"Nothing doing!" bellowed Pa, his voice rising above the din. "He's doing fine, taking every drop of the rodeo into his bones!"

She pulled at the baby, but he threw his arms around Pa's neck, held on, and himself bellowed. "See!" roared Pa, shouting laughter. "He's Texan, knows his own mind!"

This irritated Rae-Ellen, though she too wanted her child to be a real Texan. She dropped her hands; Vic still held on to his grandfather, but stopped crying. With a shrug, Rae-Ellen turned to the other women in her party and they found seats in the grandstand.

The din now was so great that they had to shout to hear one another though they were in a close group. Adah, at her first rodeo, was looking everywhere at once.

"That arena where the events are to be," she

screamed, "looks as if it's been ploughed over and over!"

"It has been!" Rae-Ellen screamed back. She could see Drew way yonder, across the arena, among all the cowboys in their big hats. "It's ploughed until the dirt begins to powder so the ground won't pack hard as cement! That'd kill a rider if he fell on it!"

Now three men, dressed and made up like circus clowns, entered the arena and ran around, falling, getting up, going through various antics. The crowd roared, whistled, clapped, and stomped.

"What are they for?" Adah wanted to know. "Just entertainment?"

"They're for bull riding and steer wrestling," Rae-Ellen shrieked, to be heard. "Remember? When a rider falls off a bull, the rope that goes under the bull and over him so the rider can hold on, falls off! The pickup men can't catch the bull, because there's no rope to fasten around their saddle horns. So the clowns come out and distract the bull, tease him and bait him and get him into a pen. Same way with the steer wrestling."

"Dangerous!" cried Adah, aghast.

"You bet!" shouted Rae-Ellen.

The whole scene reminded her, painfully, that it was a rodeo that had made her a widow. Then Adah asked another question, she shouted an answer, and after that the events began and she, along with the hundreds of other spectators, was caught up by them.

Tower was down at the pens with the other men; she could see his big hat showing above the others, on smaller men. She willed him not to put his name in the hat, told Adah so, and Adah wanted to know what that was, too.

"The cowboys put their names in one hat, and the officials put the number of each animal in an event into another hat," Rae-Ellen shrieked above the din. "Then a name is drawn from the first hat and a number from the second hat. That's how a rider finds out what animal he'll compete with."

Now the announcer sang out over the loudspeaker, and the crowd hushed. "Ladies and gentlemen! The first event will be calf roping. We got four calves just begging for it, and four cowboys itching to go at 'em, one at a time! Eyes on the center—here comes Number One!"

The hushed crowd watched. The cowboy sat his horse behind a rope barrier for the calf to be set loose. He gave the calf a head start, then kicked his pony toward the calf, fast, twirling his lasso in the air.

Like magic, it settled over the calf, the rider jumped off his horse, threw himself onto the calf, grabbed it by neck and belly, throwing it onto its side. He yanked a rope from where he'd held it in his teeth and tied three of the calf's legs together, the crowd roaring. While the rider tied, his horse pulled against the rope, which was fastened on the saddle horn, and kept the calf from getting up. Last, the cowboy remounted, let slack into the rope, and allowed the calf six seconds to free itself.

"Dawson . . . six seconds," intoned the man at the loudspeaker.

The crowd went mad. Good as they were, the next three ropers could not better his time. The first cowboy had won.

The excitement of the performance, the mood of the crowd, filled Rae-Ellen suddenly. The sight and smell of rodeo and the danger the cowboys faced, had got into her blood, and she waved her hands above her head and shrieked right along with everybody else.

"Next will be bareback riding," intoned the loudspeaker. "You'll see that these horses are smaller than most, because they're required to buck for only eight seconds!"

"Come on!" Rae Ellen urged the other girls. "Let's go to the pens, get a closer look!"

They went fast, winding through the crowd, and managed to find a vantage point. Here the smell of rodeo was pungent, adding to the excitement.

Tower was there immediately. "It's too dangerous for you here," he told them. "Go back to the grandstand."

"Why do you stay here, then?" Rae-Ellen demanded.

"I may put my name in the hat," he replied.

"You're my manager, not a rodeoer!"

"I let no woman dictate to me, remember? Travis thinks it's okay, thinks it's fine. If I want to ride."

"That's right," Pa himself said, appearing from nowhere, Vic still happily riding his arm.

"How can you be that way," Rae-Ellen cried, "when your own son died of a broken neck before the bronc got out of the chute? Stomped him to death?"

"Life goes on, girl. Rodeos are a part of life here, and rodeos are going to be in this boy's blood just like they were in Burr's!"

The announcer was singsonging about the bareback bronc ride coming up. Angrily, Rae-Ellen put her attention on this, being where she could see not only the event itself, but the way it started.

The bronc was in the starting pen. The rider stood on the top edge of the pen, straddling the space above the bronc. The only way he had to stay on the bronc was to grip, with one hand, a handle fastened to a leather belt rigged around the animal's shoulders.

Quickly, the rider dropped onto the bronc, gripped the handle, ran the small, dull-edged spurs along the animal's shoulders, and they were in the arena.

The bronc bucked, kicked his hind feet into the air, dipped his nose to the ground, then tried to stand on his back feet. The cowboy clung, working his spurs along those shoulders, irritating, not hurting, and the bronc whirled, then stood up again for a second, before trying another nose-stand.

When the rider fell, he'd stuck it out the full eight seconds. The screaming, whistling crowd proclaimed him winner even before the judges did. The pickup men trotted out on their horses, caught the still-bucking bronc, got him into a pen as the announcer sang out the bucking time.

The events followed, one after another. There was steer wrestling, in which the rider leaped from a quarter horse that was going twenty-five miles an hour onto the back of an eight-hundred-pound long-horn steer. He grabbed the steer's horns and hung on, twisting the fighting animal's great neck strongly to the right.

The cowboy kept twisting that neck to the right, as the steer rushed and raced. His hat fell off and was trampled to bits, and still he clung to the great, wide horns.

During one whirling turn, the steer plunged to its knees. Swiftly, the rider wrestled him over to his side. The clowns ran out, ready to distract the steer when he was let up. Spying them as the rider let go the horns, he chased them murderously into the chute, where two gates dropped and he was penned as the clowns scrambled over the side of the chute.

Dust stood man-high in the arena, swirled, settled heavily. The spectators went mad; the noise they made seemed to double. Now the show was in full swing. The next event was saddle-bronc.

To Rae-Ellen's surprise, Tower loomed up beside her again. "Just so it won't be a shock," he said, "I'm riding this one. Riding Drew's Diablo. I put my name in the hat."

"You can't!" she screamed above the noise.

"My name was drawn. Drew's pleased."

It wasn't that she didn't want Drew pleased. It was that Jess, the big fool, hadn't the experience. And his legs were too long. He'd get himself killed and she'd be responsible, because he was her employee.

"Don't you know," she shrieked, "that only the most experienced riders try saddle-bronc, that it's the most dangerous bronc riding? Haven't you sense enough to know your legs are too long for you to run your spurs on the bronc's shoulders?"

"I'm aware of the hazards, sure."

"You're supposed to be a manager, not a show-off!"

"As I said," he shouted, "no woman bosses me!"

Pa Travis, standing there with the happy, squealing Vic, who was smearing a cookie over his face, grinned. "I gave my okay," he said. "This is the star bronc. He needs a powerful rider, and Jess has got the power. He rides!"

Fuming, Rae-Ellen watched two cowboys wrangle Diablo, who looked as mean as his name, into the starting chute. He tried to buck, but they fought the gear onto him. Grant and Drew, on the far side of the chute, handed gear in, but she hardly noticed them, not even Drew, she was so upset over Tower's insubordination. It even spoiled the pleasure she should be feeling in Drew's fine bronc.

The bucking saddle was settled onto Diablo's back, rocked into position. Diablo looked everywhere, eyes protruding. He fidgeted and stepped and whinnied. A cowboy slipped the girth under him, pulled it up top, straddled the space over the bronc, boots in the slats of the chute, and slid the strap through the ring on the saddle, where he tied it off.

Next, he took the bucking reins, drew them back from Diablo's head, watching where they struck the pommel of the saddle. He glanced at the small wooden stirrups.

"Watch it, folks!" boomed the loud speaker. "Jess Tower aboard Drew Knight's Diablo, the meanest bronc ever foaled! Watch close... this is tops in saddle-bronc riding!"

Jess, now crouched atop the chute above Diablo, began easing himself down on the bronc. Diablo jerked. A tremor ran over his black, sleek body. A cowboy reached in and shook him by the mane to get his attention off Jess.

Jess eased first one boot toe, then the other into the stirrups. Last, he let his full weight gradually onto Diablo's back. The bronc jerked again and tried to jump, still in the chute. Rae-Ellen's breath snagged. That was what happened to Burr.

Diablo quieted some, and Jess pushed himself down tighter in the saddle, took a firm grip on the reins, slid his spurred boots up to Diablo's shoulders. His long legs had to bend at the knee, but he managed the spurs in spite of them.

The gate opened and Diablo came out of the chute like a bullet from a gun. Jess worked the spurs on the shoulders as required.

Diablo went into a rocking-chair motion. Jess hung on to the reins with one hand, the other out at his side, touching nothing.

Diablo jumped, feet bunched, came down, feet spread, and then he went into a furious spin. Froth from his mouth hit Jess in the eyes, half blinding him.

The spectators were silent as the bronc got twice as violent. He stood on his hind legs, brought his front feet slashing down, spun again, trying to bite Jess even as he bucked and twisted and jumped and landed.

Rae-Ellen held her breath until it seemed her chest would burst. Jess was still in the saddle. *How long was this going to last?* Eight seconds...ten...? she couldn't remember.

Suddenly a stirrup went flying away from Diablo and with it Jess, thrown off balance. He hurtled through the air, the bronc still bucking like crazy, the crowd screaming again. He hit the ground hard, slid, lay inert, with Diablo whirling and kicking near his head.

Chapter Twenty-four

RAE-ELLEN scrambled into the arena like a madwoman. She pushed and shoved and yelled at others who entered, to get out of her way. Someone kept screaming in her ear; everybody at the rodeo was screaming. She stumbled on, aware that the loudest scream was coming from her own throat.

"*Jess!*" she shrieked. "*You big fool!*"

She clawed through the last of the crowd, cowboys and all. She sped to where cowboys surrounded Jess, there on the ground.

The clowns and two pickup men were trying to subdue Diablo, she saw. And then the bronc was coming at her, and a hoof caught her shoulder and threw her, spinning, to the dust.

She fought off helping hands; she knew they'd

caught Diablo, were taking him away. She staggered on, blood staining her shirt, fought her way to Jess and dropped to her knees beside him. There was blood on her face too, and kept getting into her eyes, but she blinked it away.

He was white under his tan. His eyes were closed. She caught her breath, held it. It was as if it were all happening over again, as if the two men, Burr and Jess, were one... dead... dead.

"*No!*" she screamed at Jess. She gripped his shoulders and shook him. Voices around her warned that she'd hurt him, that the ambulance would be here soon. Beyond, the crowd was still roaring, but more quietly; there was sound from the animals, the bawling of cattle and the high-pitched neighing of horses.

Despite the warnings, she wouldn't let Jess alone. "Lift him!" she ordered the cowboys. "Get him on his feet and he'll be all right, you'll see!"

She tugged at him, and he stirred. He tried to sit up, and she lifted mightily to help.

"Want... stand," he muttered.

Pa showed up then, without Baby Vic. "Do what he says!" he roared. "He ain't at death's door, not when he wants to get on his feet!"

Rae-Ellen stayed close, right in the way of the cowboys who did the lifting, but they got Jess up. His eyes were open now, and he looked dazed, but he was alive and on his feet.

And then his right leg crumpled and the cowboys eased him to sit on the ground. He stared up at them, bewildered. And then he saw Rae-Ellen.

"What are you doing here?" he asked groggily.

"Seeing what foolishness you've got yourself into

this time!" she snapped. She was so relieved that he was alive and talking, she wanted to cry. But she'd never let him find that out. He'd put his own interpretation on it, when actually she'd only been upset because he might be dead. She'd feel the same about any rider, even one she didn't know, who'd looked like Jess did when she got to him. A human being is a human being.

"He's got a busted leg," Pa said. "Where the hell's that ambulance?"

Jess got his eyes under some control, and first thing he did was look square at Rae-Ellen. There was blood trickling from her forehead, and blood on her shirt front that came from inside.

"You're bleeding!" he accused.

"It's nothing!" she spat. "A scratch! Maybe two scratches. I'll put something on them when I get home."

"You'll go to the emergency room," he said, gritting, and looked his meanest. "Talk about tetanus...it's worse around horses and cattle than anyplace!"

She put her fingers on his leg to find out for herself whether it was broken. Before she'd exerted the least pressure, he howled at her.

"Hands off! All I need is some rest and I can get up and walk away! You're the one, blood all over the place! Diablo get you with a hoof?"

"I—it's none of your business!"

He struggled to reach his hip pocket, drew out a clean bandana, laid it, folded, against the place on her forehead.

"You stop that!" she snapped, jerking back. She

saw that somehow, her doing that, had hurt his leg, because pain crossed his face.

She asked the nearest cowboy for his pocket knife, and he handed it to her, opened. Forcing her hands to be steady, she began to slit Jess's boot, sawing at the leather.

That hurt, she could tell from his stiffness, but he was too stubborn to say so. Ignoring Pa Travis's objections, she continued to saw, being as careful as she could. She wasn't half through, Jess ordering her to stop, Pa Travis helling and damning and trying to get the knife away from her, when she felt the bandana come to her forehead again. Jess, propped on one elbow, swiped at the blood once, before she jerked away, fighting Pa over possession of the knife.

And then the ambulance was there and Jess refused to be lifted to the cot. "The girl," he told the attendants, "the one that's bleeding. Take her. She has a chest wound."

When they tried to lift her, she sprang to her feet. "He's the one!" she cried, pointing at Jess. "His leg... it'll probably have to be amputated! Stop wasting time, get him to a doctor!"

While the attendants lifted Jess to the cot, he did some fancy helling and damning. "I'll sue!" he threatened. "The girl's a hellcat, but she's bleeding to death! Put her on the cot with me, and get going!"

She struggled, but the attendants did what Jess said after Pa Travis turned the air blue. They laid hands on Rae-Ellen, lifted her onto the cot, put the cot inside the ambulance. One attendant drove; the other sat beside the cot and listened to the two jammed onto it quarrel, accuse each other of dying, and himself tried to examine their injuries but couldn't because they fought him off.

Arriving at the emergency room, they lost all control of the situation. They demanded to be taken to the same treatment room, and were ignored. Orderlies lifted Jess and put him on a gurney and rolled him away. Other orderlies put Rae-Ellen on a second gurney and rolled her a long way off to a curtained cubicle, where she was lifted to an examination table.

Every time she tried to get off and go looking for Jess, they pushed her down. Finally they stuck a needle into her, and then she was suddenly so heavy she couldn't even sit up.

Inside, she was boiling, battling mad. Jess was her manager. It was her duty as his employer to see that he was properly cared for. If she could only get to his doctor, she might keep them from amputating, crippling him for life.

She paid very little attention to what her doctor did to her shoulder and head. He seemed to dig with a small instrument, mutter about embedded dirt, and then he swabbed with something that burned, and gave her two shots after he'd bandaged both places.

"You're a very fortunate young lady," he told her. "If that horse's hoof had landed on your neck instead of your shoulder, you'd have been in trouble."

She asked him where Jess was, what they were doing to him. He said he didn't know, that she'd find out before long.

When she was released, walking a bit unsteadily because she was still groggy from the first shot, she

253

found her party in the emergency waiting room. It was filled with the injured and sick and their anxious families.

Pa Travis carried Baby Vic, who was tearstained and asleep. All of them drew in anxiously about Rae-Ellen, and she explained her injuries offhandedly, then asked for Jess.

"He'll be out soon," Drew assured her. "It takes a while to X-ray and then put a cast on."

"Unless they amputate," Rae-Ellen fired back. "That can take forever."

They sat and waited, Rae-Ellen's shoulder aching dully, though she'd had a capsule for pain. Her head hurt, too. She wondered how a shattered leg must feel.

Then Jess came swinging out, his leg in a walking cast almost to the knee, his jeans cut and folded up as far as the knee. He had a crutch and walked along pretty well. Even though this relieved Rae-Ellen, it also irritated her. So his leg hadn't been amputated! He still had to show off how macho he was, walking along on cast and crutch!

Still, he might be in future danger of amputation. Suppose gangrene set in. He'd spotted her now and was swinging toward her, eyes bluer than she'd ever seen them.

"It's a simple, clean break," he told her. "The bone in the foot. I have to wear the cast four weeks, and that's it. I can work the whole time."

He saw her looking at the curious-looking sandal on his foot. "To protect the bottom of the cast," he said.

When she would have asked more, he gestured

254

abruptly. "What happened to your chest? How deep did that bronc cut you?"

"It's my shoulder, not my chest! It's been dressed, and I've had shots. It'll heal fast, give no trouble."

Pa intervened. "Rae-Ellen," he said, "we all voted to come to your place. Nobody wants to go back to the rodeo, not even Drew."

Rae-Ellen smiled, glad to have them. Though she didn't want to admit it, she was badly shaken. Relief that Tower had nothing worse than a broken foot, and that she hadn't taken Diablo's hoof in the neck, leaving Vic an orphan, made her almost weak.

They gathered in the big living room. Bertha Mudd hunted out a big ottoman for Jess to put his foot up on. Rae-Ellen tried to watch, but Leah was so busy getting her into a chair and feeling her ears to see if she had a temperature, she couldn't even see Tower. Dots took the now-awakened baby and carried him to the kitchen for a cookie when he began to cry.

He's all off schedule, what schedule he has, Rae-Ellen thought crossly. This cookie business has got to be cooled. He can't grow up thinking a cookie solves every problem!

When they were all settled, Drew produced a small wooden stirrup. "This is what came off your gear, Jess," he said. "And threw you. See? It's got a clean break in it."

They passed it around. All examined it.

"It was brand-new," Drew told them. "It's impossible to tell whether it just broke clean or was sawed.

255

I personally examined all my rodeo gear last night; it was all brand-new."

"Accidents happen," Jess said, looking the stirrup over the second time. He ran his thumb on both sides of the broken place. "It doesn't make sense that anybody cut it through to make me personally have an accident, because rider and animal are drawn by chance at almost the last moment."

"And you'd have no reason to do it, Drew," Keith said. "It's your horse, your rodeo."

"He'd be a fool to do a thing like that," Grant agreed. "Put suspicion on himself. That he'd cheat to keep a rider from sticking onto his new, expensive bronc."

"The idea's laughable," Jess said, returning the stirrup to Drew. "But you might have a talk with the manufacturer."

Drew laid the stirrup aside. "It's the same as the others, I'd swear," he said. "Same brand, same style."

"Let's not make a big thing of it on my account," Jess said. "No real harm's been done. I have something else to bring up, now that we're all together and can vote."

"Ooh, that sounds excitin'!" cried Dots. "Tell!"

"I'm inviting all of you who can spare three or four days to visit me in California," Jess said. "I have a farm there, family place, raise a few thoroughbreds."

"Why," Rae-Ellen blurted before she knew she was going to speak, "I didn't know you owned *anything*!"

He grinned, infuriating her.

"I own enough. You want to buy two silver fillies, young ones. Well, I have two that are perfect. But if you consider them, I'd like for all of you to see them, maybe vote. They don't come cheap."

Stunned, Rae-Ellen tried to absorb the fact that Tower had been a man of property—some property—all along. And had kept it secret.

He moved his leg a bit on the ottoman. She was so mad at his underhanded secrecy she didn't even care if his foot did hurt.

Chapter Twenty-five

RAE-ELLEN'S fury that Tower had hidden the fact that he owned a farm and bred thoroughbreds swelled. He'd as good as lied. Those times they'd talked about his background, he'd never mentioned a farm, even this small family place to which he now confessed!

She glowered, watched him take the vote about the trip. They all voted to go: Pa with a big grin; Drew after a nod from Susie; Keith, first getting Rae-Ellen's stiff okay; Grant and Link. So did Susie and Dots and Bertha Mudd, expressing delight at the prospect. Adah reluctantly had to refuse because she was scheduled to fly home.

Only Rae-Ellen's vote hadn't been cast.

"What about you?" Tower asked directly.

"Since I'm the one to buy fillies, I suppose I have to go," she snapped. "But I'm taking my son along."

Pa Travis looked downright smug, and Rae-Ellen knew why. He was exposing her to men, ramming men down her throat.

Now, as usual, Pa took charge. "I insist that we fly out in my Learjet," he said. "I've just had it done over again in bright purple. You can't say no."

To Rae-Ellen's chagrin, everybody accepted.

The Learjet set down at the local airport, taxied to a stop. Before they got up from the big chairs, Tower said, "My farm's near Arcadia."

"That's where the Santa Anita racing track is," Pa muttered to Rae-Ellen. "Hope we get to see it."

She pulled Baby Vic's thumb out of his mouth. He squealed, stuck the thumb back in. She sighed. It was either the thumb or a cookie.

They took taxis to the farm. Somehow Rae-Ellen ended up in the taxi with Pa Travis, Tower, and Baby Vic. Tower made no advances to the baby, who chewed his thumb contentedly and stared at the big, sickeningly handsome man.

"He remembers," Tower said. He was in the backseat with Rae-Ellen and Vic. Pa was in the front with the driver.

"Remembers what?" Rae-Ellen asked.

"That he bit me. Looks like he's waiting for a second chance."

Pa chuckled. "Told you the boy has Travis spirit! Next time, bite him back, show him who's boss!"

"I don't fight yearlings," Tower said. Then, with a wave of his hand, "Tower Farms begins here, with the white fence. The fence goes all around the farm. Makes it sort of a landmark."

Rae-Ellen stared. It was a sturdy wooden fence, and looked as if it had been newly painted. It stretched ahead as far as she could see, and, when she looked across pasture land where horses grazed and colts ran, tails high, she couldn't see even a blur of white marking the opposite boundary.

"How many acres?" Pa asked.

"Four thousand. Dad said that was enough."

"Reckon so, for this part of the country."

Rae-Ellen's breath hooked. Four thousand acres! Why, he'd led them to believe... he really had... that all he had was a small family place. Maybe two hundred acres. And that he'd raised a couple of thoroughbreds that he was now willing to sell.

"How many horses you run?" Pa asked.

"A hundred. Mostly bays. I was tempted, for a while, to switch over to silver, then decided not to. I have a steady market for the bays, could sell every one of them tomorrow if I wanted to. There didn't seem any reason to change, not then."

Now, what did he mean by that? Rae-Ellen wondered. Had he secretly fallen in love with her silvers and decided to change over? But if that were so, why would he now be selling two silver fillies?

She almost asked him. Then she studied his darned handsome profile as he watched his fence flowing past, forever past, and decided she'd ask him nothing. Give him no satisfaction whatsoever.

She watched the fence some more. Vic's head got heavy on her shoulder, and she knew he was asleep.

She pulled his thumb out of his mouth, and he didn't rouse.

At last they turned in at a white-painted, wide gateway with a sign above it: TOWER FARMS. Like something out of a plantation movie. She wondered if the farm had been used for movie settings.

The taxis pulled up in a circular driveway before a great, one-storied, wooden white dream of a house. It had a central core with floor-to-ceiling windows and long, graceful spreading wings at each side. There was also a rear wing; that would be the kitchen and dining room section, Rae-Ellen thought.

She compared this to her own ranch house. Dog-trot and all, her house could be set down intact in one wing of this. It made her so furious she wished she could scream at Tower. To think that he'd be so deceptive! That he'd deliberately led her to believe that he'd been a sort of drifter, while he owned and lived in—when he chose—this palace!

Everything breathed of wealth. The more she saw, the more furious she was at Tower.

Susie had edged up to her now and whispered, "Isn't it *gorgeous*? I knew California was wonderful, but never dreamed there'd be a farm like this! Jess is one lucky man!"

"He *would* be a millionaire in disguise!" hissed Rae-Ellen. "I'll bet he's even got his own movie studios!"

Pa, overhearing, got hard-boiled. "Don't low-rate Jess," he rumbled. "I like the way he throws himself into hard work as a favor when he owns this! Admire him for it!"

262

"Did you know," Rae-Ellen asked, still hissing, "that he had a place like this when you hired him?"

"Hell, I knew he was a millionaire. Burr told me that. But common as an old shoe. Not a stuck-up bone in his body."

"Ha! You deceived me, didn't let me know he was rich! Hiring him over my head, then bragging that he does what you tell him!"

"Which is what you need to do, young woman."

The one comfort Rae-Ellen had was that Pa thought Tower's setup was so perfect. It showed in his talk, in his admiring looks. One thing, at least, was settled.

Pa would never try to get her to marry Jess Tower. And for one powerful reason: any woman Tower married, he'd bring to live in this flashy place. And Pa'd never consent to having Baby Vic taken out of Texas. It was a great relief to know he wouldn't scheme to marry her to Jess. For some reason, this made her feel cross. And even madder at Tower.

Tower herded them onto the front veranda and into a vast, sand-colored entrance hallway made beautiful by murals of palm trees and azure sea. Near the door, waiting to greet them, was a couple in their forties, neatly dressed and with placid features.

"This is Fred and Hazel Briggs," Tower said. "Fred manages the place when I'm gone, and Hazel runs the house whether I'm here or not, and with only two Mexican girls to help."

The pair inclined their heads and smiled. And then Pa, bossy as ever, took charge and introduced everybody individually. He ended with Rae-Ellen and Baby Vic, who was now awake and looking unhappy.

Hazel was all smiles for the baby. "Maybe he'd like a bath?" she asked Rae-Ellen. "I've saved ducks and boats from when our boy, Freddie, lived here. He's in movies now, may get married, and I'll have a grandson like this."

Rae-Ellen couldn't help smiling at Hazel. She liked the woman instinctively, trusted her. "I'm sure Vic will love the ducks," she said. "And he needs a bath!"

Hazel showed them all to their rooms. There was a private room for everyone, even Vic. There was even a baby bed.

"Even a baby bed!" Rae-Ellen exclaimed.

"Yes. Freddie's. Jess phoned, said a baby was coming, so we got this out and shined it up and here it is."

"That's kind of you," Rae-Ellen said gratefully.

"It's Jess should get the thanks," Hazel said. Her plump little body stood foursquare and her brown eyes glowed as she spoke. "He's the kindest soul on earth, Jess is. Does more good than anybody dreams. Gives to charities, not the big-name ones, but the struggling ones. And he's sponsoring eleven children— eleven, mind you—all over the world. Means to see them educated, too."

This information dazed Rae-Ellen. It was so directly opposite of the Jess Tower she knew. Stubborn, high-handed, rough, almost a rapist—yet he was sponsoring eleven children! She wondered if any of them were babies, wondered how they'd react if they met him in person.

Hazel asked to bathe Baby Vic, and he let her. He did his usual splashing, was toweled dry and dressed in a fresh suit and taken to his grandfather. Hazel handed him over to the old man proudly.

"We've been waiting for this boy," Pa boomed. "Rae-Ellen, Jess has had them fillies caught up. Come on, everybody, let's see them and get business over with so we can enjoy this fine place! Jess has got a pool table I plan to spend my time with—what time's left from Vic, that is!"

They went down to the stables. Here Fred paraded the two fillies, one after the other, then together.

Rae-Ellen fell in love with them on sight. They were perfectly formed, their color was superb, and they were so gentle that they nuzzled her cheeks. She wondered who had taught them that, Jess or Fred. The fillies looked like twins, though when she examined their papers in the library where a grandfather clock swept its pendulum lazily, she found that they were from different bloodlines.

"How much do you want for them?" she asked Tower.

"Fifty thousand for the two," he said coolly.

"Sharp deal," boomed Pa Travis, "but a bargain."

Rae-Ellen took her checkbook out of her handbag. She didn't even glance at Pa, who had set herself and Burr up with a one-hundred-thousand-dollar account.

She wrote the check calmly, handed it over to Tower.

He accepted the check as if it were his rightful due. He was altogether intolerable. She had just given him every cent she had in the world.

Chapter Twenty-six

SHE told this to Adah by long-distance phone. Lance came on as soon as Adah told him Rae-Ellen was broke.

"We'll advance you as much as you need," he said. "Travis, lovable as Adah thinks he is underneath, is not to have any money leverage over you. We'll keep you solvent until you have an income."

Rae-Ellen felt a great wash of tenderness for her brother-in-law. "I need quite a lot, Lance. Salaries and feed and general running expenses."

"Whatever you need. You can repay as you begin to sell yearlings, though we're in no hurry."

Rae-Ellen choked up. Lance and Adah were kind beyond description. "I accept, and with gratitude," she said. "It's going to take time. I may even have to lease a ranch if Pa gets really tough, but my herd will pay off!"

It was after dinner that night that Dots, cuddled to her Sammy, spoke of her desire to just see Burton Chadwick, the movie star. Jess looked at her and grinned.

"I guess you could call Burton my best friend," he said.

Dots clasped her hands. "Oh, Jess...would you, pretty please...fix it so I can meet him?" She hugged Sammy's arm, dropped a kiss on his fiery sideburn. "Not for romance, darling, but to *meet* the biggest star of all! *Think* of it!"

Sammy grinned, and kissed Dots full on the lips. "If Jess says the word," he agreed. "After all, we're in movie country, so why not see the stars? If," he added, "they consent to see *us*."

"Burton and his pals will be happy to meet friends of mine," Tower said in the arrogant-confident way Rae-Ellen detested. "We date from way back. They're all a little wild, like to have fun, but they're a decent bunch. They haven't forgotten their roots, no matter how excited they get when they throw a party. And they work at their acting seriously."

Rae-Ellen seethed. The last thing she wanted was to meet people who smoked grass and sniffed cocaine. What she was thinking showed, because Tower, who had been watching her, went on talking.

"They're lively," he continued, "and a bit heavy on the booze, but no drugs. They think too much of their careers to go into that scene. I'll give Burton a call," Tower announced. "He'll throw us a house party. All of you'll have a chance to know plenty of stars!"

"It's a miracle!" breathed Dots. She squeezed Sammy, then Susie. She smiled into Rae-Ellen's eyes. "Isn't it fabulous?"

Rae-Ellen said stiffly, "Burton Chadwick lives with his co-star, Veronica Swann. That doesn't speak so well of them."

A brief silence took the room. Rae-Ellen felt uneasy, wished she hadn't spoken. After all, she herself, less than two years ago, had planned to be Burr Travis's live-in girl, but things looked different now. She'd been married and was a mother. She glanced defiantly at Tower, insanely burned for him, knowing that with his cast there'd be no opportunity to grind the burning out and away.

Tower called Burton Chadwick. They had a short conversation, then Tower hung up.

"Tomorrow and next day, one night and two days," he announced. "He's giving a house party for us and his sidekicks."

"What if they won't come on such short notice?" Rae-Ellen asked.

"They'll come. They're wild about Burton's parties. And his house. It's right on a cliff edge in the Beverly Hills area."

"You going to be chicken?" Pa asked, with a wicked grin. "Stay here while the rest go?"

"Certainly not!" she cried, goaded. "I'm going!"

It would serve him right if she came back engaged to an actor. See how he'd like that!

"Me, I'll stay here with Vic," Pa said.

Rae-Ellen's instinct was to say no. Then, not want-

269

ing her child mauled by a bunch of boozing actors, she nodded and it was settled.

The mansion was enormous, garish, lavish, and perched on the edge of a cliff. The view all around was breathtaking, hills and trees and the glint of a stream, and when they looked straight down there was a vista of sloping, dark-earthed hills and green saplings and, at the bottom, a scatter of house roofs, all of them spreading and tremendous.

Burton Chadwick greeted them at the door as they dashed inside to get out of the pouring rain. Though she'd seen him many times on the screen, Rae-Ellen was taken aback by his virility.

Twenty-seven, he was almost six feet tall, had hair even redder than Sammy's, red eyebrows and auburn eyes. His build qualified him for the title of Mr. Outdoors, and his features were a godlike-human blend which took her breath away. He was much more macho offscreen than on.

She let him hug her the way he'd hugged Bertha and Susie and Dots, and found it not unpleasant. He was such a happy guy, his rich, melodious voice a pleasure to hear. He even hugged all the men in the party and, surprisingly, they hugged back.

The inside of the house was aswarm with famous stars, all dressed in western fashion—expensive jeans, fancy shirts, costly boots, and ten-gallon hats. They were all talking and laughing, hugging and kissing, greeting the Tower party warmly, exclaiming over their authentic Texas garb.

Tower swooped a shapely platinum blond off her

270

feet and hugged her before he set her down, one arm around her, then introduced her to his party.

"Veronica Swann," he said, "the loveliest thing on the silver screen! And the most talented! She's the kind to be a star when she's an old, old lady!"

"I like the sound of that!" Veronica laughed, voice silvery. "I *am* going to use Garbo for my model. I'll never marry, but just work . . . work . . . work!"

"But she ended up so lonely!" cried a black-haired star whose face Rae-Ellen recognized, but whose name couldn't remember.

"Ah, but there's the difference!" replied Veronica, and she wasn't laughing now. "I won't retire, I'll work on and on, and do it so well that only the grave can rob the world of my talent!" The words were mock-heroic, but her tone showed intense sincerity.

Her listeners applauded, and many of them hugged her.

Rae-Ellen watched Veronica embrace all who came to her, and herself returned the star's embrace when it was her turn. Veronica was twenty-six, she knew, was naturally platinum-haired, exquisitely formed, with silvery eyes and chiseled features.

"This rain," she called out, "is just in time for our party! The forecast says it's going to rain and rain! I hereby declare this to be a rain party!"

Everybody agreed, their laughs and shouts rising in volume. Rae-Ellen said nothing, but sat in the corner of a sofa and watched.

The vast living room, garishly done in rose-colored velvet and satin, gold and blue cushions everywhere, astounded her. The mahogany tables with marble tops, each with an arrangement of rose or gold

271

mums, were lovely but overdone. The bar was in an alcove. There seemed to be a horde of people, yet the room wasn't crowded.

Keith sat down beside Rae-Ellen. "I've counted," he said. "Chadwick and his guests come to thirty, and our party to ten. Forty of us, penned in by the rain. They all look happy, though."

She nodded. She'd never been with so many hand-some people. Most of Chadwick's friends seemed to be younger than Veronica and himself. They had four things in common: they were famous; they wore western clothes; they were exceptionally good-looking; and they were high on pure happiness.

Rae-Ellen didn't even try to keep names and faces sorted out, though she mingled, conversed, wandered on. She had an eerie feeling that this was a movie set, she and her ranch friends and all the guests were extras, with Burton and Veronica the stars. And Jess Tower. Wherever she looked, there he was, talking to someone different, handsomer than anybody else.

No drinks were served before lunch. This was a buffet, everyone carrying his plate to the living room or conservatory. Rae-Ellen sat with two dark young actors and a bleached blond, found herself chatting easily with them, hoped the rest of the house party would go as smoothly—and soberly—as this.

The rain fell from the sky in gray walls. Rae-Ellen tried, but couldn't see through a single window, the rain was so thick.

"It's never going to let up!" someone laughed.

"Who cares?" said another. "Suppose it doesn't?"

Someone turned on TV in the middle of a special storm report, and they all quieted.

"... and because of this storm system, which has become stationary," the newscaster said, "the heavy rain we are now experiencing is being held over the area by a second storm system. Until the second system moves out, forecasters say, the rains will continue. All persons living in the area are advised to move to level ground to avoid possible mudslides and flooding."

"Drinks!" called out a male voice. "What we need is booze!"

There was laughter and movement toward the bar. Rae-Ellen, concerned by the storm, turned down a drink for the third time, smilingly. Once she accepted a glass of sparkling water, then set even it down unobtrusively.

The afternoon grew late; the rain continued, and so did the drinking. Cards were played; there was some dancing. The noise level increased. Rae-Ellen wished she were back at Tower Farms with Vic.

It wasn't until after dinner, also buffet, that Rae-Ellen, at Burton Chadwick's charming insistence, accepted a Bloody Mary. While he watched, she took one sip, then, as he turned away to circulate, bearing his tray of drinks, she set her glass on the table beside her. She watched the rain, watched the chattering, laughing, drinking guests, tried to listen to the stereo. She spotted one after another of her Texas party; they held drinks but didn't sip. Even Tower didn't drink. The Hollywood people, however, were drinking steadily.

Not one of the men would be a fit husband or father, she thought idly. By contrast, the Texans were perfect; even the thought of Tower was almost bearable. She saw that he accepted one drink and nursed it. This made her cross, though Drew did the same, without arousing her irritation.

They danced most of the evening, some of the movie folk not quite steadily. Rae-Ellen danced, but only with Link and Grant and Drew. Tower couldn't dance because of his cast.

After dancing, the house quieted. Some guests slept in beds, some on couches. A few of the tipsy young men wrapped themselves in blankets on the floor. Rae-Ellen and Susie and Dots shared a bed, giggling.

The rain sluiced down. The inside of the house felt clammy. It was too warm to turn on the electric heat and dry the air out.

Next morning, the drinking began right after breakfast. Rae-Ellen took nothing but toast and coffee and orange juice. She stayed near Link, listened to the endless, drumming rain, chatted with two young female stars who were drinking and cheerful. Burton Chadwick was drinking more than usual, they giggled—this rain would make the Pacific Ocean drink! A couple of the younger men were getting out of hand, cursing the rain, and tossing back drink after drink.

At noon, one of these—a small, darkly handsome fellow called Cat—noticed that Rae-Ellen didn't have a glass. He reported to Veronica, who was tipsy, and she cried, "But darling, you must have *something*! Please, to make me happy!"

Rae-Ellen accepted a Bloody Mary, and then she saw Tower take a Bloody Mary, too. This irked her and she was ready to speak to him about it—this was his second one—when Cat and a swaying male companion accosted her.

"Drink it up!" Cat urged. "Bottoms up!"

"Yes," said the other one, "can't come to a rain party and not booze!"

They loomed over her, Cat burly and strong, the other larger, stronger. They suddenly had ugly looks on their faces.

Rae-Ellen set her glass down on the floor. "I won't drink!" she cried, angry. "I hate the stuff! I—"

"You'll drink if we have to pour it down you!" snarled Cat. He picked up the drink and came at her. His partner came along, hands out to hold her.

Link set down his glass and gave Cat a shove in the chest. Cat staggered backward, the Bloody Mary flying from his hand. He fell hard, his head cracking against the carpet. The other one charged Link, swung from the hip and landed a blow on his chin. Link tried to keep his balance, failed, pitched sidewise.

"Fight!" a voice cried. "C'mon, fight!"

Outside, the rain poured dismally.

Rae-Ellen fled to the back end of the room among the other girls, but not before someone's elbow, drawn back to deliver a blow, caught her painfully in one eye. Every man present, including Cat, who lunged to his feet unhurt, began to throw punches.

Glasses turned over, broke. Whiskey, cocktails and Bloody Marys sank into the carpeting, and still the fight went on. The Texas men were right in the middle of it. Even Tower, the big fool, was swinging his fists, hobbling on that cast, getting knocked down, struggling up, jumping into the melee again.

The fight lasted for perhaps five minutes. Then

Veronica called out, laughing, "We've had our fun! Didn't even know why we were fighting! Fight's over! Let's have a drink and forget the rain!"

Unbelieving, Rae-Ellen watched the men stop the battle, go arm-in-arm to the bar, laughing and shouting. There were some bloody noses, some cut eyebrows and lips, a good many bruises. Tower wasn't the only one who limped now.

Rae-Ellen blinked. So this was how movie people were! Drink until befuddled, fight over nothing, quit as if a bell had been rung, press toward the bar. Why, the fight had been part of their fun! All of them were laughing, even dabbing at one another's bleeding faces with handkerchiefs!

Link found her, made sure she was all right, went in search of a bathroom to wash his face. The corner of his mouth was bleeding, and he'd already ruined his handkerchief mopping it up. He promised he'd find gauze and tape and cover it.

It was then that Jess Tower loomed beside Rae-Ellen. He looked all right in the quick glare she gave him, except for a lump on his forehead and the scowl on him.

"You could have sipped the damn drink," he said. "You didn't have to gulp it all down."

"You drank enough! Why should I drink at all?"

"You could have pretended, seeing the condition they were in. All they needed was an excuse to fight. That and the damn rain."

She remembered how she'd drunk with Drew, hating every drop. But that had been for a purpose, a serious matter. This had been maudlin foolishness.

"Well?" he asked. "You know I'm right!"

Without another word, she turned and walked away. He watched her being stopped by one of the actors as the stereo began again, and couples paired off to dance. She went into the arms of one. Jess fumed. If she wouldn't drink with them, why dance with them?

She's higher-stepping than any filly, he thought. He yanked his eyes away from her, sought and spied Susie dancing with Drew. Susie had pretended to drink; she hadn't sparked any fight. He moved his look back and forth between them. No, Susie didn't have Rae-Ellen's hell-hot temper, not her. She was the complete lady.

Weary of the steadily sheeting rain, he peered out a window. The driveway was covered with slick mud. Rain fell on it in huge drops, dimpling the mud, making tiny lakes which flowed together. He wondered how long they were going to be trapped at this infernal party.

Not for the first time, he was ready to leave his pal Burton and get back to his own place. Back to horses and acres and quiet. He stood at the window a long time, watching the rain lessen. He heard a weathercast; the announcer said streams had overflowed, that mudslides were starting, that everyone should get to solid ground.

He stared glumly through the rain. Over yonder lay flat, safe land. If the time came, the party had only to go there—get thoroughly wet of course—but they'd be away from the cliff's edge on which they now perched so dangerously.

Chapter Twenty-seven

RAE-ELLEN, feeling on the edge of going stir-crazy, slipped away and searched closets. She found her rain togs, put them on. Then she went out a side door into the rain, holding her face up to let the water sluice off the residue of cigarette smoke and soothe the elbow-poked eye, which was beginning to throb.

She closed her eyes. When she opened them, Jess Tower stood there, also in rain gear.

"You followed me!" she accused.

"Not exactly. Let's say we both had the same idea."

"That'll be the day! Your idea is to carouse, to—"

"If you're referring to the fight, you started it."

"Because I wouldn't drink!"

"You could have pretended. Kept things peaceful."

"The fault goes way back from me, clear to you!"

"How so?"

"You arranged the party!"

"For you."

"Not for me!"

"For my other guests, then. I didn't expect even you to start trouble."

"If you hadn't phoned Chadwick, if you hadn't arranged—"

"I didn't arrange a damned thing. The minute I said I was here with guests—"

"You phoned, you can't deny that! Otherwise we wouldn't be here in this rain!"

"It's raining at Tower Farms."

"Just the same, the atmosphere would be different!"

"So you prefer my place."

"I didn't say that! I said—"

"I know what you said. Well, you didn't have to come here. Nobody dragged you by the hair that I noticed."

"I came only to be polite!"

"Then ruined it. Deliberately."

"The day I have to kowtow to a bunch of drunks—"

"Come on," he said, taking her arm roughly. "The rain's getting worse." He half marched, half pushed her back into the house.

To her surprise, the movie folk were all napping. Some were sprawled on sofas, some lolled in chairs, and the rest were curled on the carpet. The Texas people were at the TV, listening to a weathercast.

Jess started for them, and as he turned Rae-Ellen got a straight look at his face. It was cut and bruised and bleeding. Outside, the rain had kept it washed off, but now blood was seeping, there was a lump on his forehead, another on his jaw, and one eye was turning dark.

"You're going to a bathroom!" she cried, yanking at his arm. "I'm going to fix that face!"

"I want to hear the broadcast!" he protested. "Find out how long before we have to get out of here, or if we need to!"

"It won't take long!" she screamed. "Can't you *ever,* just one time, do what you're told? Are you stubborn to the *bone*?"

He gave her a look, but then blood ran into his eye and she got him moving while he couldn't exactly see where he was going. When he could see, he found himself shut into a bathroom with her, him sitting on the closed lid of the commode, her running water in the basin so hard it splashed over the edges.

He let her wipe his face with a warm cloth so he could see. He spotted her swelling eye.

"Who hit you?" he demanded.

"How do I know? Maybe it was you!"

"I was at the other end of the room. Let me up from here! I'm going to get raw beef for that eye of yours! You've already got a wounded shoulder—"

She pushed him, hard. He sat back down.

"You first!" she cried. "Then get raw meat for both our eyes!"

A thousand wonders, he gave in.

He had his reasons. He had to have the bleeding eye taped so he could see to her. He wasn't giving in to her at all, though she thought he was. He let her bathe his face, let her tape above the eye, add a Band-Aid here and there.

Outside, rain poured. It had a roar to it now. The house quivered. The rain worsened; the house quieted. Jess knew it had solid underpinnings, steel through rock. Still, he wasn't going to trust it.

Rae-Ellen's fingers were gentle. That was a surprise.

Suddenly he heard his own voice. "If we were both penniless," he asked, "would you marry a guy like me?"

Taken by surprise, her fingertips rested lightly on his face. Forgetting Drew for the moment, she heard herself reply, "Maybe I would, except for one thing."

"Which is . . . ?"

"My baby. He doesn't like you, and you don't like him."

"That kid's another Burr," he heard himself growl. "I liked Burr more than any other human being. Ever."

She tossed her head. Her fingers resumed their bandaging.

"You mention your baby," he said maddeningly, "but leave out the love bit you've always yammered about. Only one reason for that."

"Pah!"

"Fact. Love is respecting the other person in all things. It's wanting to be with that person and no other. It's giving up what you want for what he wants. It's . . . well, sticking to him through whatever, whether you feel like it or not. It's loving him in spite of his faults."

"You don't know what you're talking about!"

"Oh, yes I do. Take you, now. You're playing the

282

mother bit to the hilt. I want you to understand I'm not in the running to be a pa for Vic—never would be. It'd be for love, the kind I explained to you."

"What's wrong with you?" she cried. "Why don't you come right out and say whether you love me or not? Or if you just like to torment me, strut around being my manager!"

"A girl like you," he said, knowing he was nowhere near ready to tie himself to any girl, especially this one, "who can't get it through her head what love is, wouldn't grasp the meaning if it was offered to her on a silver platter three times a day!"

"It's Susie!" she accused. "You've got yourself so mixed up about her, you don't even know if you're capable of love! Well, let me tell *you* what love is—it's making up your mind what girl you want and going after her and not being rough and r-raping! It's being decent!"

"Meaning I'm not decent?"

"I didn't say that! I said—".

"That's what I heard."

"*Oh!* If you want to call what you've done to me decent, I can't stop you! All you've done to me is bad things! And you go out of your way to make me mad! You—"

"And you," he grated, "have matched me, act for act. You've tried to claw my eyes, too. You want to dictate whether I can marry Susie, when it's none of your business. You—"

"And another thing! You *hid* from me how filthy rich you are! That proves you're a born deceiver, that deceit is in your *bones*! Any real man wouldn't try to make me think he came from some little dirt farm when he practically owns the State of California!"

He got up from the commode lid so fast that he almost knocked her over. She had to catch her balance with no help from him.

"I'll get that raw meat," he said stiffly. "What you do with it is your affair."

When he'd gone, she wandered back into the living room. People were waking up, stirring about. The rain was worse. The TV announcer warned that the number of mudslides had increased and urged all viewers to get to level ground without delay.

The house gave a tremendous groan. Like magic, Jess was beside Rae-Ellen, without the meat.

"We've got to get out now!" he shouted. "Don't stop for coats—get out the side doors and run! Run for that level ground, back from the house!"

Stricken silent, the crowd made for the two doors. They jammed the openings, began to push and shove and fight. Jess grabbed Rae-Ellen's arm and started for the front door.

"This way!" he roared. "Link...Grant...Susie...all of you!"

Some of the still-drunk guests crowded back in, saying they'd take their chances. They didn't want to be drowned by the rain. Jess started for them, shouting, pushed and rammed at them until they turned and began to go outside, into the rain, and stumble and slip toward the level ground beyond the cliff edge.

It was then that Keith leaped to Rae-Ellen. He gripped her hands, face stark. "Darling," he cried, "promise to marry me! I want the right to stay with you, save you!"

She pulled free of him, shook her head, made her way to Jess, helped shove people through the doorways into the downpour. The rain was so thick that the daylight was like dusk. The figures already on their way to safety were moving blurs.

Now the house moved under their feet. There was a loud, sucking noise. Beams cracked and popped. Those remaining in the house burst gratefully out into the rain.

Rae-Ellen and Jess plunged into it. He gripped her arm, and they negotiated the mud, him hobbling along on his cast, crutch lost, slipping, catching his balance, slogging on. She pressed against him, trying to brace him. They headed into the level area, stumbling, half falling, rain all but blinding them.

The panicked crowd ahead pushed through the slanting, hurtling rain, falling and struggling up, falling again, clawing back up. Somehow, Jess and Rae-Ellen gained on them, overtook them, and they all went on, away from the cliff, as fast as they could.

From behind came a tremendous sucking noise. The earth beneath their feet tried to pull them backward, but they fought desperately on. Rain was smashing Rae-Ellen's face, driving pain through her battered eye.

Jess slipped again, and she braced him, hard. They stood motionless, pressed together, until he got his balance. The sucking came again and again. People screamed.

Rae-Ellen and Jess moved on, him hobbling on that cast, managing, somehow, to slog as fast as she did. Then she felt all the earth under her feet slide, pulling her back, the relentless pull filled not with silence but with a great ripping noise from the house, and screams from those who had been behind herself and Jess.

Chapter Twenty-eight

She looked back in time to see the great house move. Ponderously, in slow-motion, it slid toward the sheer edge of the cliff. Sliding herself, Rae-Ellen caught at a passing bush, held on; its stems cut into her hands. Jess grabbed for it, too, missed, went sliding on back. The house crept over the edge, then was gone.

"People . . . people down there!" Jess shouted. "Going . . . help . . ." Now he was not only sliding toward the brink, but was on his feet, making for it, limping and trying to run.

"*You come back here!*" she yelled, but the screams of others drowned her out, and the drumming, bouncing rain swathed her voice.

All around was bedlam. Shrieking people fought

toward the broad level space. Some threw themselves on the puddled mud, clutching at it for purchase. Their hands slipped, and they tried to crawl, an inch at a time, away from the cliff. The sucking pull ceased. The rain howled and whirled and beat the earth, hammering those flat in the mud so that they couldn't move.

There was a far, heavy thud and the dulled noise of splintering timbers as the once-luxurious house collapsed. Clinging to her bush, Rae-Ellen felt the ground suck once more toward where the house had stood.

She could still see Jess going for the cliff, a blur in the rain. He was going at a sliding, slogging hobble. Dimly she made out the other Texans, following him.

Gradually, the earth quieted, lay still. Rae-Ellen saw Jess go to his knees at the edge of the abyss, peering down into it. Shrouding rain fell over him, on and on.

"Jess!" she shrieked. *"Come back!"*

He didn't hear. He was too stubborn to do what she said anyway. Clinging to her bush, she watched him climb over the edge.

He was gone. Of course he'd go. He might be high-handed, but he was no coward. Members of the house party had slid down there, were possibly injured or even dead, and the crazy fool was trying to save them. She saw the other Texans go over the edge, too.

Well, one thing was certain. She couldn't hang on to this wet bush forever, wondering what was happening. Using the bush for a handhold, she turned so she faced where the house had been, alert lest the earth again begin to slide.

It remained steady, though the rain was thicker. How *could* it be thicker? she wondered. She let go of the bush with one hand, rested it, palm down, fingers clutching for any slight hold, digging into mud. She dug forever, it seemed. Her hand was in mud beyond the wrist before she found damp earth. Cautiously she braced herself, cautiously let go the bush and began to dig through mud with the other hand.

When both hands were braced, she started with her knees, hampered by her slicker, pressing and digging first one, then the other, as deep as she must. Her arms ached with the weight she put on them, but finally, with agonizing slowness, she started to crawl toward the abyss.

Maybe she could get to her feet and go at a slow trot. No, the danger was too great. Her slight, running weight might start the mudslide again. Better to creep, feeling for handhold, kneehold. It wasn't too far. She could do it. Had to do it. Had to get down into that chasm and find Jess, help him get others out so he himself would climb to safety. On she crawled.

One last, extra slow, extremely careful effort, and she was at the edge of the cliff. She waited seconds, holding her breath lest one slight move send her hurtling to the muddy, raining depths below.

She ventured to look over the edge, down and down. She peered until her eyes ached, rain streaming over her. In the wet, dawn-colored light of midafternoon, she made out moving figures. Some were

climbing a slope on the far side, sliding back two
steps for every three they labored up.

At one side beyond the piled debris of the house,
the Texans seemed to be trying to dig someone out of
the mud. She looked harder; pain shot through her
straining eyes.

One by one, she identified the Texans. They were
all digging, all but Jess. She stared desperately,
trying to identify the person they were trying to free.

And then she did, and her heart stood still. Jess!
Jess was bogged chest-deep in that sucking mud, and
it seemed the more the others dug, the deeper he
sank.

Frantic, she sought some bush, some protuber-
ance, so she could climb down there and help. They
needed every available pair of hands.

Her gaze lit on a tree root. It grew sidewise,
thrusting through the treacherous earth. She had to
trust it, had to use it to lower herself to that tiny,
rock ledge below.

She grasped the root with one hand, pulled on it,
and it held. She pressed on it, and still it held. Not
breathing, she gripped the root with the other hand
too, and carefully let her weight come onto it.
Miraculously, it remained firm.

The rock ledge was just below. She dare not drop
onto it; it was too mud-and-water slick. She hung,
the root bruising her hands, felt about with her feet
until, blessedly, they touched the ledge. And she
stood on the ledge, arms strained far up to retain her
hold on the root.

Squinting through rain, she made out a network of
tiny roots at waist level. Slowly, testing them as she

worked, she got one hand dug in so she could hold on to them. She pulled, and they resisted.

Moving slowly, she got the other hand around the network and slowly lowered herself to the ledge, and there, below, was an outcropping of rock that gave her not only a landing place but a handhold.

She looked down again. It was still a distance to where the men were digging. She sought another foothold, another handhold. Desperate, expecting every moment to fall, she found what she needed. She kept telling herself that Jess had found a way down, and so had the Texans. She could find it, too. It might take longer, but she'd get there.

Foot by foot she descended. She could no longer risk looking down. It was all she could do to find the next root, the next half-solid bush, the next ledge that would hold her. Once she fell, slid forever, somehow grabbing on to a sharp edge of rock that cut her hands, but she held on and found a place at last, where her feet touched the bottom of the canyon.

She glimpsed the shattered heaps of the house. Rafters stood up from the mud like uprights; decorative stone, mud-covered and rain-slick, littered everything. She was aware of glass buried in mud, scattered on everything.

Slipping and falling, she fought her way to the Texans. Jess was only waist-deep in mud now. He tried to scoop mud away from himself as she reached the laboring group, but someone—Drew—shouted, "Don't move, Jess! It'll make you sink! Stay still!"

And he did. She had one quick look at his face, which was covered with mud and rain, and still he was handsome. She began to scoop mud into her hands, fling it away, scoop again. She was aware of the Texans: Drew, Keith, Grant, Link, Sammy, all digging. They were using broken boards, and after forever, while mud slid in around Jess as fast as they dug it away, Keith found a broken shovel—it had no handle—and went to work with that.

"How did he get in so deep?" Rae-Ellen asked Drew.

"The mud here acts like quicksand!" Drew exclaimed. "He fell into the worst part!"

Rae-Ellen scooped a double handful of mud, flung it away, scooped again. She could feel the sucking of the mud and knew that they were all at the edge of the quicksand.

He remained still, very still. She glanced at his face as she approached to dig again. He spotted her.

"What are you doing here, dammit?"

"Digging," she cried grimly, flung away her mud, stooped for more.

"I left you where you'd be safe! This ... bog ... whatever it is, can suck in the whole mess ... house, people and all ... . until you can't see a board or a roof tile!"

"Shut up!" she shouted. "Don't talk! The vibration can make you sink!"

"So can the digging!" he howled back. "However you got here, get out the same way! And fast! You've got a kid, remember?"

"Let her stay!" shouted Drew. "We're making progress! We're below your waist now. You'll soon be out and we can all get to solid ground. The others have. They're waiting at the end of the canyon."

Suddenly Burton Chadwick joined them. He too

had a shovel, and began to dig. "Everybody else is safe!" he shouted. "Some broken arms and sprained ankles, but none of them will budge until we get all of you out!"

So the movie people did have courage, Rae-Ellen thought, scooping. Even two hours ago, she would have expected them to run, each thinking of his own safety, but now that they were near to safety, they wouldn't leave until all members of the house party could join them.

"No one missing?" Jess asked.

The big fool. Standing in that killing mud, himself a near-casualty, worrying about the others! Rae-Ellen scooped faster, jaw rigid.

"The ones who left by the side doors," Burton said, "joined those who slid down with the house. Scared to death, but sticking together. I had to throw my weight around to make them promise to wait where I left them. They wanted to help."

Inch by inch they got the mud down to Jess's hips. Then the Texans gripped him—Keith and Grant at his armpits, their own feet sinking, the others standing ready to grab his legs.

Keith and Grant heaved until the cords of their necks stood out, clothes sodden—they'd shed rain gear to dig—rain streaming over them, over Jess, over the world, and they couldn't budge him, even a fraction of an inch. When they stopped lifting and pulled their feet free of the mud and stood back, he sank a few inches more, and they had to dig again.

"This time," Keith panted, working his shovel, "we get to his knees. Then we can pull him out, quagmire or no quagmire!"

Rae-Ellen was in the way with her scooping. Besides, a double handful of mud wasn't enough. She searched the wreckage for a board and found a short one, covered with mud. She held it up, let the drenching rain wash off the top, turned it so the bottom was cleaned.

Now she began to dig. The board didn't hold much, but every scoop counted. Her shoulder hurt every time she dug in, but she ignored it and pressed harder, deeper.

It was only then, so panicked had she been, so furious at Jess, that she realized the rain washed most of the mud off all the boards as the men dug. The shovels Keith and Burton had produced were the only things that moved any appreciable amount of mud.

"Let me have a shovel!" Drew cried. "Take turns! We'll move faster!"

They did as he said.

On they dug, and on. Rae-Ellen, deprived of the chance to help, watched anxiously. The shovels, wielded by those strong Texans and by Burton, were making headway. Slowly, the mud level fell from Jess's hips to mid-thigh, to above the knees, to below them.

Jess, holding still as ordered, watched Rae-Ellen through the rain. Her face was drawn, and the thought struck him that she did have one good quality—she wouldn't want to see her worst enemy die. What he couldn't figure out, seeing she hated him so, was why she was always ready to jump into bed with him.

Not that he objected. He enjoyed it while it was going on. But afterward—he never got rid of the feeling, even now, watching her look so anxious—that she was using him for some female purpose of her own. And he couldn't think what that purpose could be. She had a reason, and he meant to find out what it was once he got out of this mess, and after that he'd be rid of that crazy yen for her, that need to get her out from under his skin.

He didn't exactly forget the Texans were still digging him out of the mud. But watching Rae-Ellen, her looking the way she did, bedraggled and muddy and pale where the rain hit her face, he got mad all over again that she hadn't stayed where he'd left her. She'd been comparatively safe there. Now, look—any minute, there could be another mudslide, burying them all, and her right at the bottom.

"It's below the knee!" yelled Grant. "Pull!"

Again he and Keith took Jess under the arms. Drew went to his knees and put his arms around the right leg, Link did the same with the left leg. Sammy and Burton stood at the ready, to jump in if needed, and Rae-Ellen did the same.

"Wait," Drew said. "Let's all lift together. One . . . two . . . three . . . lift!"

All four men lifted, straining. Slowly, with torturing reluctance, the mud let go its prey. The Texans lifted Jess, set him down on the more or less solid mud beside Rae-Ellen.

"I hope you're satisfied!" she flared, relief making her tremble. "You could have been safe, we all could have been safe! But no, you had to stick your nose in, be a great big hero! See the mess you got us in!"

"Rae-Ellen, now," Drew said, "Jess did what he thought was needed. It's over. Burton, if you will, lead us to the others so we can get to high ground. We're still not in the clear."

Chapter Twenty-nine

THE rain came harder, as if to push them all into the mud. Jess's cast was covered with mud, also his other leg. The rain began to wash some of it off.

"Did mud get inside the cast?" Rae-Ellen demanded.

"I guess so," he said grimly. "It's like liquid."

"It'll poison your foot!"

"First things first," Drew cut in. "What we've got to do now is follow Burton out of here before there's another slide. Jess, can you walk with that muddy cast, or should we make you a chair of arms and carry you?"

"The chair!" cried Rae-Ellen. "Then we can go faster."

"I can keep up," Jess growled. "You run on ahead if you're nervous."

So they went, single file, Burton leading. Jess followed him, limping heavily, but keeping up. Rae-Ellen stayed behind Jess. Drew was back of her, then came Keith, then Grant, with Link and Sammy last.

They had some slippery climbing to do at the end of the canyon, and once Jess almost fell, but righted himself and went on. A flight of steps so covered with rain that they looked like a waterfall, led up to level ground, and they slogged through that.

"They're all waiting at the top," Burton said. "Watch out for these steps. It's only water, but it's fast water and can sweep us back. I tumbled coming down them, bumped clear to the bottom!"

Moving with utmost care, they all reached the top. Someone came running from the clump of cheering, rain-drenched people beyond.

It was Veronica, her platinum hair dark with rain, clothes bedraggled, plastered to her body, streaming water. Only her patrician features and silvery tone identified her, and the way she went into Burton Chadwick's arms.

"I thought you'd never get back!" she cried. "We've been so worried, but you said for us to wait here, and we did!"

"Good girl," Burton said, holding her close. In that instant Rae-Ellen saw that these two loved each other, and her heart gave a pang at the thought that she had no one who loved her.

"You found trouble?" Veronica asked.

"Real trouble. Quagmire. We almost lost Jess."

"Not the way you worked . . . no chance," Jess put in. "You should have seen them dig. No quagmire could beat these Texans or Burton!"

298

Rae-Ellen's heart swelled. Jess had carried it off very well. He *could* be decent. And the men who had saved him, bless them, began to shrug as if it had been nothing.

"Did us good to dig, gave us a workout," said Keith.

"We were bound to win," said Drew. "The way Jess helped."

"You mean he *dug?*" cried Veronica.

Burton kissed her streaming cheek. "I mean he stood still when we asked him to. He's got a cool head, I've told you that. Another man, caught like he was, would panic. It takes guts to stand stock-still, up to your chest in mud, and just *wait* to find out whether your rescuers will win or whether the mud will get you first."

"How did you get stuck in the first place?" demanded Rae-Ellen.

"The mud nearly got Harriet," Veronica cried. "She was up to mid-calf. Jess grabbed her and threw her—actually threw her—into the rest of us. His broken foot slipped, and before any of us could get hold of him, he was nearly to the waist in the quagmire! Harriet's ever so grateful... she's with the others up there, crying. She's got a broken arm, but otherwise she's fine."

So. He'd got himself into trouble showing off. But he'd saved a life. Grudgingly, she had to admit that. No one—not even she who knew his faults so well—could criticize him for what he'd done.

"Well," Burton said, "we've got to move along. Everybody pair off, and we'll walk until we find shelter."

He put himself at the head of the party, Veronica holding his arm. Jess was next, and Rae-Ellen ran to be his partner. He was her manager, her responsibility. Behind them came Bertha and Grant, then Drew and Susie, Sammy and Dots. Keith helped the injured Harriet, and Link escorted other actresses. Thus, two by two, the bedraggled, bruised and battered actors and actresses and the Texans made their way slowly and carefully, bent into the rain.

It was now late afternoon, and the rain made the world look like late dusk. Doggedly, the party of forty passed uprooted trees and bushes, passed small mudslides and big mudslides, their path filled with debris of crushed houses and crumpled automobiles. They passed other refugees headed in the opposite direction, stopped to pass a word with them, proceeded without turning back.

"We just have to keep going," Burton called out, "until we come to streets that haven't been torn up."

"But are there any?" wailed Veronica. "It looks as if all California's one big mudslide!"

"There'll be solid parts," Burton encouraged, "and we'll find them. We just have to keep going."

That was all they'd done since this began, Rae-Ellen thought. Kept going. First, out of Burton's doomed house, then into the abyss and the job of digging, the breathless trip out of the canyon, and now.

Weary hours later, after a nightmare trudge through the punishing rain, they were able to find a hospital where the worst-injured members of the party could be treated. Chadwick, on the phone, found space for the out-of-towners and the homeless in a nearby hotel.

They had to wait more than an hour for taxis. They stood around in the waiting room, every seat being filled. Outside the rain fell viciously. Rae-Ellen was content to wait. Even know-it-all Jess couldn't insist on walking now, him with a brand-new cast that would melt if he got it wet.

She accidentally caught Jess's eye.

He grinned, unexpectedly.

She wished she could claw him, he looked so cocky standing there in his new cast, face battered, eye swollen and purple, but still handsome.

She wondered how she looked to him with her own black eye and bruises.

Chapter Thirty

THE next afternoon, the rain having stopped, leaving behind a soggy world, the Texas party climbed into the Learjet for the flight home. Tower, ignoring Rae-Ellen's suggestion that he remain behind until his foot healed, boarded in silence.

He took the armchair next to hers. She was holding Vic, and Tower acted as if the boy didn't exist. Baby Vic, on his part, occupied himself by watching the others and chewing on the gold chain of his mother's handbag. Rae-Ellen had determined to consult her baby book. Vic was fifteen months old now. When would he stop cutting teeth, why didn't he walk except where he had furniture to hold on to, and why didn't he talk?

She placed her fingers on his jaws, turned his

head, looked into his eyes. He grinned suddenly, broadly, and the chain dropped from his mouth. "Ma!" he said distinctly. "Ma!"

While Rae-Ellen was hugging and kissing him, the others, all but Tower, were exclaiming and jubilant that the child had spoken his first word. He then proceeded to shock them by saying, "Vic want cookie!"

Pa Travis shouted for someone to produce a cookie.

Dots had tucked a small bag of the sweets into her handbag. She gave Vic one and, while he gnawed at it blissfully, raved about how precocious he was.

"He could have talked all this time!" she declared. "He's been listening and learning! From now on, he'll talk in sentences!"

Rae-Ellen said nothing, but agreed with Dots and with Pa, who was booming, "He'll walk the same way, just let go the furniture and *run* wherever he wants to go!"

Pa wanted to hold Vic when he got sleepy, and Rae-Ellen let him. She almost felt her old warmth for Pa, he was so elated. But that didn't mean she'd let him run her life.

While Vic slept, the couples aboard murmured. Drew and Susie seemed cozy, and Grant and Bertha. Jess and Rae-Ellen sat rigidly silent.

After an hour, he asked, "You afraid of me?"

"Why ever should I be afraid of you?"

"I don't really know, not after all we've done. We certainly should be well acquainted. But you act so feisty, it makes me wonder. Only explanation I can come up with is you're afraid of me."

What conceit! She went hot all over. Then a cold shiver took her. She realized she really was afraid of

304

him, because he was all wrong for her, impossible for her baby, yet had this power to make her burn. He'd put her into a state she couldn't bear. She had to escape from it, but there was only the one way, and he had a cast on his leg, making contact impossible.

Despite this logic, the yen for him gnawed. Well, she decided angrily, he was so super-macho, she'd have sex with him tonight in spite of the cast. She'd prove that what she felt for him was lust. And everybody knew that no solid relationship could be based on lust. Even if it lasted, say a year, it was doomed to fail.

And failure she was going to avoid. Once she'd proved—again—what sex with Tower really was, she'd be cleansed of him and could concentrate on Drew. Because, until Drew actually put a wedding ring on Susie's finger, Rae-Ellen was never going to give up.

As if he'd read her thoughts, Tower nudged her and indicated Susie and Drew, who were holding hands.

Rae-Ellen seethed, favored Tower with a glare.

"With them like that," Tower murmured, "you're going to keep on beating your head against a stone wall?"

"What I do is no affair of yours!"

He grinned, sobered. "It sure-hell isn't."

"You know I don't like cursing!"

"Sorry. Somehow, you bring out the worst in me."

"It's the other way around! You bring out the worst in *me*!"

They sat angrily silent. Watched the clouds go by,

stared at the intense blue that surrounded their white, fluffy, powder-puff shapes.

"You're being a little fool, you know," he said.

"In what way, know-it-all?"

"To chase a man who wants another girl. Especially when you can have anybody else you want. There isn't a man on the plane, except Knight and me, who wouldn't marry you tomorrow. And be a good pa to your kid. Sammy, even. Crazy as he is for Dots, he'd come across if you blinked at him once."

"That's not so!" she hissed. "I don't see how you can say that!"

"You have looks, money, you raise thoroughbreds, you'll inherit millions from your own father, more from Travis, or your kid will. Nearly any man'd want you."

"All but two!" she snapped.

"That's correct. Like I said, Drew Knight. And yours truly."

"You think you're better than the others, smarter," she hissed. "You name good qualities I have, then ignore them! Even when you give me what sounds like a compliment, it's a slap in the face!"

He shook his head. "I left out your faults," he reminded her. "That temper, that headstrong streak, that—well—passion, which could get you into real trouble, the way you can't control it."

"Ha! You admit you're not man enough to control it!"

"No such thing. I just don't want to be bothered."

"No, you want Susie! Well, if she and Drew do get together, you're as big a loser as I am! If I can't have

306

Drew, neither can you have Susie! You'll have to look elsewhere for your quiet lady-type!"

They glowered. His jaw looked like a piece of rock. Her jaw felt like stone. She noticed that others in the plane glanced at herself and Tower, but forgot it in the sheer, loin-aching hatred she had for the man.

That night she passed lightly along the dogtrot to Tower's rooms. She didn't have to touch the door knocker; he must have sensed her presence, because he was there, opening the door.

She marched in, suddenly not knowing what to say. This enraged her. He didn't seem to know what to say, either. He looked at her in lamplight and waited. Well, she could outwait him.

At last he spoke. "To what do I owe this honor?"

She blurted out the first thing she could think of. "Vic's begun to walk, he's been going at a *run* all over the house. I had to catch him to put him to bed, and then he screamed."

"He needed to get his run out of his system," Tower said. Not a word of praise. Just criticism of her way of handling it. "What else did you come for?" he asked.

The flame reached through her body. Her nipples went hard. Well, he had to know, if she was to get him out of herself.

"You know damn well!" she heard herself swear. "To get you out of my system for keeps!"

He yanked her into his arms, ground his lips against hers, forced his tongue into her mouth. Her arms encircled him almost naturally, and she pressed

307

against him, tongue-kissing as fiercely as he did, and waited for him to take her to the bedroom.

He didn't carry her. Instead, he gripped her shoulders from behind and, hobbling, marched her to the bed. "Undress," he ordered. "Make it fast. I'm not in the mood to wait."

Fingers like sticks, she managed to bare herself. Even though she hurried, and he had the cast, he was ready first.

"Get on the bed," he ordered.

She obeyed because this was the last time. This was the encounter that would get him out of her forever. After tonight, she'd be free. A great load would be off her; she could proceed with life.

She opened to him and he came in fast and hard. They struggled and fought, cast and all, a passionate, hurting fight which they both won or both lost, whichever way they looked at it. They peaked at the same time, moaning. They lay touching, breathing hard. Rae-Ellen's heart was knocking; she wondered if his was doing the same.

She tried to sense if she'd reached her goal, if she was rid of him. For some crazy reason, she got the idea he was trying to sense the same thing. She hoped so. It was only fair that he feel some discomfort over their situation.

Suddenly she was very angry at him.

"Why don't you say something?" she asked fiercely.

"What is there to say?"

"Whether, all this time, you've been . . . well, driven to this. The way I've been driven with you."

"Suppose I have? What does it prove?"

"That we need to get over it."

"I've been doing my best. You're the worst kind of woman. Get under a man's skin and no matter how he scratches, won't get out!"

"So! You think of it as scratching! You don't even dignify it by the word *sex*!"

"It's never been what you'd call dignified. In fact, no sex is dignified, not even when there's love on both sides."

They quarreled on. She accused him of being the aggressor; he accused her of creating situations that forced him to take her. They fought about Baby Vic, whether she should have let him run around the house until he was exhausted instead of forcing him to go to bed. He accused her of being soft with the kid—all those cookies. She wanted to know if he hadn't eaten his share of cookies when he was a little boy, and he shouted angrily that he had, but because he liked them. They hadn't been a pacifier. She screamed that Vic was cutting teeth, and besides, he loved cookies.

On they raged, even while they dressed. He followed her to the door still quarreling, and she went out, telling him that she never wanted to see him again.

All day, slow fire glowed in her. Late at night, hungering for him, believing this time really would be the end of what last night had begun, she went to his rooms clad only in shorties. She was barefoot.

When he opened the door, he was nude.

"I just got ready for bed," he told her. He spoke quietly, as if they'd never fought.

She'd avoided him all day. Now, she felt, they'd

both simmered down and could finish this thing quietly and for keeps.

"I . . . I'm here," she whispered.

"Come on in."

"Last night shouldn't have been like it was," she said. "It's no fun to fight."

"No, it isn't," he murmured, and she knew that was as near as he would come to an apology.

They stood facing each other in the dim light. She felt her heart pounding, wondered if his was doing the same. Standing there, she shed her sleeping garments.

"We need to make up for last night," she whispered. "We can part decently at least."

This time he carried her to the bed. He caressed her, trailing kisses from her lips, across her breasts, to the nest between her thighs. He entered slowly, and she received him, savoring the delight ahead.

Their motions fitted perfectly, though the cast hurt her. They went faster, more ardently, and when they soared away into ecstasy, they both cried out. She called him Jess and he called her darling.

They lay in each other's arms getting their breaths.

He spoke first. "You've changed," he said.

She realized this was true, then couldn't decide whether it angered or pleased her. She had changed because tonight, in sex with him, she had recognized what could be—if he'd bother to cultivate them— good qualities in Jess Tower. And she had been astounded.

He could, if he wanted, be tender. He could be kind. Even thoughtful. All these qualities he showered on the horses; she'd watched him do it. Listened to him. Tonight, a tinge of these things had come to her as they moved together in this bed.

The pity was, it wouldn't last.

Hungering for what could never be, she nestled closer. He made love to her this time—gentle, amazing love. The kind he'd give Susie if he had the opportunity.

A sudden thought struck her, ruined the nice things. His gentleness was only because he was hampered by the cast on his leg; that was why he hadn't been like an animal. Last night he must have hurt his foot, when he was so rough.

"Did you hurt your foot last night?" she asked.

"Not at all," he said.

She was relieved. She'd never want to hurt him, no matter how mean he was. She put on her shorties, scurried back to her room. Only time would tell if she was, at last, free of him.

The silver fillies arrived from California by air just before dark. Rae-Ellen and Susie, who still looked troubled—which indicated she hadn't yet confessed about Grant—and Dots and Keith and Compton and Johnny and Grant watched as they were unloaded from the trucks that had brought them from the airfield.

They recognized Tower at once, lipped sugar out of his hands, followed along smartly when he led them into the stable.

"You've got to name them!" sang out Dots.

"Didn't you have names for them, Jess?" Susie asked.

"No. I thought it'd be better if their new owners named them. One name's enough for them to learn."

"What's it going to be, Rae-Ellen?" Dots cried. "Tell us... this minute! You'll put 'Silver' into both names, won't you?"

Rae-Ellen gave one last thought to the names that had been going through her mind. "I think this one," she said, stroking the face of the nearer one, "will be Silver Streak."

"That's a lovely name! And the other one?"

Rae-Eller stroked the second filly. "Silver Lightning," she said.

The girls exclaimed in delight, and the men nodded. All but Tower. She couldn't tell whether he approved of the names or not.

"What do you think, Jess?" Dots asked.

"The names fit. They'll look good on a racing program."

"If I sell them for racers," Rae-Ellen said stiffly.

Just because he'd raised these beauties didn't mean he was the expert on them, now that they'd been sold to her. She was, however, vaguely pleased that he approved of the names.

They stayed in the stable during feeding. Rae-Ellen thought she'd never seen anything as beautiful as that double line of horses—all silver, every one of them—content and munching. She even loved the smell of the stable, of clean horses and hay and oats and corn.

Darkness fell. Grant left, saying he had a date with Bertha. The rest of them lingered with the horses for quite some time.

They all walked back toward the house together,

312

leaving only Keith and his helpers in the stable. Jess walked even with the girls, some yards to their left. By now, except for the glint of early stars, the night was black.

"Ouch!" Tower exclaimed, and the girls stopped.

"What's wrong?" Rae-Ellen asked.

"Knife," he said. "Almost went into my arm, got stuck in my sleeve here, instead. Some damn fool threw it at me out of the dark."

They ran to him and walked him back into the stable, where there was light. Keith was alone, Compton and Johnny having gone to their quarters to fry up some supper.

Rae-Ellen was trembling. What was it with Tower? Was he accident-prone? She rushed to him, rolled up his sleeve from which he'd pulled the knife, saw that it looked like a dagger.

"Not a mark on your arm," said Susie.

"There is, too!" Rae-Ellen challenged. "See... that scratch!"

"It could have gone into your heart," breathed Susie. "You could be dead!"

"Only I'm not dead," he said grimly. "Keith, get Compton and Johnny—we'll look into this!

All of them, supplied with strong flashlights, searched the area. They found nothing, saw nothing, heard nothing. There wasn't a car hidden anywhere.

"Think it's the ones that turned the horses loose?" Compton asked Tower.

"Could be. But pretty risky this time. I don't take to being killed."

"We'll go to the police!" declared Rae-Ellen. "Tell

them about both things! Get them to give us a guard, or something!"

"I'll post my own guard," Tower said. He stuck the dagger into the belt of his jeans. "Grant will let one of his men help, and the other fellows will, too. We can catch our troublemakers and turn them over to the law."

Rae-Ellen was set on having police. She got Tower off to one side and told him so.

"It's only some stoned teenagers," he said. "Bound to be."

"Haven't you got any sense at all?"

"Sure, I have. A number of things have happened since I came here. Looks as if somebody's trying to scare me off."

"And you think I'm the one!"

"These things aren't your style. You're too open, frank as hell."

He speared a look at her and she wondered if he really thought, secretly, that she was the instigator of everything—the broken girth, the horses' being spooked, the broken spur at the rodeo, his getting almost swallowed by mud in California, and now this knife.

And after the way he had lied to her! Well, same as lied!

"Just why did you take me to your farm?" she asked hotly.

"To show you the fillies. And my home and background."

"I have no interest in the way you live! None!"

She flew at him and he caught her wrists. Both flashlights landed on the ground.

314

"You push into everything!" he muttered. "My kitchen, my bed, what I do or don't do! That doesn't mean but one thing! Want to make it a relationship—you and me?"

"I've told you I wouldn't marry you—"

"I didn't say marry. I said the other."

She slapped him. He grabbed that wrist back and she couldn't budge it.

"But you might *marry* me?"

"Not if you were the last man on earth!"

"The feeling remains mutual."

"Then it's finished, done with!"

"Oh, but it's not over," he said quietly.

He marched her to his apartment; the others didn't see, having gone on ahead. He hobbled, but he had her under control.

At his door, he half dragged her into his living room, then to the bedroom. This time he helped undress her, skinned off his own clothes, and eased her onto the bed.

She resisted, but he held her easily. She tried harder but somehow her heart wasn't in it. He took her with that new gentleness, subdued her with lovemaking. Clinging to him in the final joy, she loved him for a moment, loved him in a wild and crazy way. She wondered what had happened to her love for Drew, then, in a flash, knew that Jess had killed it, stolen it, brought it to raging life in her again, then proceeded to stab it to the core. But the Drew-love would revive, oh, it would!

"Why am I not good enough—just *me*—no ring?" Tower gritted against her lips.

"I can't shack up! I've got to have a father for Vic!"

315

Jess now felt a change in her, the female fighting for her young. Regardless, a man needed a test period. He couldn't jump into marriage with a hell-cat, to say nothing of being a real father to her kid. Even Burr's kid.

Foolishly, Rae-Ellen began to want that relationship with Jess. But all she could have was this. Until his six months were up and he went back home.

She almost cried.

"Better dress," he said. "Get inside before the girls catch on."

Silently, she dressed and left. She'd never been so miserable in her life.

Chapter Thirty-one

THE first of November came, passed. Fall was on the land. Tower's time at the Double T was half gone. His foot was out of the cast. There had been no more accidents, no further acts of mischief. The nightly watch on the horses was now kept only by the Double T men.

It was time for Silver Girl to foal, past time. Rae-Ellen remarked worriedly about this to Keith and Tower as the three of them stood watching the beautiful filly strip an ear of corn.

"What can we do?" Rae-Ellen asked. "She's a week past due now. It's been three hundred forty-seven days; she was supposed to foal in three hundred forty days."

"It's her first foal," Keith reminded.

"That's the thing," Tower agreed. "I've had even mares to foal ten days late, and everything was all right."

Rae-Ellen sniffed. Know-it-all! Mention horses, and Tower put himself forward as expert. Sure, he'd been raising horses, keeping it a secret from her, for years. But so had other men. His personal experience didn't make him a walking textbook!

Compton and Johnny rejoined them and Tower began to issue orders. "Disinfect the foaling stall again," he said. "It's stood too long for us to use, over twenty-four hours."

"This'll make three times," Compton said. "You want it same as before?"

"Exactly the same. Don't miss an inch. It's got to be as sanitary as possible and kept that way."

He went into Silver Girl's stall, felt along her belly, peered at her rear end. "Looks like she's going to foal soon," he reported. "So get right at that stall."

The others left, Keith going along to help, and Rae-Ellen was left alone with Tower. She was anxious about the filly and irritated at Tower's manner.

"Can't you make up your mind?" she asked. "One minute you talk as if Silver Girl will be ten days overdue, and the next you're in a great big hurry to disinfect the stall!"

"We need to be ready for anything," he said shortly.

"Is she going to foal, or isn't she?"

"Not this minute, no. By evening, possibly. The first signs are there."

Crossly, she left him and went to the house, ready to deal with Vic should he demand a cookie. She

318

didn't need a man to manage this cookie situation. She was the mother; her son would do as she said, like it or not. It was essential that he learn he couldn't have things simply because he wanted them.

She found him playing with plastic blocks in the nursery. Leah reported that Dots had given him breakfast an hour ago, and he hadn't even asked for you-know-what. Rae-Ellen sat on the floor and built towers of blocks, which Vic knocked over, squealing with delight, until she was weary. Usually, by this time, he'd be demanding cookies. Today, though she stayed with him until lunch, which he ate eagerly, he never spoke the word *cookie*.

He even went down for his nap, not saying it. Rae-Ellen ate her own lunch in disgust. Vic, baby though he was, behaved like all males! You couldn't depend on them to say what you thought they'd say, so you could deal with them!

Like Tower. He'd promised to send word when Silver Girl went into labor. And so far, she'd had nothing from him but silence.

She started for the stable. Halfway there, Johnny burst into the open, yelling, "She's ready... Silver Girl's ready!"

Rae-Ellen ran for the stable, kept empty of other horses for this event. She burst in. The scene was one of quiet, purposeful activity.

Keith already had Silver Girl in the newly disinfected stall, her tail completely bandaged. She was stepping nervously about, nostrils distended, shaking her head now and then.

Tower gave orders in a low, singsong tone. "Compton... Johnny... bring the soap and buckets of hot and cold water. Bring the antiseptic solution, cotton, navel paint, and powder. And the enema bag and hose."

"Have you called the veterinarian, Keith?" Rae-Ellen asked quietly.

"I told him not to," Tower said. "I'm a veterinarian."

"When did *you* ever . . . ?"

"Went to vet school way they all do. Keith, maybe you'd better come out of the stall. She's too uneasy. Give her a chance to quiet down on her own."

Rae-Ellen, about to enter the stall, turned away. She moved to the front of the manger and stood watching the filly, who continued to step about uneasily, and to toss her head. Once or twice she whinnied, low.

"She's hurting!" Rae-Ellen exclaimed. "Do something! Give her something!"

He shook his head, indicated the disinfected bench where Compton and Johnny put the supplies, motioned them away. Keith had already gone to the far end of the stable and squatted on his heels to wait.

"*Something* has to be done!" Rae-Ellen insisted.

"You've seen other fillies foal."

"Yes, but they—it seemed so natural! Silver Girl—"

"—is going to take longer. Come on. We leave her now. It's best to let her foal by herself. We'll look in on her now and then."

Unwilling, but knowing that fillies and mares did like to foal alone, Rae-Ellen followed Tower to where Keith waited. Compton and Johnny joined them, and they all squatted and sat on the stable floor and waited.

320

But Silver Girl didn't foal. On their third trip, Tower admitted she was going to have a hard time. Instead of moving about, she was lying on her side.

Tower went into the stall, got her onto her feet and walked her around awhile, then let her lie on her side again. Keith joined him, and in murmurs Rae-Ellen could scarcely hear from outside the manger, discussed the problem.

"What's the trouble?" asked Keith.

Tower felt the filly's sides and belly. "The foal is supposed to come out feet first with the head between them, but she's turned in the opposite direction," Tower said. "We'll walk her again. Maybe the foal will turn."

Breathless, Rae-Ellen watched the two men get Silver Girl back onto her feet. They walked her back and forth, over and over.

At last Tower shook his head. "We're stuck with a caudal—backwards—presentation," he said. "We've got to induce a very rapid birth because the navel cord may break too soon and the foal will smother before it's born."

He poured hot and cold water into a disinfected pan and disinfected his hands, not drying them. Then, carefully avoiding the bandaged tail, he waited until the filly again lay on her side.

Swiftly he put one hand up the filly, felt carefully around until his fingers touched and identified the foal's legs. Gently but urgently, he pulled on them.

Rae-Ellen, unaccountably weeping, saw the legs emerge, then the hind quarters, the new little midsection, the shoulders, and, at last, the head on the front legs. She saw Silver Girl raise her head, her big dark eyes on her foal.

The newborn was a wet, dark silver and looked to have its dam's good head.

"What is it?" she called softly, still weeping, almost liking Tower because he had brought forth the foal. "A colt or a filly?"

Tower grinned. "A perfect little filly," he said.

He was as excited as Rae-Ellen. He could even understand why she was crying. They might have lost this little beauty; it would have been so easy to lose her. And Silver Girl, as well. He became aware of the sweat that filmed his body, and even then only half realized the strain he'd been under.

Hands steady, he broke the cord and tended the stump, the afterbirth. Keith was there with towels to dry the foal. Compton and Johnny stood ready to carry out any order.

In moments, the new, beautiful little foal was struggling to her legs, her feet, was standing. Silver Girl got to her feet, nuzzled her young. Rae-Ellen wept on at the perfection of this birth.

The men shook hands all round. Keith came to Rae-Ellen, put his arm around her. "Don't cry," he said. "It's over. All you need do is name the foal."

She let his arm remain because it was a comfort. Also, she noted that Tower had stiffened. So. He didn't like it! He had the idea he was the only male who could touch her!

But then he turned away, ignoring her, and started telling Compton and Johnny how to clean up. He disinfected his hands again, then took the bandage off Silver Girl's tail and disinfected her. From a bag

Rae-Ellen hadn't noticed, he took a hypodermic and gave Silver Girl an injection.

Rae-Ellen pulled away from Keith. "What's that shot for?" she demanded. "Is she in danger?"

"Not now. Just a precaution, a measure I like to take. After all, I had my hand up her. I'll feel better that she's had the shot. And so should you." He clipped out those last words.

"I do, certainly," she retorted. "I want her, and the foal, to have everything just right."

"Jess is tops," Keith put in. "Too bad he isn't going to set up as a vet hereabouts. He'd be the best. The vet we have could have delivered the foal, but not as fast as Jess. And he's not hospital-clean, either. We owe Jess a vote of thanks."

"Yes, we do," Rae-Ellen agreed. She dried her tears, faced Jess. "Thank you for bringing Silver Dart into the world safely."

"That's her name? Silver Dart?"

She nodded, gazed into the stall lovingly. "I know it's best for me not to touch her just yet," she said, "but it's a temptation."

"Better wait until tomorrow," said Jess. "Silver Girl's still keyed up. New mother . . . and she had a hard time. She needs twenty-four hours to get over it. Tomorrow she'll be fine, they both will."

Jess was amazed to hear himself carrying on so softly to Rae-Ellen. It made him sore at himself. However, she had cried over the foaling; she did have tender feelings. They were there in her, though so deep no man on earth would be able to coax them past that temper that stood guard.

Rae-Ellen gazed long at the new mother and at the

new foal. Then, still moved by the drama of birth, she looked at Keith and Jess, smiling. Her eyes met Jess's eyes, and he smiled back. It lighted his face with a new handsomeness, one that didn't make her angry, and she almost liked him.

As for him, the smile shocked him to the bone. Then he realized it meant nothing, really. It had been for the foal, not him. Yes, that was it. His mouth went into a straight line.

Rae-Ellen made for the house, wishing the feeling of liking Tower might last, knowing it wouldn't, that it couldn't.

She and Jess Tower were poles apart.

IV

Blue Norther

Chapter Thirty-two

It was late November. Silver Dart was growing fast and gave promise of being even a greater beauty than her dam. Rae-Ellen put warm, long pants on Vic every morning when it was chilly, and a red sweater, and took him to see the foal.

She had decided that Silver Dart was to be first in a line of thoroughbreds that were to belong to her son. When she announced this in the stable one day, Tower frowned.

"What's wrong with the idea?" she asked sharply.

"Nothing I can put a finger on. Except he might want to be a race car driver, not a horse breeder, when he grows up."

"Then I'll buy his horses from him," Rae-Ellen said. "He's to be what he wants, do what he wants."

Keith, listening, chuckled. "My money says he'll breed horses," he said. "Look at him now, trying to climb the manger to get at the foal! Okay if I take him into the stall?"

Rae-Ellen shot Tower a look, smiled at Keith. "Why not?" she agreed. "It's his foal, he's entranced by her, kisses her! Later he may change, but for now he's as horse-crazy as his mother!"

"Suppose I take him in," suggested Tower.

"Sure thing," agreed Keith. "You don't get much chance to make up to the boy." He looked at Rae-Ellen. "Okay?"

She nodded. She wasn't exactly crazy about the idea of Tower handling her son. Further, she didn't know how Vic would react. Lately he'd been staring at Tower; Tower had spoken to him easily, asked him how he was, as if the child were a grown man.

Now Tower stepped to where Vic was trying mightily to get a foothold for climbing the manger. He gripped one small foot and lifted it to the next board, held him while the boy pulled the other foot up beside it. In this manner they proceeded until Vic fell into the manger and lay wide-eyed on the soft bed of hay. When he tried to get up, he fell over and bounced. Then, delight on him, he bounced up and down, laughing.

"Vic horse!" he squealed, bouncing.

Keith doubled with laughter. Tower grinned. Rae-Ellen couldn't keep from smiling.

He bounced and bounced, cheeks rosy. Finally Tower swooped him up, ignored his instant scream of rage, got his hand away from the little mouth that was trying to bite him, and settled him on his shoulders. Vic was still screaming as Tower made for the stall, but stopped abruptly when Tower opened the gate and entered the stall, where Silver Girl stood, the foal nursing.

"Silver Dart," Tower told the child quietly, "is hungry. She nurses."

The boy turned wide eyes on Tower. "Dart eat cookie?" he asked.

"Not cookie. Milk."

The baby's wondering gaze fastened on the nursing foal. When he became restless and wanted down, Tower squatted, held him on one knee, and went into the singsong he used on horses, telling how hungry Silver Dart was, that Silver Girl was her dam and took good care of her.

"Pretty soon," he singsonged, "she'll take her into the pasture and they'll eat grass together."

Vic regarded Tower. "I not eat grass. I eat cookie."

"Not all the time, you don't. Two cookies every afternoon." He held up two fingers. "No more. They'll make your teeth hurt."

The boy stared at the man. Rae-Ellen waited. Give him another moment and he'd be screaming for a cookie. Rage at Tower swept her. Didn't he have sense enough not to mention the word *cookie*, much less talk about it, tell Vic he couldn't have one any time he wanted it?

Astoundingly, Vic pointed at the foal. "Touch," he said. It was as if cookies had never been mentioned. For a second, Rae-Ellen felt that Tower had some influence over her baby, then realized it was an accident, that Vic was simply more interested in the foal than in a cookie.

Tower set Vic on his feet beside the foal, which had stopped nursing. He kept one arm around the boy, who put out his hands and patted the silvery face of his own baby horse. His own little face was split in a grin that made him look homely-handsome.

Tower guided his hands to the foal's nose, and he squealed at the softness of it. Then, for just a moment, he set Vic astride the foal, and Vic gurgled and laughed.

Rae-Ellen watched this show Tower was putting on with emotions tangled. Never had Vic responded to any man with this enthusiasm with the exception of Pa Travis. He responded to Keith, of course, but in a different manner. Keith tossed him in the air and caught him, the way Pa did. Both men tickled his ribs, and both fed him cookies. Their relationship with him was one of fun and merriment.

Tower, to do him justice, had made a lucky approach. But Rae-Ellen felt Vic was too young for it. Sure, he understood that Silver Dart drank milk when she nursed. And he'd *seemed* to understand that the foal couldn't eat cookies, even appeared to accept the statement that he himself couldn't eat all the cookies he wanted.

That was ridiculous, she decided. A lucky accident for Tower. This knowledge enabled her to stand quiet and watch him continue to show off. This was a one-time thing only. He hadn't the experience or, she knew firsthand, the patience to deal with a headstrong child. It was absolutely infuriating. If Baby Vic only knew what a heel Tower was, he'd bite his finger to the bone!

Finally, Tower let Keith take Vic. Rae-Ellen noted

how gently Keith put the child astride the foal, how carefully he held him. She glanced at Tower to see whether he noticed Keith's gentleness as compared to his own near-rough handling of the child, but Tower was down at the other end of the stable, helping Compton and Johnny herd the horses out into the corral and beyond to pasture.

By the time he came back, Keith had turned Silver Girl loose and she had led her foal, gamboling at her heels, to the pasture. Keith offered to take Vic to the house. "Isn't it about time for his morning snack?" he asked.

"Yes, please do take him up, Keith," she said, smiling. "I have some things to go over with Tower."

When they were gone, Tower came long-legging to her.

"What did you make of that?" he asked.

"Make of what?"

"The way your kid acted with me."

"He was interested in the foal."

"He didn't try to bite me, not once."

"It was Silver Dart."

"Not altogether. We talked some. You heard."

She maintained a dignified silence. She was going to admit nothing to this night-prowler, this conceited show-off.

She saw him getting mad, saw him actually force a casual look onto his face. She watched his mouth. If they didn't hate each other so, she would have thought there was a touch of softness on his lips.

"That relationship I mentioned once," he said. "It'd work out between me and the kid. It's up to you—it'd work out between us too."

331

"Like those movie friends of yours? A relationship a month, and call it love?"

"Some of them love. They do."

"Like Veronica and Burton? For how long?"

"Long enough to have kids, marry."

"The marriages don't last."

"Ours would. If we took it that far. Because we're farm people, not keyed-up actors. And you can't judge by Veronica and Burton. She's set to be another Garbo."

"Because we're farmers, we'd succeed?"

"Or have a pretty good chance."

"Not good enough, Tower!"

"Meaning I'm still not good enough?"

"If you want to take it that way, yes!"

"Come to my rooms. Let me demonstrate. I dare you."

If he hadn't dared her, she wouldn't have gone. But she'd not back down from him. As it was, she spun on her heel, ran to the house, passing Keith on his way back to the stable. Inside, she checked on Vic, who was with Leah.

Then she checked the house. Susie's car was gone and so was Dots's, but she wanted to make sure they themselves were absent. Then she went running down the dogtrot, chin out. She got to Tower's rooms. He was waiting on the bench outside.

Not speaking, they went in, undressed, lay on the bed. If she hadn't been so mad at him for showing off she would almost have admitted the tenderness of his sex, which verged on lovemaking. There *was* tenderness in it.

She was always in bed with him now, it seemed,

moving with him, couldn't seem to end it. Sex between them had become both stimulating and soothing. But it solved nothing, she thought miserably, changed nothing.

One big fact remained: Jess Tower was an impossible man who was messing up her whole life. Yet, knowing this, she felt herself soar again to ecstasy with him and suddenly, inexplicably, wanted to cry. And would not, because it would only lead to another fight.

Jess, because she acted the same as ever, decided he'd proved nothing to her at all. Well, let her go. There was no getting through, not to this hellcat.

Chapter Thirty-three

AFTER that, Rae-Ellen went to Jess Tower every night—only, she told herself grimly, because she had to get him out of her blood. Then and then only would she be free to really go after Drew while there was still time. Or, for that matter, to consider marrying one of the other men with whom she'd had sex.

Again and again she went over the list. Drew was perfect. He'd been created to be her husband, to be father to her baby.

Keith Belisle had shown her, in lovemaking, all the warmth and tenderness any woman could desire. He was honestly affectionate toward her son, and Vic responded. Keith would be a splendid father.

Grant Miller too had his good points. With him she had discovered that sex could be a healthy, clean, delightful experience. Life with him would match the sex. If she grew to love him. This she considered often, pushing away the thought of Bertha Mudd. Probably, if Rae-Ellen married either Grant or Keith, she'd come to feel friendly affection for him. Which was more than many married couples had.

There was Link Bradley, with whom she'd been unable to try out sex. Because he was so thoroughly decent, had treated her so kindly, she hadn't been able to experiment with him. Now she regretted it. Instinctively, she knew their sex would be above average.

And he and Vic would get along. That she saw every time Link came to the house, for the baby went running to him and wanted to ride horse on his foot and Link tirelessly obliged. Never, not once, had Vic tried to bite Link or any of the others.

Only Jess Tower. That itself put him out of the running. She needed only to cleanse herself of the unholy hunger he roused, and he'd be finished business.

And if she couldn't? She'd cut him off abruptly, go after Drew like mad. With a twinge, she realized that if she won Drew, her frienship with Susie would be destroyed. She set her jaw. Susie had only herself to look out for. Rae-Ellen had to procure, not only a husband, but a respected and suitable father.

Thus she arose, next morning, into a hot, brassy sunrise, her mind made up, spirits high. Of course Drew would love her! She'd so far surpass Susie that he'd be helpless to do otherwise. She'd win him, oh, she would!

Because the late November weather was unseasonably hot, she put on a pair of electric-blue shorts and a sleeveless shirt to match. She dressed Vic in a red sunsuit and sandals. After breakfast, they started for the stable to see Silver Dart, this now being a ritual, and saw Keith first thing.

"Thought you'd be out early," he said, grinning. He picked up the boy, who was chattering about Silver Dart, hoisted him to his shoulder for the trip to the stable.

"Why did you think we'd be early?" Rae-Ellen asked, laughing. She was in love with the world because she simply *was* going to win Drew. Beginning today.

"The weather," Keith explained. "Last hot day of the year, all that. I hate to see cool weather come on."

"I like the changing seasons," Rae-Ellen declared. "Oh, I enjoy a hot day like this, even love to go to Florida during the winter season, but not to live."

"Texas is where you want to stay, then?"

"Oh, yes! I used to think North Carolina, back home, was best! But now I'm a confirmed Texan!"

He looked into her face seriously, and she felt a throb of alarm. Was he going to propose again? But he only smiled and said, "Nothing could drag me out of Texas. Or off this farm. Unless you personally fired me."

She laughed again. "As if that'd ever happen!"

"I sure hope not. I've got aspirations, remember."

Her pulse quickened, but his tone betrayed that he expected a response. And he deserved one; he'd asked her twice to marry him, and that was an honor.

337

"What are your . . . farm aspirations?" she asked, careful to avoid any hint of romance.

"Why, to be manager after Tower goes back to California," Keith replied easily. "I'm learning from him; he's generous about teaching me things."

This praise of Tower rankled Rae-Ellen. "What is he trying to do, give you a crash course in everything he learned in college?" she snapped.

"He's not like that. Look, I know you don't get along with the guy, but he's not too bad, you know."

"I never said he was, Keith."

"It's just that your dispositions don't hit it off. You look at each other, and sparks fly. He's good with the horses, and he's teaching Compton and Johnny a lot, too. Time he's gone, if you see fit to make me manager, we'll be in top-notch shape."

"Consider it settled," Rae-Ellen said quietly. "You'll have to hire a new foreman, I suppose."

"No, Compton can be foreman. I was thinking it'd be good to hire a couple of younger men, train them, and, as the herd grows, hire another man and train him."

"Whatever you think," Rae-Ellen agreed. Surprised that she didn't feel a keen interest, she decided it was the heat or the fact that she hadn't yet devised a way to get in Drew's company, or both.

She saw Tower come out of the office at the far end of the stable. He was forever studying the bloodline charts. It was too soon for the almost mandatory farewell party for him—he had two months yet—but she could give *a* party. That was a way to be with Drew, to launch her final campaign. To steal him from Susie.

By the time they'd reached the stable, had gone inside and played with Silver Dart and petted her dam, Rae-Ellen was sweating. Baby Vic was covered with a film of perspiration. Keith wiped his brow with a bandana, saying this was the hottest day he'd ever seen in November.

Rae-Ellen took Vic outside to cool him off. There wasn't a breath of air stirring. The sun bore down, unbearably hot, and she moved into the shade of the stable and wiped Vic's sweat-streaming little face with her bandana.

Keith followed. Tower came to where they were standing, and said one of the fillies was ready to breed. Vic ran to him, wanting to ride on his shoulders, but Rae-Ellen caught him up into her arms and carried him toward the corral where Tower said the filly was penned up for her inspection. Vic struggled, then quieted, eyes on Tower, his damp face solemn.

Platinum was the filly in question, and Rae-Ellen stood quietly while Tower pointed out all her good qualities. "She may turn out to be one of your best dams," he said. "Look at that head on her, those hindquarters!"

She had to agree. He was right.

"How about Thunder Boy for the sire?" she asked.

"He's the one I had in mind. I've just checked his papers, and Platinum's. They're a good match. Also, he could stand at stud over the county, on a selective basis. Unless you take him to Florida to race."

"I've decided against that," she said coolly. "I don't choose to mix racing and breeding. This is to be a breeding farm only."

He nodded, and this irritated her. "That's the way

339

I feel about my place," he said. "I've never raced one of my horses."

They returned to discussing Platinum and Thunder Boy, Vic playing at their feet. Jess had given him four corn cobs and he was happily trying to stack them on top of one another, chortling and squealing and laughing when they fell and rolled. Over and over he did this, getting hotter by the moment. Rae-Ellen wondered if Tower noticed what perseverance her son had, but he wouldn't mention it and she certainly wasn't going to.

Suddenly Rae-Ellen noticed that the sun, which before had been so hot and glaring, had disappeared. Right then the wind blew in, ruffling her hair, and she smelled the wind, cold. The sky was dull above them and a dark, bruised blue in the north. Leaves scuttled along the ground. Gooseflesh stood on the sweaty Vic, and Rae-Ellen shivered.

"What's going on here?" Tower asked. "What makes it so cold, of a sudden?"

"Feels like a norther...a blue norther," Keith said. "Looks it, too."

"How do you know it's a blue norther?" Tower asked. He scooped Vic up and carried him, shielding him, as well as he could, from the wind as they hurried toward the house.

"Pa Travis told me," Rae-Ellen said, anxious to get warm clothes on Vic. "It comes without warning, out of nowhere—like this."

"And gets bad?"

"Terrible. It's a murderer of a storm that blows snow before it, unbelievable amounts of snow, piles it

340

deep. Then it whistles across the snow and paralyzes everybody and everything for days!"

Tower whistled, shook his head.

"And then," Rae-Ellen continued, "it blows away and the sun comes out as if it had never even been cold, and melts the snow. Am I right, Keith?" she finished.

"Absolutely," said Keith, walking on the other side of Tower. "Mr. Travis is expert on these storms. Most of us get to know them—we've been through our share."

"A blue norther," Compton, who had come along, now said, "will drop the temperature more than forty degrees in forty minutes. You can hardly believe it, it's so fast."

"You can watch a thermometer and see it," Johnny, who had also followed, added. "I've done it myself!"

"It gets so cold you wouldn't believe it," Keith said. He watched the ugly sky, began to trot, the others keeping pace. "Looks like this could be a real bruiser," he said. "We'll use the whole crew to get you and Vic inside, see the windows are tight, start the furnace. Then we'll see to the horses! That okay, Jess?"

"That's for sure!" Jess exclaimed. "I need all the help and instructions you fellows can give me!"

The wind blasted, scuttling them along. Dry leaves swirled around their shoulders, swept into their hair, plastered their faces.

"Looks like we're in for it!" shouted Keith. "Got to get ready right away!"

Inside the house, Tower set Vic down and he ran for the kitchen. Keith switched on the furnace and

Compton and Johnny tested the windows, locking them to make them tighter.

"I need more information about the storm itself," Tower told Keith. "Tell me, then we'll make a dive for what's to be done."

"Well," Keith replied, "there's the wind, like we said. Icy wind that drives through towns and across rangeland, lashes the herds that bunch together, goes through every crack in the shanties and the hides of the people inside. Kills some of them. Kills cattle. Piles snow everywhere. Right in Texas, we get killer snow with these northers, hard as it is to imagine."

"Let's get the horses inside," Tower said.

He opened the back door. The wind came in a hard gust, an icy wind that cut, and on it were hard, piercing flakes of snow. While Tower was fighting the door, a new gust brought softer snow, and more of it.

Jess personally fought Thunder Boy and Silver Fox into their stallion stalls and saw to it they couldn't budge their gates to get at Platinum. Then he put the filly into the last stall and fastened her in securely. While he was doing this, the other three got all the horses, including Silver Girl and Silver Dart into their stalls and began to feed.

After this, following the pattern Keith laid out, Jess had Compton put a big metal floor pad in the stall next to Silver Girl and her foal. Johnny set a large electric heater on the pad and plugged it in. While this was being done, Jess fastened a blanket on Silver Girl, a smaller one on the foal, while Keith and Compton put blankets on the other horses. Johnny continued to set up heaters on metal pads in vacant stalls, until, when he finished, there were six of the stoves throwing out heat.

"Do the heaters help very much?" Jess asked.

"A whole lot," Keith said. "Travis uses them for his prize stock every norther. They don't make it warm, but do keep the temperature up enough that, with the blankets, the cattle—and here the horses—will come through fine."

"What about the rest of Mr. Travis's cattle?" Jess asked.

"They use those hay-filled shelters on the range," Keith replied. "They serve as windbreaks, the cattle he leaves out are hardy, and they hunker together and survive. He's only lost a very few."

When all the horses were blanketed, the men brought in buckets of drinking water and sacks of feed to use along with the hay from the big loft. A bit of warmth began to emanate from the stoves.

Inside the house, Leah and Susie and Dots kept the furnace regulated. They ran buckets of drinking water, then Leah turned the water off outside so it wouldn't freeze and burst the pipes.

All the while, snow blew on the wind, thickened, built up on fence rails and at the edges of buildings. Already the falling snow was so thick it was hard to see through.

Rae-Ellen dressed Vic in his warmest clothes. She herself hustled into woollen slacks and laced boots. "How long does a blue norther last?" she asked the other girls.

"Two days, three, a week," Susie said. "And they're so lonely! Jess and Keith will stay at the stable, I

343

know they will, and it'll be just us females in the house. And the baby."

The phone rang. Rae-Ellen grabbed it, to find Pa Travis on the other end. "Got things all set here," he told her. "I'm coming over to your place for the duration. Rosita too."

"But what about your cattle?"

"Under control, with my foreman in charge and plenty of men to help him. Tower's never been through one of these. He needs more than just Keith to protect all that horseflesh you've got there!"

They hung up. The phone rang again. This time it was Drew, saying he was coming if he was allowed. His sheep and work crew were prepared for the worst; he himself wasn't needed. Joyously, Rae-Ellen told him to make it fast and hung up again. She was trembling. Was Drew coming for her sake, or for Susie's? Well, no matter. He'd be here; that was what counted. She didn't have to wait for the party.

The next time the phone went, it was Link, asking permission to ride the storm out at the Double T. "None of my clients will be in," he said. "And I might make myself useful out there."

Rae-Ellen gave him permission gladly. And when Grant called, said his place and Bertha's were secure and he'd like to be at the horse farm, again Rae-Ellen consented. She asked about Bertha, but he said Bertha wanted to stay at her own ranch and sent her best wishes to all.

Dots then insisted on inviting her Sammy. "It's turning into a house party!" she declared. "And it won't be like the one in California! This'll be a good one . . . we can even have popcorn and apples!"

Rae-Ellen laughed and hugged Dots. She counted mentally. There would be seven men: Tower, Pa Travis, Drew, Grant, Keith, Link, and Sammy. And Baby Vic for the eighth. As to women, there would be Rae-Ellen herself, Susie, Dots, Leah, and Rosita.

There'd be time—she'd make time—to be alone with Drew. Tenderly alone.

Chapter Thirty-four

BEFORE any of the storm people arrived, Rae-Ellen, peering out a window, saw Tower, wearing heavy clothing, making for the house lugging a coil of new, heavy rope. Behind him came Keith, also carrying rope. And still farther away, Compton and Johnny were moving from the stable to the other buildings, also carrying rope.

"Watch the baby!" Rae-Ellen told Dots. "I'm going outside to see what they're doing!"

She put on her short, heavy leather coat, pulled on woolen gloves, tied a scarf over her head, and hurried outdoors. Tower was on the back gallery, uncoiling his rope, and Keith was just arriving with his.

The wind hit Rae-Ellen in the face full-blast. She

brushed away the snow and blinked. "What's that for?" she cried, pointing at Tower's rope.

"Guide ropes!" Tower shouted above the howling wind. "This one goes to the stable! So does Keith's rope!"

"Guide ropes?" she shouted back.

"Ropes tied between points, from house to stable, from stable to granary, and so on. To feel your way in the dark and when the snow gets really thick."

"We've lanterns for that!"

"Lanterns aren't good enough!" Keith shouted now. "See how thick the snow is on the ground already...an inch, at least. When it gets so thick in the air you can't see through it by day or by lantern, the ropes are the thing to have. Jess is rigging the south rope to the stable; mine will be the north rope. That way, if anything happens to one of them, we'll still have a guideline between house and stable!"

Bewildered, Rae-Ellen looked from one man to the other. Tower shot her a look.

"Keith says the snow comes down in blankets!" he yelled. "Says by morning it'll be a couple of feet deep on the flat, and piled as high as the windows at the house!"

"It gets *that* bad?" cried Rae-Ellen.

"Worse, even!" Keith called. "And this is going to be one of the worst! That's our job now, to rig a network of ropes so we can follow a rope and go where we need to, storm or no storm!"

Grant appeared with a coil of rope to run from house to garage. Meanwhile, Tower tied the end of his rope securely to one of the slim pillars. Rae-Ellen watched him pull on it with his great strength. The

348

knot tightened. Then, uncoiling the rope as he went, he moved toward the stable through the snow. Rae-Ellen followed, the hard-driven flakes stinging her cheeks.

"Better get in out of the cold!" he warned.

"I want to watch!" she shouted. After all, it was her job; she couldn't tie those intricate knots and pull them tight, but she could examine every knot and see for herself that it was tight. It wasn't that she didn't trust the men—she even trusted Tower—but it was her ranch and she was responsible.

The wind gusted, blew steadily, gusted again, blew harder, bringing a heavier onslaught of snow. She ducked her head sidewise into it, laid her body against the wind, and pushed.

Jess wished to hell she'd go into the house. This was the kind of action on her part that got under his skin. She was always doing something bullheaded, or popping off, aggravating him and making him down-right furious. No wonder she was so hard to get out of his mind—she kept on and on. Never acted the way a normal, feminine woman did. Sure, she owned the horse farm, but she had no excuse to stalk him while he ran his rope.

Rae-Ellen stayed so close to Tower that she nearly stepped on his heels. Snow cut at her cheeks, made her lips wet and cold. She licked them, and that made it worse, because it felt as if the wind were freezing the dampness on them. At last, when she'd decided this trip was going to take an hour, they were at the stable.

Tower stopped at the south entrance and looped his rope around a post that kept the door from slamming open against the outer wall. The rope was too long, and he took out a pocket knife, opened it with his teeth, sawed the rope off. He hitched the end around the post, making the knot very tight, then anchored it with half the rope he'd cut off.

Rae-Ellen surveyed the long, long rope path leading from stable to house. The snow was already so thick she could barely see the rope, which was waist-high to her.

Tower started back along it. She followed.

The wind was gustier, colder, with heavier snow. She saw the other men going toward other buildings, playing out rope. When she and Tower reached the back gallery, it looked as if it had a rope knotted to it.

Grant was tying a short length to one of the ropes, strengthening it. "I finished the one to the garage!" he yelled. "This one goes to the granary!"

"Fine!" Tower shouted back. He took the short length he had left and reinforced the knot on his post, securing the south rope to the stable. "We'll have a network of ropes, time we finish! Nobody'll get lost, no matter how thick the snow or dark the night! Just grab the right rope and follow it!"

"You bet!" agreed Grant. "And even if you grab the wrong rope at first, all you have to do is keep changing ropes, and you'll end up at house or stable, one or the other!"

Rae-Ellen kept following as the men strung ropes. On she tramped, leaning into the cold wind, face numb, snowflakes blinding her. She practiced, followed the rope from house to granary; from granary to stable; one rope from stable to house, the other rope from house to stable. She followed the network to

350

the smokehouse to the chicken house, to the pig-pens, to the garage.

What a system! They could go from place to place in utter safety, didn't even need lantern or flashlight. And everything led to everything else. Suddenly, though she admired the plan, it struck her as a bit ridiculous.

She suggested this to Link, who had arrived in time to help. "Wouldn't just one rope from house to stable be enough?" she asked as they walked into the wind.

"No," he shouted. "Mr. Travis does it this way, and he's had less trouble than ranchers who don't take such pains!"

At that moment the norther really whirled down upon them, and it was worse than Rae-Ellen had expected. She stood outside a moment. In that short while the snow on the ground deepened and stood higher on the gallery rails. It threw itself against the windows of the house. She could see it thickening along the bases of buildings, growing into mounds there. She went inside when she could no longer see through the wind-driven curtain of white.

"How long does this part last?" she asked Grant as they took off their snowy wraps in the little back foyer.

"Hours, even days. We're in for a siege this time. It'd be certain death, even now, to wander outside if we didn't have the ropes."

In the living room, Baby Vic was shrieking. He was beating against a window, face covered with tears. There was nothing to be seen through the window; it was plastered solid with snow. He ignored

Pa Travis, who was trying to get his attention, jerked away from him, and roared at the mysterious outrageous swathe of white against which his small hands were trying to beat.

"Go 'way!" he shrieked, and wept and pounded on the glass.

Rae-Ellen scooped him into her arms and he struggled, roaring and kicking.

"He's afraid of the snow," Leah said.

"Afraid, hell!" snorted Pa. "He's plain mad at it!" He pulled the yelling child from Rae-Ellen's arms and she let him. He carried him into the kitchen, yanked the shades down, and shut out the sight of the snow.

"Damn fool windows in this house," he rumbled. "No shades in the living room, just them see-through curtains!"

"That's for sun and light!" Rae-Ellen retorted. "Vic loves those windows!"

"He'll quiet in his playpen," Pa said, making for where it stood in its corner. "Get him a cookie, Rosita!"

Rosita gave Vic the cookie Leah produced. He let up screaming, took a bite, then flung it away. He sobbed mightily, just once, flung himself onto his back and lay gnawing his thumb, eyes wide and accusing.

"Outgrowing cookies," Pa said.

Leah produced a small, wool-filled comforter and covered Vic. Rae-Ellen turned away, grateful for the respite. Knowing her son, she was certain he wouldn't remain quiet for long.

With Pa, she made for the living room where Dots

352

and Susie were talking with Sammy and Drew, both of whom had arrived in time to inspect the network, then, finding there was nothing for them to do immediately, had come inside. Rae-Ellen smiled a greeting at Drew. He'd come, she thought, to be with Susie. But she herself fully intended to take advantage of being snowbound in his company.

She asked, "Is everybody comfortable? Leah has a cake and says she's going to make coffee. She'll keep a pot of chili simmering for the duration."

Drew and Susie looked up, smiled, resumed their murmuring. Rae-Ellen's impulse was to join them, break up their cozy closeness, but she overcame it and turned to Grant, who had followed her. If Susie was now in the very act of confessing about her affair with Keith, and he was forgiving, it was too late.

She chatted with Grant and the others automatically. Of course Susie wasn't confessing! Not here, not now. It would be foolish for Rae-Ellen to assume that and give up any effort to entice Drew. Later, she thought. Later I'll get him alone. I will!

She kept an eye on the vast windows. The snow was plastered solid against the glass. Even when she went to a window and tried to see out, there was only the ever-thickening coating of snow. She wondered how deep it was at the stable.

The men were in and out constantly, even Compton and Johnny, knocking snow off their shoulders, stamping it off their boots. Pa Travis, Keith, Link, Grant, Sammy. Even Drew tore himself away from Susie, went outside and was gone a long time before he returned. He reported that the horses were doing all

353

right, that the foal was lying against her dam, who was nuzzling her.

The foal! Rae-Ellen thought, jolted. She'd been so stunned by the sudden vicious storm, so intent on the network of ropes knowing the horses were in the stable with heat going, that she hadn't gone inside to see them. Could Silver Dart survive the merciless norther? Rae-Ellen's impulse was to wrap up and follow a rope to the stable, but Pa set up such an uproar that she decided to wait. She'd go when he was at the stable and couldn't hell-and-damn about her leaving the house and Baby Vic.

Why hadn't Tower come to the house as the others had done? It was just as well. He'd never been through a norther; he was liable to do some crazy, dangerous thing. Wherever danger was, he had a talent for getting into trouble.

She longed to be at the stable, but for once Pa was right. Baby Vic took priority. He was out of his playpen, tired of playing in the kitchen, and back in the living room, staring at windows. He began to scream and cry when he found they were all blotted out with white stuff. Rae-Ellen and the other women, Pa Travis and whatever other men were inside, tried to quiet him and failed.

At times they got him into the playpen with toys and there was peace. But he didn't sleep, just grew more irritable, shrieked until he was hoarse. He was tired, there were circles under his eyes, but he wouldn't relinquish his battle with the windows.

Hours passed. The men took a thermos of coffee to Tower, and a bucket of chili. He wanted to keep a close watch on Silver Girl and her foal and on the other pregnant filly. He sent word that he'd be up later.

Darkness came early, still filled with driving snow. The men said it was dumping out of the sky now, that they'd never seen such a snowfall, even in the worst norther.

"And I remember a good lot of 'em," Pa declared. "This one's got 'em beat a mile."

Grant, on one trip in, reported drifts up to four feet along some of the buildings. Even the ropes were snow-covered.

Susie, getting Rae-Ellen alone for a moment, confided that she'd told Drew about herself and Keith. "He was disappointed, said so, but he said it makes no difference. He still wants to marry me!" she whispered shakily. "I'm the luckiest girl in the world!"

Defeat rolled over Rae-Ellen. Somehow it wasn't as crushing as she'd thought it would be. Because, for some reason, she was upset about Jess. Why hadn't he, in all this time, made one trip to the house? They came and went so much she couldn't keep track of who was in the stable, who was following a rope somewhere, only of who was in the house. And it was never Jess. And there was no need for him to just *stay* out there; even Pa said all the horses were in top shape, warm as toast.

She sat in a living-room rocker and tried to cuddle Vic, but he wouldn't be cuddled. He stared at the white windows and sobbed; sometimes he roared. She put him down, he toddled to a snow-clogged window, small face furious, and set his palms against the icy glass. The biting cold made him jerk his hands back and he screamed, "No . . . no!" and began to screech again and they couldn't quiet him.

Jess, snow-covered, came in on this uproar, swept the screaming Vic up and shouted with laughter. With Rae-Ellen crying out that Vic hated the snow, Jess took some from his coat, put it on the baby's hand and said, "Snow." Vic stopped screaming, hiccuped, and stared at the snow on his hand.

"Snow, nice snow," Jess told him quietly. "Nice snow melts, goes away." And it did.

The boy stared at the wet spot on his hand, stared at Jess, who chuckled and put his finger out. The baby stared at it. A breath quivered through his sturdy little body. He grasped the finger, drew it to his mouth, and began to gnaw contentedly.

Jess shot a look at Rae-Ellen, infuriating her. He looked so . . . so triumphant. He dropped the baby into her arms. Vic reached out for Leah and quavered, "Cookie," and Rae-Ellen let him go to the housekeeper. She glared at Tower, unable to decide whether she was grateful, dismayed, or simply cross.

"Just came in to report," Jess told her. "All animals are in good shape, the foal too. And the pigs. And the chickens."

She nodded.

He started for the door, and Rae-Ellen followed. "Wait," she said. "I'm going with you."

"The hell you are. That snow's a solid wall. How else do you think it's mounded so fast? It's all I can do to keep my hand on the rope. Half the time, I wasn't even sure I had the right rope."

"I want to see my foal!"

"Vic's foal."

356

"You know what I mean! I want to see with my own eyes—"

"You're not going out in this storm!"

"Manager or not," she whispered, "you don't manage me! I'll come to the stable when I choose!"

"You do that," he growled, "and I'll drag you back by the hair! That's a promise!"

He stomped out, and she stalked into the living room. She collected Vic from Leah and, with Dots and Susie helping, put him to bed. He fell asleep instantly, worn out from his day and evening-long battle with the snow.

Chapter Thirty-five

Ess, who had a strong hunch that Rae-Ellen, hellcat and fool that she was, might indeed come to the table, hunched into his coat, pulled his earflaps tight, and gripped his flashlight in one gloved hand. With the other hand he located the rope leading to the south end of the stable—having told the men at both ends that that was the rope he would use—and stood for a second drawing the cold air into his lungs.

It pierced like icy needles, stung his nostrils and forehead. He'd never experienced such cold weather.

Carefully, he went down the gallery steps into above-ankle snow. It had got deeper during those few minutes he'd been in the house. He wondered how deep it would get, on level ground, before it quit; thought of the cattle hunched in shelters, hoped they'd be able to root through the snow and get at the hay piled there.

The constant wall of snow hit him broadside, hurling out of the darkness. He drew another breath, and it was half air, half snow. He coughed, ducked his mouth toward his coat collar and breathed carefully, using it as a makeshift filter. He kept a careful hold of the rope, his hand already freezing cold, and began to move along it toward the stable.

Snow enveloped him in an endless, freezing blanket. He wished he'd stayed in the house a bit longer to warm up. But between quieting Vic, who settled right down as soon as he had snow explained to him, and then getting into a fight with Rae-Ellen, he'd even forgotten to limber up his hands. Now they were like ice chunks, both the one sliding along the rope, and the one pointing the flashlight uselessly at the falling snow.

The flashlight's rays shone no more than two inches into a world of ink and whiteness. He moved on, his feet, already cold when he started for the stable, now chunks like his hands. He couldn't take proper steps, had to push and drag them through the snow.

Now he sensed someone on the rope. He shouted: "Who is it? Tower here!" But the only reply was a howl of wind and a mouthful of snow.

He swallowed the snow, moved on slowly, carefully. This was the most dangerous situation he'd ever been in, worse than the mudslide. There he'd had people helping him. Here he had only a rope and a virtually useless flashlight. He wasn't alarmed, but he was completely aware of what could happen should he lose that rope.

If he fell, as he might easily do, and rolled to one side or the other of the rope, he'd be in a real mess. Because, feeling for the rope, he could go too far to the right, too far to the left, and never find it. He could stagger, shouting, forever looking for the lost rope, forever trying to make himself heard by those who weren't present.

He'd only imagined he'd sensed someone on the rope, he thought. No point in waiting to make sure. It was too cold to stand still. He needed to keep moving.

He moved with total care. When he was perhaps a third of the way to the stable, as best he could figure, he stopped. He'd better go back to the house. Have it out with Rae-Ellen. Get her promise that she'd not come out on the rope. They'd have a big fight, sure, but that didn't matter. He had to see to it that she stayed inside.

Then he remembered that Mr. Travis had been inside. While Jess was quieting Vic, he'd heard Travis say none of the girls were to go to the stable, that he was going to stay inside and see to it that they didn't.

Jess pondered, snow beating and wrapping him head to foot, swirling around him, biting his face, piling up on his eyebrows. Would Rae-Ellen listen to the old man? She hadn't wanted Jess for her manager, but Travis had hired him and he was still on the job. Yes, he decided, the old man would keep her safe if he had to tie her up.

He moved again, slowly making for the stable, pulling his leaden boots through the deepening snow, taking the force of the snow in his face. He closed his eyes as he walked, and the rope was the only connection he had with the house, the stable, with life.

At about what had to be halfway to the stables, he stopped again. Suppose Travis didn't tie Rae-Ellen up if she needed it? What if all of them there in the house—and whoever might have traveled the north rope—failed to convince her? Would any of the men be fool enough to let her go to the stable with him, on the rope? Or would they leave her, as he had done, and she'd start out—sneak out—on her own?

There was only one thing to do. Turn, fight his way back to the house, persuade...order...threaten...do anything to make her stay inside, not to risk her life in this hell of snow.

Or, at worst, after he thawed out, if she went bullheaded on him, bring her along on the rope himself, make sure she got to the stable, then keep her there until the storm ended and they could see where they were going. That might be two days, even three, the world blotted out with falling walls of snow, but at least she'd be safe.

And raising hell to get to her kid.

It was then he heard his name. "Jess!" somebody called, a voice thin in the windy night. "Jess...you out there?"

His pulse lunged. Rae-Ellen? "Here!" he bellowed. "South rope! Where are you?"

There was no answer. He shouted again. Silence and snow and freezing blackness. He started toward the house. If it was Rae-Ellen, that was where she'd be, between here and the house.

He tried to move faster, shone his light, could see

nothing but whiteness. Snow clogged his eyelashes, got into his eyes. On he moved, calling her name.

There was no answer, but he kept going, shouting.

Suddenly, from behind, he was attacked with such fury that his flashlight flew away and he lost his grip on the rope. He went staggering forward, slammed facedown in the snow, fought to his knees, to his feet, numb hands in clumsy fists, and waited.

He could hear panting. More than one person panting. Blindly, he drove his lump of right fist at the panting. It crunched into what might be a jaw; he heard someone grunt, felt that someone brush him as he fell silently into snow.

Two men, his alerted brain reminded him. There are two men. He listened for the panting again, didn't hear it, but instead heard the first one staggering and grunting up, and swung his fist again.

This time, he missed, but one of them, the panting one, landed a fist on the side of his head and he plummeted backward into the snow. He rolled, got to his knees, his feet, stood in a crouch, fists ready, listening, sensing, waiting his chance.

Something crashed down on his head, hard; he felt the pain to his heels. He was aware of a scratchy bag being yanked over his head. And then he was drifting into utter blackness.

He felt nothing as two bulky figures fumbled for the rope, found it, took turns gripping him at the back of his collar, dragging him. They stumbled and staggered, fighting to keep the rope, to keep themselves oriented, but when they reached the stable, they didn't drag Jess inside.

Instead, they changed to another rope, and after that rope followed a third one.

He wasn't aware that they dug a trench in the mounded snow, tied his hands and feet, that they rolled him into the trench, covered him with snow, scooped snow over him until he was only a mound among other mounds. He knew nothing of how cleverly they retraced their ropes to the stable, where they reported that the storm was worse, much worse.

Over all the shanties and ranch houses and shelters in the pastures, the storm rampaged. It dumped the white, freezing blanket, spread it ever deeper, kept spreading and mounding, along the fences, along the buildings, over the already thick mound where Jess Tower lay in total unconsciousness.

Chapter Thirty-six

RAE-ELLEN could tell the storm was getting worse. She kept opening the back door, peering out across the gallery, the floor of which was now thickly covered with snow.

"What you popping in and out for?" Pa Travis asked.

"To see how things are."

"Don't hatch any ideas about going to the stable. I heard you and Jess."

"Then you heard for yourself how bossy he is! You can see why I want him fired!"

"He'll not be fired, not by a long shot. Take tonight. He may be new to a blue norther, but he catches on fast! He knows they're killers and he's ready to fight."

"That's just it! How can he fight? He's never been through one before! It's not safe for him even to go along that rope by himself!"

"Safe as it is for the others."

"Oh no it isn't! They're experienced! You notice Sammy doesn't run back and forth! He'd got sense enough to stay inside!"

"Jess's got sense. He can follow a rope. Hell, anybody can."

"Including me! It's my farm, and they're my horses, and—"

"You're staying put," Pa said. His tone was grim. "I ain't having my grandson's ma traipsing around in this norther!"

"You think I'd get killed, maybe *drown* in snow? Don't be ridiculous!"

"I know for sure you could die if you lost the rope. It's bad enough that my grandson lost his pa and you're too bullheaded to... I ain't about to let you risk him losing his ma, too!"

Rae-Ellen's teeth clicked together in surprise. She hadn't thought of that! Trust Pa. As usual, he'd put her into an impossible position. Now he was making her choose between staying in the house with her baby or going out to make sure that crazy Jess wasn't in some kind of trouble again.

She glared at Pa. She didn't know what to say or do. And then her mind began to function, and she could reason. This was a blue norther, and it had wind, yes, but she'd been through a really bad hurricane in Florida with terrible winds over a hundred miles an hour. And with trees uprooted, branches

366

and debris flying through the air and rain sluicing down. Talk about killer storms!

This storm, actually, was no worse than that. Just different. All she had to do was hold on to the rope, slide her hand along, let the wind cover her with snow, endure the cold, and in just a few minutes she'd be in the warm stable. And stay there, to make sure Tower did nothing foolish. What foolish thing he might do, she couldn't think, but past events had taught her that he had a talent for getting into trouble.

Hotly, she tried to explain this to Pa. And that also she wanted to see with her own eyes how her horses were getting along.

"You're crazy!" snorted the old man. "Jess can take care of himself *and* the horses! He finds out you think he can't, he'll quit his job and you'll be without a manager!"

"That's no threat," Rae-Ellen said fiercely, hands on hips. "I've wanted him fired all along, remember? If he wants to quit, that'll make me very happy!"

And it would. He'd be gone, and there'd be no need to try to get him out of her system. And he'd not be trying to ride in rodeos and breaking his foot, he'd not be sinking in quagmires, and getting a knife thrown at him. Of if he did, it would be someplace else, and no responsibility of hers, none at all.

She told Pa Travis all this, too.

He gave her a straight look. As if he were reading her, to the bone. As if he knew the emotional trouble Tower had caused her and knew, but didn't care, that her dearest wish was to be rid of Jess Tower.

"Only time a woman ought to feel responsible for

them things," Pa drawled, "is for her man, her husband. Not for somebody whose guts she purely hates."

The only thing that saved her from having to give him some kind of answer was that Drew came in the back door. Pa went striding to him, and Rae-Ellen followed. All the other women—Leah and Rosita and Susie and Dots—had gone to bed.

"Things at the stable okay?" Pa asked Drew, who was shrugging out of snowy coat and cap and gloves.

"Couldn't be better," he said. "I've got those same heaters in my sheep barns. They really cut the worst of the chill, make it almost warm."

Pa gave him a look from under his brows. Drew had spoken the hated word sheep. Pa's dislike of the animals went so far he didn't want them mentioned in his presence. Rae-Ellen wondered what his reaction would be if only she had the right to tell him that she was going to marry Drew Knight, sheepman.

Because Drew looked so cold, Rae-Ellen gave him chili and coffee. He said he'd left Grant and Link and Keith, along with Compton and Johnny, at the stable.

"What about Jess?" Rae-Ellen asked. "He was on his way out. Didn't he get there?"

"I took the north rope in," Drew said. "Jess was probably on the south rope. You can pass that way and unless you yell at the right time never know the other fellow is there."

On edge, Rae-Ellen refilled Drew's chili bowl and coffee cup. Pa decided he'd have some, too. Rae-Ellen downed a scalding cup of coffee, making plans of her own, which she'd put in operation when Drew left and she could slip away from Pa.

When she thought she'd scream if he didn't budge, Drew finally left. Rae-Ellen put the dishes in the dishwasher, which couldn't be used until they turned the water back on, told Pa she was going to bed, said good night, and went to her room.

Here she put on her warmest slacks and laced on fleece-lined boots. She put on two wool shirts and her new lamb's-wool-lined leather jacket and two pair of heavy knitted wool gloves. She pulled on a stocking cap, winding the long end of it around her neck and up over her mouth.

Knowing Dots would be up at the first whimper out of Vic, she slipped out of her room into the dogtrot, flashlight in hand, but not turned on yet. Wind-driven snow blasted into her face, took her breath even through the protective stocking cap. Trailing her free hand on the house wall, she went slowly along the dogtrot, snowy wind whistling through it as it would through a funnel, piercing, cold, until she reached Jess's rooms. There, still following the wall, she turned left, moved the width of the apartment, stepped down into snow halfway to her knees, dropped her flashlight, floundered, searched, couldn't find it, went stubbornly on.

She followed the house wall until she reached the back gallery and eventually located the south rope to the stable. Light shone from the kitchen where Pa, unaware of what she was up to, sat keeping vigil.

She put her right hand on the rope and moved away from the house. Cold sliced into her nostrils and through her head; it pierced into her lungs and she held it there. On she moved; when her held breath ached until she could stand it no longer, she gasped in more icy air, this time through her mouth, covered by the stocking cap, and it was fully as cold.

Steeling herself, she inched along, hand on the icy rope that swayed in the wind so she had to grip it firmly or lose it. She didn't know, after a blowing, snowy eternity of swaying rope, whether she'd been caught into this great, dark freezer of the world an hour, a night plus a day, or even a week. There was only the cold, the wind, the snow, the stumbling, dragging movement, the icy knives of cold stabbing her lungs, her vitals, numbing her body more and more, turning it into a ponderous, frozen clod.

Somehow the wind tore the long end of the stocking cap loose and it moved and whipped, and wind shot icy fingers past the collar of her coat. When she snatched a breath, snow got into her lungs, and she coughed. And then snow got into her mouth. Once it clogged her nose.

"Jess!" she screamed over and over. "*Wait!*" Surely he was ahead of her on the rope, had to be. "*Jess!*" But his name didn't come out as a scream. It was a whisper only; she couldn't hear it herself.

She wondered, frozen, how far she had come. And then she ceased to wonder, ceased to think, and inched along as she'd been doing forever and ever. She let the norther wrap her in unending swathes of snow.

Abruptly, the rope ended. There was a post. She let go the rope, put her hands on the post, then took it into her arms. The stable. She'd got to the stable. She staggered toward dim light from a tiny window, found the door, fought it open and stumbled inside, to be enveloped by the absence of cold and the presence of warmth. She could hear horses, could almost smell them, but her nose was too cold.

She was aware of movement. She blinked in the lantern light at the men surrounding her. Drew, of course, and Keith. Grant and Link. Compton and Johnny.

No Jess.

"Where's Tower?" demanded Grant. "How come he let you make the trip on the rope by yourself? And what are you doing here?"

"L-looking for Jess," she told them. "Didn't he get here?"

"No," Drew said. "We thought he'd used the south rope. I used the north."

"He did, but he didn't stay long," she gasped. "He took the south rope back. And I came on the south rope, and he wasn't there!"

The men stared at her.

She was warming up a bit, but hardly noticed.

"You're playing some kind of joke!" she cried, in a panic. "He did come back! I know he did, because I got here on his rope, don't you see, and he wasn't—"

"Did you step into any of his tracks?" asked Drew.

"No. Or maybe... I don't know... once I fell!"

Though the stable air was warm, she could scarcely breathe. Suppose he'd frozen, walking, lost the rope, got up, tried to find it, wandered goodness knew where? Suppose he was out there now, dying?

"Jess is a competent man," Drew said. "I know what you're thinking, Rae-Ellen, that he fell and lost the rope. Jess would operate efficiently. He'd stay right where he fell and feel above and about himself for the rope. Do you understand?"

She nodded. "I fell. That's what I did."

"He may have decided to go to the granary before he came into the stable," Grant said. "He wanted to get in some more corn for Silver Girl, let it warm up before she ate it."

"Then I'll go look! Which is the rope to the granary?"

"That's out of the question," Keith said. "You've just had a long, hard trip out from the house. And you took a spill."

"The sensible thing," Drew said, "is to wait a few minutes. Jess'll show up any time with that corn. He'd feel like a fool if we came rushing out, looking for him."

"I agree," Link said. "After all, he's the manager. He'll feel called upon to do more than we do."

"You don't understand!" wailed Rae-Ellen. "He's been gone a *long* time . . . he left before you got there, Drew, and you ate chili and drank. Something's happened to him! Don't tell me he'd make the rounds of the whole place!"

"He might just do that," Grant said. "He's the manager, and a capable one. Conscientious. In fact, I'd almost bet he *is* making rounds. And that he'll do the same thing tomorrow."

Drew was nodding agreement. Rae-Ellen could almost believe them. It was like Jess to poke his nose everywhere. The way he was made, he'd feel he should see to everything in person.

The men all consulted together. All agreed that Jess was making rounds. But they also agreed, bombarded by Rae-Ellen's passionate declaration that they'd already waited too long, to start a search in fifteen minutes.

While they waited, Pa Travis and Sammy Soose stumbled in. Pa glowered at Rae-Ellen, but didn't speak.

Sammy, however, was more talkative. "You upset us all, Rae-Ellen," he said. "Sneaking out to see your foal . . . Mr. Travis was set on coming to see if you're safe, and I came to keep him company."

Pa sensed something was wrong. He glanced about, demanded, "Where's Jess?" and they told him. They also told about the fifteen-minute wait, which was now ended, and still no Jess.

Pa Travis, being the most experienced in these storms, assigned ropes to the various men to search. Compton was to take the north rope to the house; Keith and Link the south rope to the house; Johnny the rope to the garage; Grant the rope to the granary; Drew the rope to the pigpens; Sammy the rope to the smokehouse; Pa himself chose the rope to the garage and the one to the chicken house.

"You stay in the stable, Rae-Ellen," he ordered. "Then if Jess comes walking in, you can explain. If he doesn't, we'll search until we find him."

They left, and Rae-Ellen was alone. She patted Silver Girl and the foal, checked all the electric stoves. She spread her coat to dry.

She paced the area between the two rows of stalls. The horses began to fidget. Then she sat down on a bale of hay and waited, and the horses grew quiet.

She thought of things she would say to Tower if he showed up. She'd point out how thoughtless he'd been to make the rounds without telling them, let him see that she, for one, recognized his conceit. That he had to do it all, get all the praise.

But under those things she was going to say to him, beat a new, strong feeling. Fear. She tasted it on her tongue. She was afraid that something had happened to him, that the men wouldn't get to him in time.

She began to pace again.

Chapter Thirty-seven

EVER so gradually there came awareness. He was. He existed. Slowly he sensed that there was a place and it was dark. The other thing, opposite of dark, was light. There was no light. He knew, dully and from far away, that he lay in blackness, and the blackness wasn't warm. It was cold, and he was cold.

That was his first sensation, the extreme cold. The next, enveloping him in a groping, gradual manner, was of being closed in. And then he identified the regular, heavy throbbing. It was in his head and coursed along his body, and for the first time he tried to move, to change things. And couldn't.

Think . . . think. The word rode his head, splitting it. *Remember.* And he drove himself to come awake, to know. And take stock, assess the situation. Find out where he was and who he was.

The pain grew worse because he was thinking, but he pushed that sluggish, throbbing mind on. And on. He was on his back, very cold. Hands and feet were like icy stone. Something over his head made it hard to breathe. Cloth.

Horses. There'd been horses. Snow. A storm. And there'd been a time when he was on his feet, pressing through snow to someplace. To horses. In the stable. Then someone—two people—had jumped him in the snow where there had been, someway, a rope. He'd fought. Something crashed onto his head, blacking out the snow.

And now there was this.

He tried to figure out where he was. Tried to move his hands. They were tied in front of him, at the wrist. He moved them as far as they would go and they came against what must be wood. A wall. His side was against a wall. He lifted his head, and snow pressed in, thumped onto the cloth over his face, and he knew he was lying in snow, was surrounded and covered and mounded in snow.

Heavily, he turned half on his side. His feet were tied at the ankle. But turning created a little space and now he could breathe. And breathing, he could almost think.

He remembered the rope now. It led from house to stable and he'd been following it to be with the horses. He'd been worried about something other than horses, but what it was eluded him. Suddenly he remembered the attack clearly—the crashing blow, the sack coming down over his head, the sinking into blackness.

He moved his head again, felt a weight slide off and an icy wind knife through the coarse weave of the sack. He pulled freezing air into his lungs, letting it bite, for it was clearing his head.

He had to get out of here, but carefully. There was something he'd known for a long time ... Yes, that was it. If a man is caught in a snowstorm and covers himself with snow, it will shield him, give him warmth, save his life.

Which meant that, until his half-frozen body was ready for action, he must not displace the snow that covered him. Prone under the snow, he drove his fingers to move; they responded like sticks of ice. He kept them moving. Sooner or later, he'd get some circulation there. He turned his feet back and forth carefully, so as not to dislodge his blanket of snow. He tried to move his toes. They wouldn't respond.

His mind was plodding, plodding. The ache in his head worsened, but he cudgeled his mind, demanding that it remember. He was something more than just a victim, buried in the snow. He was a man, he wanted out, and he wanted to know who he was.

Rae-Ellen! The name jolted through him.

He knew it all now, remembered how angry he'd been at her, recalled his concern that she'd venture into the storm, remembered the other men out in the stable, taking care of the horses.

When would they miss him, start a search? Or would they miss him? Would they think he was in the house, and themselves remain in the safe, warm stable, never dreaming he was here, in this condition?

He worked harder at restoring circulation. After he got it back, he'd lunge onto his side, knocking the snow away, get onto his knees, jump onto his bound feet, hop until he found the side of this building, until he found the rope that led to it. He'd keep that rope touching his hands as he hopped, following it, and it would lead him to people, and he would be freed.

Free to go to Rae-Ellen. To let her know what a fool he'd been. To explain to her that she was spirited and perfect and that her match was not to be found. To beg her, if he must, to overlook his past roughness. To apologize for telling her, in the plane from California, that he didn't want her.

Mind going in circles, hands and feet working, lying in what could well be his snowy grave, he realized his deep and burning love for Rae-Ellen. She was woman incarnate. She was warm and thrilling and exciting. She was tender when he gave her the chance to be tender. She was like Texas itself, the very soil of Texas, fertile and tempting, primal and open-armed.

Only he'd been too stubborn, too blind, to admit what she was. He'd treated her as no woman, not even a wicked one, should be treated. And there was no wickedness in her. Only that glorious spirit and that overflowing love waiting for the man with wits enough to go after it.

He tried to slide his feet toward his buttocks, to push himself up, but they wouldn't move yet. He lay turning them, forcing them, without a second's rest, back and forth. He kept working his fingers inside the gloves. He breathed deeply, the wet sacking

oming against his face as he inhaled strongly, not
moving away as he exhaled.

Then, suddenly, he blacked out again. All his
efforts to move ceased, and he lay in his snow-grave
while the wind thickened the white shroud over him.

Chapter Thirty-eight

PA Travis burst into the stable as Rae-Ellen paced. A blast of snow came in with him, and he fought the door shut.

"Has he showed up yet?" he demanded.

"No," she said tightly. "And you . . . ?"

"Not a sign. But some of the others'll find him, bound to."

"It's all my fault," she said tightly.

"How come?"

"I wanted to come with him and nobody would let me. If I'd done it anyway, we'd have been together!"

"Which proves what?"

"Oh, don't be dense! Together, we'd have kept on the rope! If one started away, the other would stop him! I'd have stopped him!"

"Why would he do that, wander away? That ain't like Jess."

"He may have fallen. Not been able to find the rope. He may have gone a step or two away from it, and then he'd never find it, be wandering out there in circles!"

He looked thoughtful.

Rae-Ellen stared at him wildly.

"Let's not go into a panic," he said. "One of the men is sure to find him."

Compton was the next man to return. "He ain't on the north rope to the house," he reported. "At least not now. And I didn't find no tracks like he might of been there."

"The snow'd cover the tracks in minutes," Pa grunted. "Chances are slim he'd use the north rope: he had a liking for the south rope."

"Maybe he *is* making the rounds, sir."

"Could be. If he is, someone'll meet up with him. Might take a spell if he found the pigs, say, in trouble. He'd try to shore them up, for sure."

The next one in was Johnny. "He ain't on the garage rope," he reported. "I tried to search off to both sides the whole round trip, but dasn't go too far from it or I'd be lost, too."

"You done right, Johnny," Pa said. "Soon as all the men get back, if nobody's found him or he ain't showed up yet, we'll reorganize and put out a real intensive search."

Keith and Link came in from the south rope to the house. "We saw nothing of him," Link said. "And he wasn't *in* the house. Everybody's up now, worried sick."

While they were all staring miserably at one another, Drew returned. He shot in at the door, snow behind him, stood knocking snow off his clothes.

"He's not on the pigpen rope. Hasn't been there, because a board was loose, letting in snow. I took time to patch it up. The pigs are doing fairly well. I fed them extra, too."

Pa scowled, lines cutting from nose to mouth. Rae-Ellen quivered. Two more to report, Grant and Sammy. She couldn't remember where they'd gone, but was on edge for them to get back. For only then would Pa mount an inch-by-inch search.

Ten minutes later, Grant and Soose were there, with nothing to report from granary or smokehouse. Both had taken tumbles and lost their ropes temporarily, which accounted for their getting back to the stable so late.

Rae-Ellen spun to Pa. "You said we'll really search now!" she cried. "Tell us what to do! The longer we wait—"

"Waiting's over," Pa said. "Compton, Johnny! Cut off three lengths of rope about four foot long!"

Rae-Ellen, not understanding, wildly impatient, began to pace again. "Stop that!" Pa ordered. "All of us in and out, and the storm, is hard enough on the horses! Think you'd know that!"

She sat down on a bale of hay, gripped her hands in her lap. It was hard to breathe. Panic balled in her chest and air seemed to be stopped by it. The condition eased off a bit when Pa passed out the lengths of rope, plus others he ordered cut.

"This time we go in teams," he said. "Tie the short rope onto the one leading to where you head, equal

383

lengths on each side. Make the noose free, so it'll slide along the guide rope. Then one of you get on each side of the long rope, hold to your end of the short one, and search that way."

"Clever idea, sir!" exclaimed Keith. "It means we can search out from the guide rope."

"You can go two feet, then you've got the span of your arms and legs. One can stay put at the long rope and the other search out four feet on his side. If he don't have luck, he comes back to the guide rope and the other fellow searches out four foot the other direction. That way, you'll not lose the guide rope."

"That's a big help," said Drew.

"And yell with no let-up," continued Pa. "Move slow. If you need to let go your short end, don't go but three steps from it, and then only if your lantern shows you your rope. And tell your partner what you're doing."

"What are the teams?" Rae-Ellen cried impatiently.

"Keith and Grant," Pa said promptly, "take the north rope to the house. Knight, you and I'll take the south rope. Link and Compton, take the granary."

"What about the garage?" asked Rae-Ellen. "Johnny and I could go to the garage!"

"You'll stay put," rumbled Pa. "The horses need somebody, don't lose sight of that. Keep your eye on the foal."

"She's safe with her dam! Jess is—"

"We aim to find Jess. And don't get the idea he's doing nothing about finding himself. You do what you're told."

He finished assigning ropes. Rae-Ellen watched

them leave. The door closed and she made certain the latch was secure so the wind couldn't blow it open and spook the horses. She paced; they stepped about nervously. She sat on her bale of hay; they quieted.

The longer she sat, the more frightened she grew. Jess could be lying anywhere along any rope, unconscious, covered with snow.

Suddenly she reached for her wraps. This time, after she zipped up her jacket, she tied the long part of her stocking cap around her face, leaving only her eyes uncovered. Then she put on her two pairs of gloves, spied a short length of rope with Compton's knife beside it, snatched them up. She closed the knife and put it in her chest pocket.

The instant she opened the door, the storm slammed her. The wind was sharper, colder; the snow was falling faster, the thickness of it beyond belief. Knowing the henhouse was last on the search route, she fastened her short rope to the henhouse rope.

Breathing through her scarf, she took the lantern that had been left behind to help light the stable, and started along the rope. Once on the ground, the snow was so deep she could scarcely pull her foot out, take a step, pull the other one out. She slid her short rope along with one hand, swung her lantern out as far as she could with the other, way out, peering keenly into the thick whiteness.

She screamed Jess's name without letup, and again couldn't hear her own voice over the howling wind. Even through the layers of stocking cap, the bitter cold burned her throat and knifed into her lungs.

She inched along the rope. Almost, she let go the

short length to range farther on either side, then dared not. If she herself got lost, she'd be no good to Jess.

She kept going, forever going. Screaming his name, swinging her lantern out, holding it out, standing in her tracks, seeking mightily to see, pulling herself on. The farther she went, the worse it got.

He was lost, she knew he was. They'd never find him, not her, not the others. He was dead, dead in the white snow, his wonderful, vital life smothered and frozen out of him. Tears ran from her eyes, hot on her cheeks at first, then icy, and now she couldn't see because of the tears.

Stumbling on, she wept. Oh, why hadn't she consented to the relationship he'd wanted? She'd had it in her power to make him happy and had refused. Now that it was too late, now, in this awful situation when he lay dead, she knew what a real man he had been—a man of the farm, of horses, of strength and tenderness, of wells of love that she had been too stubborn and blind to plumb.

Staggering, searching, she kept going. How could she ever have mistaken her crush on Drew for love? This, the shaking, bone-deep emotion she felt for Jess, was the real thing. And she'd had it in her hands; she could have lived with him, slept in his arms, felt his lips on her, could have luxuriated in his man's love. That, too, she realized now that it was too late. Jess had loved her. That was why he'd come to her again and again, just as she'd gone to him. He had given her love, and she had mistaken it for sex.

The wind froze her tears. Grief filled her laboring heart as she fought the storm. Maybe, by some

386

miracle, he *had* gone into the henhouse and was getting warm before coming back to the stable or going to the house!

After forever, her gloved hand bumped into the knotted rope at the henhouse. Feeling her way along the front wall, she found the door, opened it, half fell inside. There was dim light from the electric heater, from her lantern. The hens, on their roosts, clucked. A rooster cackled, then, when she didn't move, was quiet.

"Jess," she called. "Jess, darling, are you here?"

Silence. Except for more clucking; the rooster became indignant.

She moved about slowly, swinging her lantern so she could see. There were the roosts, filled with sleepy, disturbed chickens. There was the electric stove, throwing off warmth. There were chicken house tools, neatly hung on the wall.

No Jess. No sign that he'd been here.

She studied the tools, wondered if she dared take the shovel along. She picked it up; it was heavy. But she was going to take it. If she found a place that looked as if there might be a body underneath... The tears started again.

The shovel was too heavy. She couldn't manage both lantern and rope if she carried the shovel. She tried holding it under her left arm, but it slid down past the lantern in her hand and sank into the snow. Sobbing, she pulled it out, leaned it against the front wall of the henhouse. She could get back to it, if need be.

Keeping to the wall, she left the rope and made her tortuous way across the entire front of the building. She stepped into the snow then, pulled heavily around the corner, followed the wall again, shining the lantern. The snow was unbroken and smooth with new snow falling onto it faster than ever.

The first she knew of the mounded snow at the rear of the building was when she stumbled over it and fell face down in it. As she scrambled to regain her footing, the mound under her moved. Her heart sprang into her neck; she dropped the lantern and began to dig with both gloved hands.

"Jess!" she screamed. "Jess, is it you?"

Something moved again, and her hands came onto what must be sacking. She knew from the shape of the head under that sacking who it was. She'd felt its outline so many times, felt it in passion and joy, in love she didn't recognize!

He was alive! Jess was alive! She dug faster, thought of the shovel, wouldn't take time to go for it. When she got him uncovered, his hands seemed to be tied and his ankles were tied.

He had a knife on him, she knew he did. She started to dig for his pocket, remembered Compton's knife, which she had stuck into her own pocket, stripped off her gloves, got the knife and opened it. She cut the rope that tied the sack around his neck. It was Jess; the lantern light flickered on him.

"Who are you?" he asked. He knew who she was, but this might be part of the nightmare. He could be hallucinating.

Then he knew he wasn't hallucinating because she snapped, "Hold still! Now turn over!" She cut the ropes at his wrists, his ankles. Then she tugged at him, helping him up.

He was on his feet, stepping out of the grave, not accepting her help but doing it on his own as he did everything. "I've been working my muscles," he said. "We've got to get to the stable. I don't know where we are, but the horses—"

"There's no need to go to the stable ever again," said a voice from the snowing darkness. "You're not going to take a step, either one of you."

Chapter Thirty-nine

RAE-ELLEN recognized the voice. It was Keith. Not the warm, intense man who had made love to her, who had wanted to make her his wife, but suddenly a hard and vicious man with death in his tone.

She felt Jess, half-frozen as he was, tense to hurl himself at Keith.

"I've got a gun on you, Tower...don't move!" Keith snarled. "So has Grant! And we can see you by Rae-Ellen's lantern!"

Rae-Ellen moved to kick out the light, but Keith reached out and gave her a shove. "None of that! It'll only make the bullets come sooner!"

Rae-Ellen caught her balance, stood against Jess. He put his arm around her, held her close.

Grant, lantern flickering on him, laughed. "What a

pretty sight! Hugging each other, standing at thei grave, the one they're going to cuddle in together!"

"You're insane," Jess said. "To kill for no reason!"

"We've got solid reason," Keith retorted. Ligh glinted on his revolver; it was pointed straight a Jess. Grant's was trained on Rae-Ellen. "As to insani ty," Keith went on, "don't the head-shrinkers say we're all a little insane about something or other?"

"Only you two are the exceptions!" mocked Jess.

Rae-Ellen winced. She knew Jess was playing fo time, goading Keith and Grant into talking. She knew he was ready to spring and grab one of those revolvers. Which would leave the other free to shoot And he was too frozen to get away with it. Her teeth began to chatter, and she bit down on them, hard.

"Since we're to die," Jess said, "we'd like to know the reason. What have we done? What have you to gain?"

"You ruined our future," Keith said. "You, Tower took the job here, rich man in your own right, and every time you and Rae-Ellen met, sparks flew. You Rae-Ellen, you've got your own bullheadedness to blame. If you'd married me, you could have put a stop to the plans Grant and I have been forced to make. Which has resulted in—this."

"You had plans?" Jess asked. "I don't see what they were."

"We were too smart for you, Tower."

"Tell me about them, Keith."

"It'd take too long."

"Not if you're quick."

"Well. No harm for you to know. When Rae-Ellen started giving off sparks about you, Grant and I took steps. He's my half brother, and we'd planned for one of us to marry Rae-Ellen. For the land and the oil and the horses. For everything."

"I see."

"So Grant and I worked schemes to discredit you with Travis, to make him fire you. That girth, over at Bertha's, when you fell off the horse. That was the first one. To make you look clumsy and careless."

"I'm the one who fixed the girth," Grant boasted.

"Next, I turned the horses loose," Keith went on. "Thought sure old man Travis would send you packing, but he didn't."

"I'm the one who tampered with the spur at the rodeo," Grant said. "Bought one like Knight bought, sawed it, then substituted it. Took the chance some other cowboy would draw the number, but I was lucky. You drew Diablo, and you took the fall. Didn't make you the star of the day, either. *Or* make you lose your job."

"Then," Keith continued, a grin in his tone, "came the mudslide. That was a natural. We were ready to give you a push, but you sank on your own. Then, worse luck, we had to help the others dig you out. You've been harder to get rid of than a horsefly!"

"Keith threw the knife at you," Grant said. "Missed. But, like the horses, it got laid on teenagers."

"Then this blue norther came," Keith exulted. "This time, it's going to work."

Jess let his arm drop from around Rae-Ellen. He was taut, ready. She tensed to help him, whatever he did.

"Explain the blue norther," Jess said.

"At first it was to be just you, Tower. Grant and I

knocked you out, buried you here. Later, we were coming back to smother you, take away your bindings, make it look like you'd died in the storm and the snow had covered your body. Now, with Rae-Ellen here, it'll look like you found each other, froze, and were mounded over. The storm will get the blame . . . not us."

"It's not that simple, Keith," Jess said. "Those guns. The only way you can hold me is with a bullet. And when I'm found with a bullet in my body, there's no way to pass my death off as an accident. You'll be caught."

"No we won't," Keith said. "We'll keep clear of suspicion, even. It'll never be pinned on us."

"And if you do succeed? What next?"

"We'll make out. Grant will marry Bertha Mudd and I'll work for Travis again and look for a rich widow too. We'll not get the Travis money to divide, but we'll share what comes from the oil wells Bertha will dig. We'll be winners, after all! You and Rae-Ellen will be the losers!"

He threw back his head and laughed.

Before Rae-Ellen knew he was going to move, Jess threw himself at the two men, hitting them both at once. All three fell, the guns flying away. Rae-Ellen jumped onto the one she knew to be Grant. He bucked and almost dumped her, but she clung, her bare fingers without sensation, but holding on to him.

They rolled, fighting in the snow. Snow covered her face and she twisted desperately and they rolled again. This time, she was on top. Like a flash, she scooped a great handful of snow up and slammed it

394

down over his face and into his mouth and he began to choke and cough. He rolled again, but in the process she got another pile of snow and slapped it all over his face and into his mouth. They kept struggling, Rae-Ellen using snow for her weapon, winding her stiffened legs around him, pulling off his cap, digging her fingers into his hair and pulling.

Jess knew that Rae-Ellen was fighting Grant, fighting for her life. Before he could save her, he had to overcome Keith, who was bent on a death struggle. Jess crashed his fist, which was a chunk of ice, into Keith's face; at the same instant, Keith landed his fist on Jess's forehead. Jess punched a knee into Keith's groin and, while the foreman was doubled from that, managed to dig his gloved hands past the coat collar and around the neck inside, and began to squeeze.

Keith tried to roll. Jess, though his whole body was a chunk of ice and impossible to handle, pressed with all his might and stayed on top. And squeezed that neck relentlessly, squeezed until Keith's flailing legs stilled and his hands dropped away. Still, there was tension in Keith. Jess lifted himself, bore with all his weight on that neck, heard it snap; then Keith wilted completely and didn't move again.

Grant freed himself of Rae-Ellen and, with her hampering and hobbling him, Jess managed to knock him unconscious. Rae-Ellen dived for the ropes with which Jess had been tied, and they began to bind Grant's wrists.

Suddenly someone else was there, helping. From their voices it was Drew and Pa Travis.

Drew shone his lantern on Keith. "He's dead," he

told them. He squatted, examined. "Broken neck," he reported.

"I did that," Jess said.

Drew next examined Grant. "He'll live," he said.

"We overheard part of what these two said," Drew told Jess.

"We better get Grant on a cot under guard," rumbled Pa. "We can put Keith's body in a storeroom. The law can come in when the storm lets up."

Jess and Rae-Ellen sat, shoulders touching, at the kitchen table, where Leah and Rosita fussed and clucked and fetched and carried. Rae-Ellen and Jess had their feet in the same tub of cold water under the table, and their hands in a great pan of cold water on top of the table. This, Leah and Rosita insited, would prevent frostbite.

All the others were in the room. Drew had his arm around Susie. Rae-Ellen thought they looked cute.

Compton and Johnny were at the stable with the horses.

"I'm anxious for the sheriff to come," said Pa. "Jess will go free because he killed in self-defense and to save Rae-Ellen. Grant will have to answer to the law for what he tried to do."

Jess moved his feet in the tub; Rae-Ellen moved hers. He covered one of her feet with one of his, pressed gently. He put one of his hands over her hand in the pan of water, and pressed.

Then, not so much as asking her consent, he spoke. "All of you," he said. "You might as well know. Rae-Ellen and I are getting married. Right away. I'll run my horse farm from a distance, and become a Texan. Thought you'd be interested to know."

Everybody gathered about the half-frozen pair, girls chattering, Drew and Link and Sammy congratulating. Pa Travis pounded Jess's shoulder mightily, hugged Rae-Ellen until she could hardly breathe.

The old darling! she thought. He planned the whole thing! Bless him!

"What changed your mind about a relationship?" she whispered to Jess.

"Marriage is a relationship," he muttered. "Also, when that kid of yours hushed his crying, then used my finger for a teething ring, I knew. We'll hit it off, Vic and me."

"And me?" she whispered, tremulous.

"And you," he whispered, his lips on hers for all to see.

ROMANCE...ADVENTURE ...DANGER...
by Best-selling author, Aola Vandergriff

DAUGHTERS OF THE SOUTHWIND
by Aola Vandergriff   (D30-561, $3.50)
The three McCleod sisters were beautiful, virtuous and bound to a dream
—the dream of finding a new life in the untamed promise of the West.
Their adventures in search of that dream provide the dimensions for this
action-packed romantic bestseller.

DAUGHTERS OF THE WILD COUNTRY
by Aola Vandergriff   (D30-562, $3.50)
High in the North Country, three beautiful women begin new lives in a
world where nature is raw, men are rough...and love, when it comes,
shines like a gold nugget. Tamsen, Arab and Em McCleod now find themselves in Russian Alaska, where power, money and human life are the
playthings of a displaced, decadent aristocracy in this lusty novel ripe
with love, passion, spirit and adventure.

DAUGHTERS OF THE FAR ISLANDS
by Aola Vandergriff   (D30-563, $3.50)
Hawaii seems like Paradise to Tamsen and Arab—but it is not. Beneath
the beauty, like the hot lava bubbling in the volcano's crater, trouble
seethes in Paradise. The daughters are destined to be caught in the turmoil between Americans who want to keep their country. And in their own
family, danger looms...and threatens to erupt and engulf them all.

DAUGHTERS OF THE OPAL SKIES
by Aola Vandergriff   (D30-564, $3.50)
Tamsen Tallant, most beautiful of the McCleod sisters, is alone in the
Australian outback. Alone with a ranch to run, two rebellious teenage
nieces to care for, and Opan Station's new head stockman to reckon with
—a man whose very look holds a challenge. But Tamsen is prepared for
danger—for she has seen the face of the Devil and he looks like a man.

DAUGHTERS OF THE MISTY ISLES
by Aola Vandergriff   (D93-929, $2.95)
Settled in at Nell's Wotherspoon Manor, the McCleod sisters must carve
new futures for their children and their men. Arab has her marriage and
her courage put on the line. Tam learns to live without her lover. And even
Nell will have to relinquish a dream. But the greatest challenge by far will
be to secure the happiness of Luka whose romance threatens to tear the
family apart.

You'll also want to read these thrilling bestsellers by *Jennifer Wilde...*